OBSIDIAN MAGIC

(LEGACY SERIES BOOK 2)

MCKENZIE HUNTER

This is a work of fiction. Names, characters, businesses, places, events, and incidents are either the products of the author's imagination or used in a fictitious manner. Any resemblance to actual persons, living or dead, or actual events is purely coincidental.

McKenzie Hunter

Obsidian Magic

© 2017, McKenzie Hunter

mckenziehunter.author@gmail.com

ALL RIGHTS RESERVED. This book contains material protected under International and Federal Copyright Laws and Treaties. Any unauthorized reprint or use of this material is prohibited. No part of this book may be reproduced or transmitted in any form or by any means, electronic or mechanical, including photocopying, recording, or by any information storage and retrieval system without express written permission from the author / publisher.

ISBN: 978-1-946457-80-6

ACKNOWLEDGMENTS

It will never change for me. I am always grateful and humbled by the people who help me through the process. I want to offer my sincerest appreciation to my beta readers: Angie "Nana" Hatcher, Kathy Beard, Kylie Kniese, Marla Maslan, Misty Chancellor, and Ryan Sundy, for their hard work and honest feedback. My friends and family who have been with me throughout the process and have always been supportive and encouraging.

I would also like to give a special thanks to my patient and wonderful editor, Luann Reed-Siegel, who works so diligently to help bring my stories to life.

Last but definitely not least, I would like to thank my readers for allowing me to entertain you with my stories.

CHAPTER 1

Three times I picked up the phone to dial the number only to stare at it without making the call. What would I say to Gareth? Was it my imagination or did Gareth, the head of the Supernatural Guild and member of the Magic Council, know that I was a Legacy? No, I hadn't imagined it—he'd whispered my real name in my ear. I took a deep breath. He'd made it seem like he would keep it a secret. And I was sure that might have been his intention, but he had responsibilities and an obligation to protect people from the likes of us, of *me*.

This time when I put in the number, I pressed send before I could talk myself out of it again.

Gareth answered in a deep, velvety voice. "Ms. Levy Michaels," he purred. How did he make his voice sound so sexy and haughty at the same time? "I didn't think it would take two days before you contacted me. You are a strange woman, aren't you?"

"Do you expect me to say yes to that?"

"I was just making an observation. To what do I owe this pleasure?"

Really? Fine, I will play your game. "I was just wondering if you were going to the Harvest Festival," I asked in a cloying voice. "I hear it's going to be really nice." Each year I went out of my way to miss this, and I had a feeling it probably wasn't on his list of things to do this weekend.

"Hmm. I hadn't thought about it. Should I? I went a couple of years ago. It's a good opportunity to try out the best bakeries in town. Have you tried the persimmon pie? They only have it around this time of year. And apparently, Claire's Bakery makes the best zucchini bread money can buy; it's at a special price at the festival. Maybe I should go and buy a couple and freeze the rest for later. Ah, and the pumpkin ..."

"You win. I didn't call you to discuss pies, bread, and cake, but I'm sure you know that." He wasn't lying. It was a mystery how Claire could take the most disgusting vegetable ever grown and make it into the best bread I'd ever tasted. "We need to talk."

"Well, you know where my office is. What time should I expect you?" he asked.

"Is it safe to discuss sensitive matters there?"

He laughed, a melodious rolling sound. "Levy, if you want to meet me privately, please don't be coy. Just ask."

I had forgotten about his arrogance and narcissism but when I heard them in his voice as he spoke, I got a much-needed reminder. "I'll be there at eleven."

"You want to do lunch, I guess? Again, Ms. Michaels, if you—"

"Give me an hour; I'll be there."

He was frustrating. I shrugged on my back sheath with sai in place and grabbed my jacket. I didn't make it far from my room before I found my roommate, Savannah, sprawled out on the floor on a yoga mat with her body contorted into an odd position. She must have decided to do double duty with

2

her worship. I teased Savannah that her obsession with fitness was very cultlike. She paid tribute to Bikram and Vinyasa. And worshipped the false idol Lululemon. Between her full-time job as an administrative assistant and yoga and Pilates, I rarely saw her in the morning and on her days off she seemed to feel the need to offer the gods additional tribute.

"What time are you going to work?"

"Later; we have several pickups and then we'll have to go through them." This was the most boring part of antique acquisitions—picking up boxes of things that we either learned about from someone contacting the company or various ads on the web and Craigslist. Usually we would find a few magical objects, but there was a higher incidence of just finding plain old junk. But that was a risk we were willing to take, because when we did get a good box, it was usually *damn* good. People called claiming they had antiques they wanted to sell. And we didn't just pick up a box or two. They pretty much waved their hand over a cluttered shed, garage, attic, basement, barn, or whatever and let us scavenge it. This happened more when it was the child of a deceased parent. I guessed their thinking was that all the valuable things were probably in the main part of the house. Many people had been wrong about that. But they essentially used us as a trash-hauling service. We gave them a flat fee and claimed possession of everything in the space named.

Over the weekend, we'd acquired a barn. We were called in by the granddaughter of the deceased who sounded as though she just couldn't be bothered with any of it. I figured it was going to be a big job.

"I fixed breakfast," Savannah said in her typical morning voice, which was a lot perkier than mine even after I'd had several cups of coffee. I smiled but groaned inwardly. I didn't want her egg-white-only, no butter, sautéed vegetable food. I

3

wanted bacon, the whole egg, and waffles with mounds of butter and syrup. And just to keep it healthy, I'd add blueberries on top.

"Muffins," she offered. My smile bloomed and my mood changed in an instant. Meeting Gareth still weighed on my mind, but life was always better with muffins.

Except for these muffins. Walking toward the table, I frowned. I reclaimed my mood, too. *What the hell is this?*

"They're egg-white muffins and only forty calories each. You can have several of them, guilt-free."

Really, can I have all of your tasty muffins?

"Mmm. Yay." Since she was watching me, I took two and wrapped them in a napkin.

"I've known you long enough to know your sarcastic 'yay,'" she said and shifted herself into another position. I remembered her calling it the Warrior II pose but I simply called it the Dying Crane.

"And yet, this is what you decided to serve me for breakfast."

She grinned, displaying the small dimples at the corners of her lips. Her pale blond hair was gathered into a messy ponytail, and I glanced at her neck looking for marks. Savannah loved vampires. She was an utter and total fangirl with an obsession that reduced an assiduous and pragmatic woman to a blustering vampire admirer prone to bouts of swooning whenever she was near one. And after having dinner with Lucas, the Master of the city, she was enthralled and enamored by him specifically.

"Where are you going?"

"To meet Gareth."

"Oh, give me a minute to shower and dress."

"Savannah, I'm going alone. I'll tell you everything when I get back. Maybe we'll go out for drinks, I'm sure I'll need one."

She stood, stretching; lithe grace commanded her movements. With each change of position it was obvious that Savannah was a dancer. "Good, we'll go to Devour. Lucas is expecting me," she offered.

"Why is Lucas expecting us at his vamp bar? Savannah, you know how I feel about that place."

"You're paranoid. It's fun." Only to Savannah. There were two clubs where mostly vampires hung out. They were also frequented by the locals who thought it was cool to party with the undead and occasionally be their meal for the night and sometimes more. Crimson was where the new vampires hung out; it was safer to me. Nothing more than a bunch of brooding young vamps who had watched too much *Angel*, *The Originals*, *Vampire Diaries*, and *Buffy* to be anything more than entertaining. Most of them were still trying to find themselves, adopting their sulky, angsty, tortured soul personas as they spent the majority of the evening trying to out brood one another. Some of them were seductive enough and played the role of the tempter quite well, but they were new, easily rebuked or ignored. And in my case, mocked.

But Devour's name was very appropriate. The moment you walked in there wasn't any doubt that *you* were on the menu whether you wished to be or not. The older vampires frequented this club. Most of them had had hundreds of years to perfect the art of seduction, and they were good. Very good. It was illegal for vampires to compel but it didn't hurt the older vampires' ability to find a willing donor. Their mannerism and words charmed you better than any spell could and before you knew it you were enthralled, giving in to anything they wanted and it was done legally and without the use of any magic.

Devour was also the residence of Lucas, one of the oldest vampires in the world. The night we'd had dinner with him, Savannah had been beguiled and I wasn't sure she had control of any of her own desires. I wasn't affected, not because I was immune to their charms, but because I'd come into his den of sin battle ready. He kept offering me alcohol to try to get me to relax. But I couldn't, I had to be on guard for the both of us. When he'd asked if we would join him for dinner again, I had to speak up before she committed us to another meal. I was convinced that this was a prelude to one of us ending up as the entree. Despite my repeated objections, he seemed to have only heard Savannah's gracious acceptance.

"Well, don't go without me," I said.

"Oh stop, you're being silly."

"I'm serious. I really want to go. I love the food there, and all the drinks are top-shelf without having to ask." And cheap. I guessed that not only did it relax us but drunk humans made uninhibited prey, which was good entertainment for them.

Us. I frowned at the thought. There wasn't an *us* because I wasn't human. I'd been hiding for so long I had assumed the human persona as part of who I was as much as I'd taken to my assumed name, Olivia—Levy—Michaels. That was who this world knew me as. Anya Kismet was me in a former life, when I was just a child. Before Trackers came after us and I realized my life was going to be different than most people's.

"Don't leave without me," I repeated before heading out the door to my car. It was nice to be confident that when I started my car it was more than likely going to work. A new feeling for me, because in the past I'd refused to spend the money to have everything repaired, so my car had been temperamental. If it had been too cold, hot, or rainy, it hadn't seemed to want to start. Relying on public transportation or Savannah's car if mine failed had ceased to be an option. It had taken a chunk of my savings to make the repairs but had still been cheaper than buying another car. It left me more money to use to hide or disappear if things ever got too bad. I had no idea what would come of Gareth knowing my birth name or whether I would need to leave for good.

I should have left the sai in the car, but I couldn't bring myself to do it. They were enchanted weapons that could be used to prevent shifters from shifting, rare magical objects that they weren't immune to. The need for self-preservation and to expect the unexpected had been ingrained in me to the point that going unarmed into a building with some of the most elite shifters, mages, fae, and witches in the city to discuss me being a Legacy—someone most were taught to kill on sight—seemed ridiculous. Even if I was only there to *talk* to the head of the Supernatural Guild, I couldn't be without them.

"Who are you here to see?" asked the disinterested young man at the reception desk, barely lifting his eyes from his phone to make contact. I was used to the kind elderly woman who'd greeted me on previous visits. Her bright smile and welcoming personality were contagious and it didn't hurt that she was a fae. If her personality didn't put you in a better mood, her magic could. Cognitive manipulation was against the law but if you worked for the people who enforced it, there was probably some leniency.

He leaned back in his chair, his emotive, stormy blue eyes sweeping over me, his tousled walnut-brown hair pulled into a messy man bun. The metallic blue shifter rings that danced around his eyes were livelier than he was and probably more excited about the job.

Where the hell did they get this guy?

"Your name," he breathed as though the very act of

requesting the information was the last thing on his extensive to-do list, right after doing nothing.

"Olivia Michaels."

"I don't have an Olivia Michaels."

"What about Levy?"

"Oh, yeah." His eyes flashed. He said my name over and over and then gave me a long, assessing look. I wasn't sure if he knew me as the Olivia "Levy" Michaels who had been charged with three murders a little over a week ago or the one who had been exonerated. The confusion was understandable. The supernatural community went to such lengths to put a nice spin on its activities and to maintain the harmonious relationship with the humans that they were justifiably cynical about the news they read or heard.

He picked up the phone. "Uncle Gar, she's here. Do you want me to send her up?"

I couldn't hear what Gareth said on the other line, but it made Nephew Man Bun scowl. "Fine, you just want her to stay down here? What's the purpose of the meeting if she's going to stay down here? Doesn't make sense to me, but you're the boss." Gareth grumbled something loud enough for me to hear his growl but not to make out his words. Again, Nephew Man Bun continued to grin when he answered his uncle. "How was I supposed to know you were being sarcastic? You didn't *sound* sarcastic."

Gareth said something else but once again I couldn't make out the words. "Calm down, Uncle Gar, it's not my fault you're not funny." Whatever Gareth was ranting about didn't matter because his nephew had pulled the phone from his ear and stopped listening.

"Go on up. Fifth floor. He's in a mood, good luck."

With a simper, I said, "Thanks for putting him in that *mood*."

He chuckled. "You're welcome. Anytime. It's what I do."

Gareth wasn't in a mood. In fact, his trademark crooked grin was nestled on his face. His handsome face, and I hated that I kept noticing it. And he looked as though he knew that I was noticing it. Crystalline blue eyes had fastened on me the moment I'd started through the door. It was getting harder and harder to ignore the features that were as defined as his arms, which his short-sleeved shirt exposed.

You're so sure of yourself, aren't you?

"Are you going to come in or do you plan to stand in the doorway gawking at me?"

"I wasn't gawking. I'm just trying to see the family resemblance. Where's …?"

I waited for him to interject a name. I couldn't believe that I'd been at the Guild numerous times and hadn't learned the name of the woman who was usually at the front desk. I waited and Gareth stood with the little kink in his lips, letting me squirm. "Sorry, I don't know her name."

"It's Beth. So, Ms. Michaels." He stepped closer. An intense smell of oak and masculine musk inundated the small space between us. I loved the way he smelled. I inhaled and then took a step back, increasing the space between us. He quickly closed the distance as soon as I did. He glanced at the ends of the sai sticking out.

"Are you expecting a fight?" He made a noise. "I guess someone like you would have to be a little more cautious than most. Right?" Then he went to the door and closed it. "After all, people are quite afraid of you, aren't they?"

"There isn't a reason to be," I said softly.

"Are you sure? After all, your kind nearly killed everyone in the world, or at least the United States. I think it's a little naïve to think you, a Legacy, are totally harmless." His voice changed, becoming cool and level. Professionally distant.

"I'm not able to do anything like that on a wide scale."

Gareth began slowly walking around me, and it made me nervous. I craned my neck to follow him as closely as possible. It was at this moment that I was aware that he was a predator, *Panthera leo spelaea*, cave lion. An animal that predated man. A massive creature with the ability to take down prey with a single swipe of his huge paw. And even with that to his advantage, I was probably a bigger danger to him than he was to me. That had to bother him. Legacy magic was the only kind that affected shapeshifters.

When he was back in front of me, I said, "Let's cut the games. We need to talk."

Again, he swallowed the distance between us and when he spoke his warm breath wisped against my lips. "Then talk."

"How did you know?"

"You have a shield on your foot." He grinned. "Remember when I checked for it in your hair? You were calm because you knew I wouldn't find it." He leaned into me, his voice dropping to a low purr. "As I said before, the body will always betray. Your heart rate increased and so did your breathing when I asked you to take off your shoes. I knew I would find it there before I even checked. But it was cute watching you think you got away with it. Only people who are hiding something pretty bad have them. You weren't in our records as committing a crime that would have caused you to have your magic restricted and I'm sure I would have remembered you, if I had encountered you before. I didn't know why you would have a reason to hide that you possessed magic. I figured there had to be a reason why you were hiding that you were a magic wielder. Then our conversation about things being extinct bothered me. You seemed to want me to really believe that. It didn't take long for me to get to Legacy."

"There's a big leap from you detecting the presence of a shield and Legacy. What about all the things in between?"

"Of course. Do you remember when you were in my bed?" he asked with a sly look, a hint of a smile playing at his lips.

"Your guest room," I offered. "I was in your guest room."

"Everything in there is mine. *My* house, *my* bed," he said, and he couldn't have made his grin more sinful if he'd tried.

I guess by that logic, I don't need to go back to his house.

His finger lightly stroked against my hand, which tingled with a warmth that was probably my imagination. I reminded myself that everything with Gareth could be reduced to nothing more than primal carnal instincts. He just seemed to elicit those in me. And that was the story I planned on sticking with. It had nothing to do with the fact that he was handsome and radiated a raw sensuality that was impossible to ignore. *Stop being a shifter fangirl!* I scolded myself.

Stepping away as his lips inched closer to mine should have been my first response, the ideal response—the logical response. But I didn't. Just before his lips brushed against mine, someone knocked at the door. I took the distraction as an opportunity to put a couple of feet of distance between us.

His nephew peeked his head in. "Beth is back, I'm leaving."

Gareth's brows rose. "Really. You worked all of"—he looked at the clock—"an hour and a half and you're ready to call it a day?"

"I have to go back to school in two weeks; you plan to have me here the whole time?" His contemptuous scowl mirrored his uncle's.

"Yes, that's my plan."

He walked in, and when he stood across from his uncle there was just a slight resemblance. The shifter eyes and the

11

sharply hewn features. He had on khakis and a button-down and looked uncomfortable and very unhappy about it.

"I just borrowed your stupid car. Seriously, don't make it a thing," he retorted, dismissing his uncle's stern look with a roll of his eyes.

"It is a 'thing'. You stole—"

"Borrowed, you knew I was going to take it. It's a Tesla, you know I love those cars, so you knew I was going to *borrow* it the moment you left me alone with it at your house." With a heavy sigh, he continued. "And I didn't enjoy it anyway—you had me pulled over five times. I had your stupid car for three hours and you had me pulled over five times!"

Gareth chuckled.

His nephew brushed off the taunting laugh. "It didn't bother me, just added to my street cred." Gareth's laugh faded into a scowl. The kid really knew how to rub Gareth the wrong way. I liked him.

"Good, next time I'll have them arrest you—that should really increase your cred."

His nephew mumbled something under his breath as he backed out of the room.

"Avery, whatever you scraped against caused six hundred dollars' worth of paint damage. You have to work it off. Go downstairs and ask Beth what you can do. At minimum wage, you should have it paid off in no time."

His glower didn't have an effect on Gareth. In fact, the entire exchange seemed to have perked up his day.

"Mom gave you a check."

"My sister didn't damage my car, *you* did."

Avery glared at his uncle under his long lashes, which really diminished the effect, and mumbled something else under his breath before exiting the room. He looked over his shoulder to shoot another furtive glare in his uncle's direction.

Gareth's teasing smile remained on his face as he directed his attention back to me. "Where were we? Oh yes, you were in my bed"—he moved closer to me—"and you told me."

There wasn't *any* way I would have told him. I knew the consequences of disclosing something like that to someone whose job was protecting the supernatural community and helping maintain the optics that supernaturals weren't dangerous to humans. He would be the last person I told. As far as the world was concerned, I was the biggest danger out there, and no amount of schmoozing or PR spin was going to help it.

My kind was responsible for the Cleanse, a spell performed that latched on to anything magic like a virus and killed off a significant number of supernaturals and humans who had dormant supernatural ability, probably as a result of a family member's liaison with a supernatural. My ilk stood behind a veil and a bastion of strong wards that protected them while the world died around them to ensure that they would be the most powerful people in the world.

My parents and a small group of resisters attempted to stop them but it was too late. It ended when the supernatural community and the humans formed an alliance; magic and science mingled, creating an unholy war that was bad enough to be considered part of our history.

With all historical wars, the villain is always in the eye of the beholder and rightfully so. There were always two sides to a story, except when it came to the Legacy. Everyone was united against us. We were one of the most hated groups ever to exist. It wasn't until a couple of weeks ago that I'd discovered that the honor was shared with Vertu, who were Legacy supercharged. Legacy were often considered to have the purest and strongest magic to exist and all supernatural magic was linked to ours. Vertu were the progenitors of magic. Some speculated that we were their doing and were the only offspring that they considered worthy of being their equals and companions. Other magic wielders were just spurious descendants that they had little to no regard for. I'd had the unfortunate experience of meeting and trying to fight one. It was a magical ass kicking that I could've gone a lifetime without experiencing.

"I call BS, there is no way in hell I told you."

Gareth was too close and his eyes azure diamonds that glinted from the cast of the ceiling light. "But you did. Remember, I had to wake you up. I kept asking you a series of questions, and the first time I asked your name you said 'Anya Kismet.' A lot was destroyed in the aftermath of the war but there were records salvaged of your existence and in them were Kismets." He stepped closer, removing the small amount of distance that I'd claimed, and his finger stroked a strand of my hair. "And you use walnut powder to color your hair—I assume because it is less damaging than commercial dyes and you have to do it so much to hide the red."

Seriously, how did he acquire that useless information? But it wasn't actually so useless. I licked my lips, my mouth was getting dry.

His gaze dropped to my lips. "Would you like some water?"

I needed more than water, I could have taken a shot of something—anything. Was Gareth this good, or had all the things I'd done to conceal who I was only worked on the pedestrian? As he grabbed a bottle from the fridge in the apartment-sized office, I tried to think of what to do next. He was the only person that knew—I hoped. I could take the memory away from him, and for a while I considered it. The chilled predacious look he gave me from the other side of the

14

room made me wonder if he knew I could do that and if so, that I was considering doing it to him.

"Now what?" I asked after taking a long drink from the bottle, appreciative of the space we had between us as he rested against the wall.

"What do you mean?"

"Do you arrest me?"

"Why would I do that?"

I shrugged. "I don't know. It seems to be your go-to move. You just threatened to have your nephew arrested and you've threatened to arrest me for less."

He chuckled. "My nephew only seems to learn when the lessons are hard. *You* were being petulant, it was necessary. You're calmer now, more subdued. Submissive." His voice dropped to a low, deep rasp. "I like it."

Gareth knew the right buttons to push and he seemed to enjoy tapping at them at every chance. The deep shadows of his arrogance and conceit just compounded the situation. I took another long drink from the bottle, reining in my sarcasm and the threat that was edging to be released.

"See, even a little ticked off, you have control of your magic. You aren't the wild and uncontrolled degenerate that the books and historians have painted you all as." He pushed himself from the wall. "I always expected Legacy to be nefarious monsters who thirst for power and are driven by their draconian desires. You are none of those things." He gave me an assessing look that lingered for a moment too long. I shifted my gaze from him, focusing on everything around the room: the large windows to my right, providing an unobstructed view of the mass of trees next to the building. When I returned my focus to him, his look had settled on an odd combination of curiosity, intrigue, and wariness. His feral interest was piqued and his smile faltered, giving way to a smirk.

"All the books really didn't prepare me for you." He studied me again and walked over to his bookcase, pulling out a leather-bound book and thumbing through it until he found what he was looking for. He handed it to me and I glanced at it. That was all I needed—just a glimpse. I knew from experience it would be a textbook account of the Legacy and our sins. Our acts against humanity were adequately documented. We had a small section in the history books because the world had changed as a result of what we'd done. For many, things were simplified to BC and AC. A new world was created by the selfish act. Defining moments in history had simply been reduced to the periods *before* and *after* the Cleanse. When no one knew that supernaturals existed and after when the whole world knew that they did.

We were depicted as creatures with a ruthless lust for magic that had led us to nearly kill off the population. Verbose, florid, and intellectual language were used to eloquently describe us as sociopaths. The Legacy who resisted were depicted in such glowing terms that they were essentially canonized.

I quickly handed the book back to him and he kept a careful eye on me as he guided it to the desk.

"I will admit it is quite interesting being in the presence of a unicorn."

"You're a cave lion. I think it's safe to say I'm not the only unicorn in the room."

He shrugged. "The spoiled young man downstairs who stole my car is one. My sister"—he looked at his phone vibrating against the desk—"who will not stop calling me, is another."

Sighing, he picked up the phone. "Yes, dear," he said in a low saccharine voice. Amused by whatever she'd said, he laughed. "Charlotte, I'm not accepting payment from you."

She said something else and the smile wilted into a stern line, jaw set in defiance, and if Charlotte could have seen his face she would have known the battle was over. She had lost.

"He damaged it. I know he has the cute puppy dog eyes and he probably turned on the charm and the guilt and you caved, like you always do. It's a good thing your husband and I have an immunity to it. You can thank me later."

He inched close enough to me for me to hear as she evoked her position as an older sibling to try to get him to do what she wanted. I'd known the man for three weeks and knew that wasn't going to work, and it didn't. A deep, melodious laugh filled the room. "Do you really think your position in getting to see the world ten years before I did gives you veto power over me as an adult? You pull that card often, when has it worked?" he asked.

"Charlotte, this conversation is over. He's working off the car this week. Love you." And then he hung up. Before I could respond, he was guiding me out the door.

"We'll finish our conversation at lunch."

I pulled away from him. It had become my personal mission to wipe the arrogance off his face and let him know that the people downstairs in the SG office were the only people he had the right to control. It was obvious he assumed his rule extended beyond the confines of the building and the organization and no one had told him otherwise.

"I can't have lunch with you. I have to go to work."

"At what time?" he asked.

I didn't want to have lunch with him. I wanted to keep this as professional as possible and that boat was slowly leaving the dock, unmanned, floating aimlessly down turbulent waters that seemed deceptively placid.

"In a bit."

"Well, that's hardly a time. Is that how you work? It seems

like there should be more structure. Why don't you call Kalen and get a specific time?" He offered a playful grin.

I looked at my watch. I had four hours before I needed to meet Kalen, and I really just wanted to talk to Gareth, see his position on my existence, tell him about Conner, the vile Vertu with the god complex, who actually *was* the type of person he'd described earlier, and then treat myself to a nice lunch. I needed to let Gareth know about Conner's plans to do the Cleanse slowly this time as opposed to the way it had been done before. He planned to work with others who would betray the supernatural community with the promise of more power and to curry favor with the Legacy. He was slowly building an army. I didn't want to have lunch with Gareth. I wanted him to help me with the coup I had to plan; perhaps he could help with the civil war I might incite as well.

"Based on the look on your face, you need lunch and maybe even a drink. Then you can tell me about Conner and what he's planning that has placed that look of fear on your face."

I stood my ground. "What about Clive and Humans First?" That small group of agitators, called HF for short, believed that humans were special little snowflakes that needed to be separated and protected from the ruthless supernaturals. They were hypocrisy at its undiluted core. The reason the Cleanse had ended with the defeat of the Legacy and millions of lives had been saved was because the witches and the mages had been able to break the wards the Legacy hid behind and get through their veils. The special little snowflakes would have lost without the help of the supernaturals. But that was a forgotten part of the revisionist history that often accompanied the HF's rhetoric.

"What about them?"

"They saw me perform magic, and Jonathan told them

18

what I am." Bringing up that name quickly brought a frown to my face and Gareth's offer of a drink was becoming more enticing. Jonathan, a mage who had sat on the Magical Council, had betrayed his kind to side with Conner just for the chance to have more power. The thirst for more power at the expense of other people's lives made me cringe, and if I had a bit of sympathy for the way his life had ended, it was eased when I considered his cruelty and betrayal.

"Jonathan is dead, he can't corroborate their story. They are a fundamentalist group who use over-the-top rhetoric to make their case about segregation. I doubt anyone will believe them."

Trackers were fundamentalists, too. Pseudo-military trained people who hunted us down and killed us, all the while telling a world that wanted to believe we didn't exist that we did. They were going to make that belief a reality. They'd killed my parents and countless others, and two had found me. I'd had to use magic to wipe their minds, and I'd given the last one a false memory of him killing me. I hoped I didn't have to worry about them anymore.

Humans First was different. They wouldn't try to kill me, they'd probably invite me out for coffee and plead their case for another Cleanse to wipe out the other supernaturals. They would probably hold their noses the entire time and do the walk of shame as they left our meeting place, but they would sacrifice anything to achieve the Utopic world where magic didn't exist. Since the Legacy and Vertu had lived separately before the Cleanse, away from the impure magic, it would be advantageous to them all. Or so Humans First would like to believe.

Gareth pressed his hand into my back, again attempting to guide me out of his office. I sidestepped, moved out of his reach, and crossed my arms over my chest. Planted in the middle of the room, I refused to acquiesce to his demands.

He stood taller, also crossing his arms over his chest, defiance etched over his features.

Come on. Just ask. All you have to do is frame it as a question. I've done my adulting for the day, now it's your turn.

I didn't think it was very hard to ask, but Mr. I Always Get My Way behaved like it was an act of treason. A betrayal to the great state of Gareth. He chewed on the words and looked as though it was glass he was crunching on rather than a *please* or *will*.

His tongue slid across his lips before they parted slightly, but the words wouldn't come out.

Take your time Mr. Reynolds, I have four hours to kill. But you will ask.

"Do you mind if we continue this discussion over lunch?"

"Thank you for asking, I would love to." I forced the light smile to remain on my lips instead of taking a play from his book and allowing it to be taken over by a smirk. It worked for nearly ten seconds and then I was nothing but smirks.

"I usually don't have to work this hard to get a woman to go out to lunch with me," he said, his tone gentle and breezy. But it wouldn't have been him if it wasn't thinly laced with conceit.

"Well, then that makes me special. I guess I am a unicorn after all."

Downstairs Avery was slouched in a chair in the waiting room, his eyes planted on his phone screen as his fingers danced across the keys. He glanced up at our approach but quickly returned to his phone.

"Is that work?" Gareth asked in a coarse voice, as deep brackets formed around his mouth as he frowned.

"Beth doesn't have anything. She's really efficient. You should give her a raise." His eyes briefly met his uncle's. The shifter ring seemed to glow for a moment before he looked back down at his phone.

"Ah, yes. Pardon me, I made the mistake of pairing you with the wrong person."

Gareth tugged him to his feet and pulled him into the large office. When he returned he had a satisfied smile on his face.

"What did you do?" Beth asked, the disappointed moue deepening the wrinkles around her mouth. Fae aged but because of their magic they did so better than others. Often the only thing that aged them was their gray hair. Had her wrinkles been magically enhanced? I couldn't help but wonder why. Perhaps she liked that they added character to her appearance, made her look genteel, demure, grandmotherly, and innocuous, which probably allowed her to get away with a lot of things. *It couldn't possibly be the sweet elderly woman who greets us every morning with an infectious smile.* But I had been treated to her fae mojo when she'd used it to manipulate my emotions. It was illegal, but I had a feeling "illegal" and "legal" magical usage weren't kept strictly separated within the confines of the Supernatural Guild. I suspected that trying to continue the peace and alliance with humans and maintain the perception that magic wasn't that bad often put them in murky gray areas.

Gareth grinned. "He's now the office assistant. That should keep him busy."

"You are putting in zero effort trying to be the favorite uncle," I offered as I followed him to the door.

"If I cared about being a favorite or popular, I doubt I'd be good at my job. Those traits rarely coexist in a good leader."

"Who are you getting your leadership advice from, Amanda Waller?"

His brow furrowed. "Who?"

"From *Suicide Squad*, the comic book. They take a bunch of misfits and use them for government operations. The leader is a little hard-ass but has to be because she is dealing with the craziest and most deranged criminals in the world," I explained.

I was met with a blank stare and the only way I could explain it any further was with other comic book references. "Never mind."

"You're an odd woman, Ms. Michaels."

I shrugged off his observation or insult—I didn't care to figure out which one it was as I headed for my car, parked across the street from his.

"Where are you going?" he asked as I opened my door.

"I'll follow you."

He'd stopped walking, was just standing on the sidewalk of the large beige structure that reminded me of a federal building because of its size. Well-manicured bushes wrapped around the building. Beds of brightly colored flowers, which I suspected were magically enhanced, trailed along the bottom of its walls and seemed to soften the ominous feel. I realized a building couldn't have a personality, but there was something cold and sterile about it. Even with people who had taken great liberties with the business casual dress code walking in and out, the place seemed stiff. An organization that dealt with the magical misfits and criminals of the supernatural world probably couldn't have a soft and cuddly feel.

"No," he said simply without an explanation. *No. Did I ask him?* I wasn't changing my mind unless he gave me one. A casually amused, defiant smile remained on his face as he stood planted just a few feet from my car. I wasn't sure why I needed to win this. Who was I kidding, Gareth had been the conductor of this situation from the beginning, wrangling every bit of control from me, and I hated it. He was narcissistic and domineering and I felt it was my personal obligation—no, my *duty*—to resist him doing it to me.

I had come to his office to talk—he'd won. I'd agreed to

22

lunch although all I'd wanted was a meeting. We were going to lunch—he'd won. I needed this to be on my terms. I was starting to think that for every inch I allowed him to take, he would definitely take a mile. I wasn't ready to concede.

I got into the car. He laughed, turned, and started to walk back into the building. I hopped out. "Where are you going?"

With a shrug and a plaintive smile, he said, "I do believe there are pressing things about our conversation that will warrant a level of privacy. I think it is as important to me as it is to you. Perhaps I was wrong. But when you're ready to discuss things, my door is always open. Have a good day, Ms. Michaels."

Tumbleweed should have bounced across the sidewalk as it did in old Westerns—I felt like this was a standoff with our hands on the triggers of our stubbornness, each waiting for the other to concede. I refused to be the one to do it. *Not going to do it. Nope. It isn't going to happen.*

Then he started walking again.

Damn.

I groaned, grabbed my sai that I'd placed on the passenger side, and walked over to his car. "Fine." He stopped walking and turned around. He arched a brow at the sai but didn't comment. For years I'd lived in this perpetual state of terror that if people ever found out who I was, they'd try to kill me. Gareth was the type of person that hunted me. I'd had Trackers that were shifters and mages come after me. He knew what and who I was and the fear, doubt, and need for self-preservation dwelled so deep in me they were hard to abandon. I could be at ease around Savannah, but it was hard to do it around anyone else.

"Where are we going?"

"Antonio's. There's a meeting room, so our conversation will be private."

"How long did you have to wait for that reservation?" I

asked, impressed. Kalen had been trying to get a reservation with them for nearly three months; it was something I had to hear about more often than I cared to acknowledge.

"A couple of hours. When you said you were coming to the office, I had it made."

"*A couple of hours?* Someone has clout in the city." I tried to keep the snark to a minimum but I couldn't help it. He usually did get the things he wanted.

He chuckled. "Or a mother who does." This was Gareth, head of the Supernatural Guild, a member of the Magic Council, and son of a business magnate who could get reservations at a restaurant with a three-month waiting list with a couple hours' notice.

At least he was a gracious winner—the taunting look of victory was just a small glint in his eyes and wavered on his face for a few seconds. "I appreciate you joining me. I don't bite, you know?" he said as I settled into the passenger side.

"You're a lion, that's *exactly* what they do to their prey. They use their claws and fangs. Is this the right time for me to point out that I've seen you *literally* bite another shifter? Yes, you do bite."

"Well, that's different." And in bemused silence, he sat next to me, and when he spoke, it was with a deep, silken rumble. "You consider yourself prey?"

"No, but I think you do."

He grinned as he pulled out of the parking lot and I attempted to pay attention to the passing landscape that whizzed by instead of the periodic glances he gave me.

"What happened to your parents?" he asked softly, as though he already knew the answer but needed it confirmed.

"Trackers found them. I was fifteen when it happened." I squeezed my eyes together, fighting tears, and tried to push away the memories and the heaviness that always accompanied them. Grief didn't help; it only made me angry and I couldn't properly direct the rage because there were so many people to extend it to. Did I blame the Legacy for their nefarious, twisted thirst for power, humans who had rightfully destroyed them but made sure the world knew that a dead Legacy was the only Legacy acceptable, or Trackers who wouldn't let the rumors of our existence die? The ones who existed were harmless, and I was tired of paying for the evils of others. It was a belief that had held steady until I'd met Conner. Conner was going to turn my world upside down and make a mess of things.

"Conner wants to have another Cleanse," I finally said after moments of uncomfortable silence.

"Yes, I gathered that from the last time we spoke. He's disappeared. I went back to the location where I found you the last time with several high-level mages and they couldn't find a veil or feel a ward."

I had gone two days ago to the very spot and I couldn't find anything, either. Could he still be there and have something like the shield I had on my foot that masked my magic so that it was virtually undetectable? Could he do the same with his wards? My parents had tried to protect me and I understood why they'd kept some things from me, but I doubted they'd ever thought that I would be trying to stop a demagogue who was aligning his army to do another Cleanse. When the panic sparked in me, it felt like a forest fire blazing in my chest and squelching it wasn't as easy as it had been before.

It was real. I had a fight on my hands and there was more at stake than just a bruised ego and hurt feelings if I failed. Before, if I failed the only person who suffered was me. Not anymore.

"He's stronger than any mage that you can use. Even if they find it, will they be able to bring it down?" Less than a hundred Legacy and Vertu had performed the Cleanse; it had taken hundreds of powerful mages, witches, and fae to bring down wards and open the veil.

"Maybe not, but at least they can—" He stopped abruptly. I immediately saw what caught his attention. In the middle of the square that we were driving through, a brawl was taking place. Bodies soared across the street, and strong magic inundated the air, lacing around my skin, pricking at the hairs on it. I felt it and pushed against it, unraveling it away from me. Gareth looked at me and held my gaze, eyes narrowed.

He picked up his phone but before he could make the call, SG cars came from several directions. Violence coursed through the air along with magic—different magic. I let it wash over me just for a second, trying to identify it, making sure it wasn't my magic or Conner's. It wasn't—it was different, but malicious and dark. I had to push it away with effort. It took a few minutes to gather control of the feelings it unleashed. Violence. Terror. Anger. Magic I wasn't familiar with and could go another lifetime without feeling again. It left a heavy, dreary haze over me.

Centre Square was probably the most diverse area in the city, filled with boutiques, coffee shops, restaurants, and specialty shops. A few witches had shops in the area but this wasn't witch magic—it was too dark, malicious, and strong. Possibly mage, but if so, they were using dark magic. It glazed the air with violence and discord.

Gareth stopped the car in the middle of the street and got out first. I grabbed the twins and followed him through the streets. Two men exchanged punches and blood splattered. I tried to pull them apart using a gentler technique than Gareth, who yanked people apart, sending them a couple of feet away. Once they were subdued, he zip-tied their hands. I made a mental note that he seemed to have a lot of ties with him. Since most of the people were human, a zip tie was enough.

Twins in hand, I ran through the street, guiding as many people as I could to the magic shops. A witch worth anything would have put up a ward. Even a weak one could at least reduce the effect of the odd magic that had incited the rage and violence. A thin woman, eyes blazing with anger, was about to smash a three-inch heel into another woman when I caught her arm. She directed her magically induced ire on me and slapped me. It wasn't her. I realized that, but I needed to get her to back off. I pushed her back; a hip toss landed her facedown on the ground while her head flailed and the threat of further injury didn't help.

As I surveyed the chaos around me, a familiar strong magic brushed against me, and I knew who it was before she spoke.

"I have this," said Harrah, her voice as soft, gentle, and angelic as her features. Calling her *just* a fae seemed too benign a use of the word. She was the PR guru of the supernatural world and a member of the Magic Council. She was the person who often played intermediary between humans and the supernatural community and the face of what people perceived magic to be: gentle, benign, and benevolent. And magic could be all that and easygoing as the *herba terrae*, witch weed; but it could also be violent, dark, and dangerous. It was her job to make sure no humans ever perceived it the latter way. Harrah made magic innocuous and palatable for humans because she represented it with a pleasant seraphic face, gentle round amber eyes, and a voice that was saccharine sweet. Magic wasn't malicious because Harrah was the nonthreatening face of it.

And if they happened to see another side of it, she made sure she fixed the situation. She was good at her job. I didn't trust her and she made me nervous. Standing barely over five three, with a narrow frame and her long brown hair pulled back in a neat, low ponytail, she was dressed in a simple dark suit as though she was ready to give a press conference as soon as this ordeal was over.

Grabbing my sai that I'd had to drop to handle the woman, I ran, trying to trace the magic, feeling large amounts of it coming from the street—the source. Three figures that I couldn't make out. They saw me as soon as I turned the corner and retreated. I ran through the street cutting through the alleyways when I could, trying to cut them off and catch them. As I moved around a corner, I got a better glimpse at them. The moment I came into their line of sight, they changed direction. I needed to stop them. I could use magic but not out in the open, in front of strangers— especially with Harrah so close. I doubted she was the under-standing type, especially after witnessing her give the order to assassinate someone and guarantee she would make the optics work, which she did.

I pushed myself harder, panting, the magic still wafting in the air, but they were too distracted trying to get away from me to be as effective as they had been before when they'd wreaked havoc on the small area. I was just inches from them when they turned in unison, and I focused on their eyes: an odd chartreuse color. Their features were similar, perhaps they were triplets. They moved as a unit and directed their magic at me, hitting me before I could form a ward. I went back but managed to plant one of my sai in the grass to stabi-lize me as I was thrashed with stronger magic. By the time I recovered they were gone.

I rested back on the ground, closing my eyes to block out the sun as the magic still rebounded around and in me. I waited until it settled and was nothing more than an annoying ache. My hands were sore from gripping the sai too tightly. I was about to get up, when Gareth hovered over me.

"Do you need help? I know how you hate to be damseled. I don't want to pull out my white knight shtick if I don't have to," he said, amusement quickly settling over his features as he knelt down next to me.

"I'm fine," I said, rolling to my feet. "Just a reminder not to tangle with the deadly mage triplets alone, or whatever they were. Is everything contained?" I brushed the dust off me. Magic still wafted through the air, strong and potent. I frowned at it, hating the weighted feel of residual stygian magic that they had left behind.

I studied Gareth, a scowl etched over his features, his nostrils flaring. His eyes lowered as he studied the area. "Did you get a good look at them?" he asked as he continued to scan the area. If by chance I had forgotten he was a predator, it was abundantly clear at the moment. Fear and apprehension rose in me and I gripped my sai tighter. I assumed he sensed the change in my mood because he took a step back and made an attempt to relax his frown. His effort at a smile failed. His lips were now pulled into a taut line. "Describe them."

"Three, two men and a woman. The men were tall, a little over six feet, thin—very lanky in build. One was a little broader and a little heavier than the other, maybe by ten pounds, and his hair longer slightly. The broader one had a scar—"

"Left cheek, just below the eye," Gareth offered. "The woman: was she about five eight, sandy hair like theirs?"

I nodded. And he continued, "Odd-looking eyes, green, nearly fluorescent, and their magic feels like a strong wind. And dark. Deadly—that's the way mages describe them."

"You've met them before?"

"I gave him the scar." He pulled out his phone, punched in

one number, and then turned and started walking and talking. He walked so fast that I was at a slow jog trying to catch up with him. There were very few words that I caught, but I didn't need to hear the whole conversation to get the gist of it. The havoc triplets had escaped. I assumed from the Haven, the supernatural prison. Not only was it surrounded by enough magical flowering vines climbing up the wall to sedate anyone if they tried to escape out of a window, there were sigils and runes on many of the rooms to restrict magic.

Gareth leaned against his car, waiting for me, assessing the area. Usually a clean and pristine area, it was now in a state of disorder and disarray with extensive property damage: shattered glass from broken windows and bottles littered the streets, clothes were scattered over the sidewalk, the doors of several stores were barely holding on by their hinges. Trails of blood covered the cement, food was everywhere. It was a chaotic mess, and as ambulances took away people who'd suffered more than just a minor cut or bruise, Harrah stood in the middle of it, her face flushed.

Behind her soft amber eyes I could see the PR representative's mind working. This would have to be handled, reduced to something that could be explained away by banality rather than the abuse of powerful ominous magic.

Find them, she mouthed. Gareth responded with a simple nod.

"Who are they and how did they escape from the Haven?" I asked as I dropped into the passenger seat after he'd gotten into the car.

"They didn't escape from the Haven."

He sighed and considered my question for a while. I thought he'd known the answer all along, but it seemed like he was trying to decide if he should tell me or not. When he finally spoke, it was slow and restrained as he chose his words carefully. "Not all people who are imprisoned are in

30

the Haven. If we suspect they can escape and are a big enough danger, we send them somewhere else, to Barathrum." His voice was low, grave.

My Latin was rudimentary, but as a magic user I knew the basics. They were housed in a place whose name was Latin for *hell*. How bad were the terrible triplets that the Haven wasn't even enough for them and they'd been sentenced to such a place?

"Technically it's not hell. We don't know what that is. It's a prison in a veil that we use. It's very strong but requires a lot of manpower to open and to keep closed—and apparently the use of darker magic. Opening it is so difficult that it's the last resort of use. But for the Maxwells we felt it was necessary. They are chaos mages."

"Okay, is that a real thing or did you just not want to call them the Terrible Triplets, because I think it has a nice ring to it."

His mood was too dour to be lifted with my lame attempt at a joke. "They are very real. As real as the Legacy and the Vertu. Mages—stronger than even high-level mages. It's not them performing dark magic—they *are* it. There are a few of them; most chose not to do magic and made an agreement with the Council to be ironed so that they couldn't. They weren't forced to do it, they agreed on their own. I can't perform magic, I know very little about the need to use it all the time, but apparently, that is true for some."

"Not really. I can and I don't have a desire."

"Why?"

"Because I can die if I do." It felt odd to admit it to him. Gareth moved his hand closest to me off the console of the car and then rested it on my leg. I didn't ask him to move it but I was very aware of it.

"I think that something can be worked out for you. I need to discuss it with the Magic Council."

"Don't do that!" I blurted.

He looked surprised. "Why?"

I just couldn't explain why. My kind were responsible for the Cleanse, how could they trust me? It didn't help my case that when I'd had the chance to disclose it and possibly work out an arrangement, I hadn't. I wasn't in a good position to expect them to trust me.

"Just not now."

"If it's a trust issue, just agree to be braced with iron for a while. We can make it as small as we need to and nearly undetectable."

"Iron doesn't affect my magic."

"I know. We need iridium. We don't need to totally disable your magic, just weaken it enough so that if things get out of hand, we have a fighting chance of subduing you if we need to."

Subdue. I really hated that word. And the amount of iridium they would need me to wear to subdue me would leave me unable to function in general. I didn't tell him that. I just didn't want him to know everything about me if he didn't already know it.

"For now, will you just keep this between us?"

Moments stretched, he spent more time glancing at me than looking at the road. The indigo shifter ring seemed darker and more defined as his eyes constricted to look at me. The tension and concern he'd had about the Maxwells seemed to now be directed at me. I'd never doubted that Gareth had gotten his position because he was as assiduous as he was dangerous, and at the moment, those qualities weren't in my favor.

"I'm not hiding anything," I offered.

"I didn't say you were" was his terse response as we pulled up in front of the Guild. I kept my sai in hand. I wasn't sure why it comforted me more to have them with me with Gareth, but it did.

"This requires my attention. We can finish our conversation later. I will pick you up at eight."

He said it with such command that for a brief moment I felt like I couldn't say no, and I didn't. It wasn't until I was several feet from my car that I stopped. *Wait a minute. He didn't even ask?*

"I have plans tonight. I can meet with you tomorrow in the morning."

He stopped, amused. "Plans? Well, you'll have to change them. Tell *him*?" He waited for me to confirm—I didn't. He relaxed into his smile; swathed in arrogance that seemed to be uniquely his, he chuckled. "Well, I'm confident that you will make the right choice about who you'd rather spend time with. Me, the head of the Supernatural Guild and member of the Magic Council who really has a lot of important things he needs to discuss with you, or some random."

"That sounds a lot like blackmail."

The devilish grin didn't falter as he turned and headed toward the door. "It's not blackmail, it's just strategic bargaining."

Hmm. Strategic bargaining sounds a lot like blackmail.

CHAPTER 2

*W*hen I arrived at work Kalen's face contorted into a look of utter derision and disgust as he gave me an assessing look. We didn't look like we were going to the same job. He was dressed in a pair of blue slacks, a white shirt, and a dark gray jacket that contrasted with his blond hair. The look of derision made his exceptionally regal demeanor haughtier as he turned his hooked nose on me.

"I really must implement a dress code. Maybe that will stop you from coming to work like this." He made a dramatic openhanded gesture over my attire.

"Maybe, I'll stop coming period if the work environment keeps being so hostile. It's work, not a runway," I responded, mocking his look of disdain. I turned my lips up at him. "Perhaps I don't want to work with such a snob."

He scoffed. "Snob. I don't think so." I was about to get the mantra. The long soliloquy about him denying his inheritance in favor of the struggle of the common man starting up a business. He didn't seem to grasp the concept that the "common man" never used that term. And when I pointed that out, I had to listen to his perceived struggle that was nothing more than the out-of-touch rantings of a trust fund kid. But I listened, with a placid smile, keeping one-fifth of my opinions to myself while I attempted to keep my eyes from rolling out of my head.

In the middle of his monologue, someone knocked on the door. The first thing we saw was thick coils of blue and black ombré hair and then a familiar face peeked in.

"Hi," Blu said as she entered the room.

"Wow, now that's what I'm talking about." And once again I was treated to another one of Kalen's looks as his gaze rolled over my pink Converses and up to my dark blue jeans that had a few rips at the thigh but actually looked more on trend as opposed to jeans that were on their last legs. Then it darted to my plaid button-down that was rolled up to midforearm. He even glanced at my neck and ears, which were jewelry-less, in his eyes the ultimate fashion sin. Last year for Christmas he'd given me a pair of earrings and a locket, which I'd worn for a couple of weeks but eventually stopped. If he'd noticed, he hadn't commented.

Blu, on the other hand, looked like she was late for the catwalk. "Her jeans are ripped, too," I pointed out with a smirk. And they were. Fitted black jeans hugged her curves. White tank top, adorned by a long multicolored necklace that had a hint of color that matched her burgundy and black jacket. And even I had to admire her boots. Each time I'd met her, she was dressed in a unique and fashionable outfit. I was mostly indifferent to it, but Kalen was clearly impressed with her. His smile widened as she stepped closer.

"Ah," he said as he brushed his hand over the jacket and then tapped on her bracelets. "I do believe we have a fan of Betsey Johnson."

She looked down at his hand, seemingly unaffected by his invasion of her personal space, something about Kalen that most people found off-putting. The sharply defined features, wide supple looks, and gentle silver eyes that accompanied his aristocratic appearance afforded him more leniency than the average person. Blu seemed flattered by his appreciation.

"No, a local designer. A friend that I went to high school with. He's having a show next week, you should go." And as Kalen took lithe, measured steps around her, taking in her whole appearance, he nodded at her suggestion. I ignored the conversation as they began to speak a language that I didn't understand—fashionista. A language I adamantly refused to learn despite Kalen's constant insistence.

I'd zoned out, focusing on the terrible triplets and the destruction that lay in their wake. Everything that had happened lately I linked to the Vertu—to Conner. If the wind felt a little coarse, I attributed it to him even though I wasn't sure whether he could control the weather. Most of my life I'd lived thinking that the Legacy had this omnipotent power —that we were all-powerful—but the fabric of that reality had been torn so easily once I'd found out about the existence of the Vertu. Legacy paled in comparison to them. And Conner wanted to do the Cleanse over, to get rid of all the other supernaturals and have a world of just humans, Vertu, and Legacy. There were a few humans that agreed with his draconian views—I believed they were victims of blissful ignorance. And some of them were part of Humans First.

Blu obviously didn't have the undying love for fashion that would lead her to discuss it for hours on end. Eventually she redirected him back to the purpose of the visit.

"The Hearth Stone, what is your asking price?" She hadn't wasted any time coming to purchase it once I'd told her that we had acquired one. It was a powerful stone giving witches the ability to use ancestral magic.

Kalen went to one of the storage cabinets and pulled it out and extended it to her. She examined it, and the wistful look and desire she evidenced weren't going to work to her advantage if she planned to negotiate. She wanted it and there wasn't any doubt. Of the various stones that we'd encountered in our job, this one was a deep granite color, purer than the others, which were often a muted gray. And it was noticeably heavier. Something Blu seemed to notice as well, which only seemed to spur her desire. It shadowed her pleasant features and I saw something in her that I hadn't before—a lust for power. It was the first time that I'd questioned Blu and her intentions, but I always questioned the motives behind enhanced power. Some people believed that increased power led to the desire for more of it. It was the undoing of my kind.

I marked my concerns as paranoia because Kalen didn't seem to possess any, and he was often just as cautious as I was.

"How much?" she asked, her deep brown eyes fixed on the stone. She pulled them away to meet our gazes for a moment before directing her attention back to it. The stone looked innocuous, but I'd learned over the years that sometimes those were the most dangerous things. Until this moment, I hadn't realized how strong she was. I'd first met her in the company of Gareth, and perhaps his intensity had masked her power. I should have expected her to be a force to be reckoned with—after all, Gareth had trusted her to retrieve memories that were magically stolen when I was set up for murder. And now with the magic wafting off Blu joining that which Kalen gave off, I found myself feeling stifled by the strong waves of it that inundated the room.

I had a moment of pause as I considered how dangerous the Hearth Stone could be in the hands of someone as powerful as Blu.

Kalen handed her an invoice.

She frowned. "I didn't expect it to be that much," she admitted in a low voice.

"I'm sorry." I inched toward her, ready to take the stone back. Before I could, Kalen stepped closer to her.

"How about we make a deal?" He suggested an amount a third less than the asking price. "In addition, you'll have to get me into that designer's show, and I would like you to make us ten protection amulets." Protection amulets were little crystals of unimpressive magic that the witches sold to humans for an exorbitant price. They were more flash and lovely impressive colors than anything else. But they sold well. They weren't something we typically carried, but I doubted we'd have any problem selling them.

She quickly accepted the offer, handing over the money and agreeing to bring the amulets in a week. She thanked him, taking his hand in one of hers and covering it with the other. It lasted longer than I expected and seemed to cross the line of professionalism rather quickly.

"I still want the agreed-upon thirty percent of the initial value of the stone. I didn't agree to give her the 'pretty fashionista' discount," I said as the door closed behind her.

"You're awfully young to be so cantankerous."

"*Cantankerous.* What happened to tenacious? Assertive? Snarky? Those are all the things you said you loved about me." I flashed him a coy grin.

"That was the honeymoon period. Now you're just my cantankerous employee with horrible taste in clothing." He grinned and his silver eyes brightened, sparkling with a hint of mischief before he lifted his finger.

"You can change my clothes but then you can be the one going through"—I stopped, trying to remember the client's name—"Ms. Neal's barn and I'll just stand back and be delicate and pretty in my new fancy clothes."

His smile flicked into a taut line. "I remember when you were fun and not so mouthy."

"That was the honeymoon," I shot back.

He grabbed his keys and headed out the door, leaving me to lock up. I did it quickly and followed him out. He went to the Infiniti QX80 parked in front of the shop. Nothing about the luxury SUV indicated that we were glorified junk collectors.

Ms. Neal's home, or rather her late grandfather's, was like most of the farmhouses we were invited to. Big white ranch homes. Wide porch with stairs that were a couple of inches higher than average and two rocking chairs in the front. A long stretch of dirt and gravel that led to two locked barns. One I assumed was for farmwork and the other for storage. Ms. Neal met us at the top of the long driveway. Her reddish-brown hair entwined into a braid that draped over her shoulder, and her glasses overpowered her narrow face. As she walked up to the SUV, her petite frame seemed smaller.

When she spoke, it was a direct contrast to her appearance: deep and forceful. "I'm glad to meet you two." She extended her hand. "I don't have much time as I indicated over the phone. You are free to have anything in there, I just ask for three items."

"Yes, about that," Kalen said, pulling out his tablet, "I need you to be specific about the items. When we have exemptions, I like it to be specific. I wouldn't want you to think we were taking advantage of you, so everything needs to be aboveboard and spelled out."

I doubted if anyone had ever gotten anything over on her, but it was the same spiel that he gave to everyone. We'd learned from experience that we'd do all the dirty work—or rather I would—pulling out all their crap, and when they saw something they thought was valuable, it always seemed to be one of the unspecified items they wanted to keep. It might have started off as a weathered book that had sentimental value or an antique ring but quickly turned into a large list of must-haves.

"Yes. Yes, of course." But it took her a while to answer. Each time I tried to hold her gaze, she'd glance away after only a minute. Something lurked behind her eyes. I couldn't figure out if it was the behavior of a grieving grandchild or something more ominous.

"What are the items?" Kalen pushed, because she'd started walking toward the barn without giving an answer.

Nice try. We've done this before.

"A knife—it's an antique and has been in the family for a long time. There should be a saddle in there I would like to keep, and a stone."

Kalen sensed it before I did. She was being intentionally vague. "What type of stone?"

"Just a gray-white one."

Seriously lady, that's what you're going with? A gray stone. No specifics. Fine, I'll bring you a gray stone. I had every intention of picking up a rock in the gravel and handing it to her.

"Gray and white stone. Anything more specific?" Kalen asked, his eyes narrowed on her, and I could feel the prick of magic coming off him. He wanted to compel her to truth, but it was against the law without her permission. It was really hard to get consent for something like that. Essentially you're telling a person: *Hey, I suspect you're lying your ass off—and wouldn't know the truth if it throat punched you—can I do a spell on you to fix that?*

Kalen's face relaxed, the gentle smile bloomed, and when he spoke it was silky and melodious. He couldn't use magic, but he had a few tricks that didn't have anything to do with it. He was charming—very charming when he needed to be, but unfortunately, he felt it was a waste of good talent to use it on me. I got eight-a.m. before-his-coffee-and-bagel Kalen. Except he was eight-a.m. Kalen all day with me.

He stepped closer. "Sometimes our memories fail us—especially at times like this. I can help you give a better description."

Liar, liar. Now let him do magic to get it out of you.

She pulled off her glasses, her eyes narrowed on him. "What are you?"

Giving her a clipped half-smile, he said, "Fae."

"You're not going to do any magic on me. Either you just mark on your little computer there that it's a gray and white stone, or leave."

You are so getting a rock. But curiosity had us both planted there. We'd done this long enough and I suspected the stone was probably one of the few things that needed to be confiscated. The Magic Council, the group who had judiciary power over the supernaturals and whom I'd met a couple of weeks ago during the time I was framed for murder, didn't allow certain magical objects to be in the possession of anyone in the human or magical community. I was pretty sure this was one of them. And no one could pretend they didn't know what they were because they were listed on the Magic Council's website and that of each governmental department in all states. Humans and supernaturals were expected to follow the rules.

Since the Cleanse, the world and magic were different. The supernaturals had been forced out of the closet, and to maintain an alliance with the humans, they safeguarded them against anything that could be considered dangerous to humans and supernaturals alike. There were few things on the list—but I bet "gray and white stone" was on it.

Kalen scribbled something on the tablet and had her sign it. While they were doing that, I grabbed my sai out of the SUV. We could never be too cautious. We walked toward the barn, and I scanned the area looking for a pretty rock, which I planned to give to Ms. Neal. In his hand, Kalen dangled the keys that she had given up a little too easily. As we continued up the long path to the barn nearly thirty feet away, Kalen cursed at the gravel that scuffed up his shoes and dust that kicked up on his pant legs. Magic— potent and noxious—wafted out of the barn. He stopped midstep.

"She lied to us," he stated as we inched closer.

"At any point, did you think that she was telling the truth?" I asked. I wasn't sure how sensitive he was to different forms of magic. You had to have been exposed to a specific magic at some point to be able to identify it. As far as Kalen knew, I was just human. It felt like a betrayal of our odd and dysfunctional relationship, and the guilt had gnawed at me for days once I'd found out Gareth knew I wasn't. Kalen was more than my boss; I considered him my friend despite his penchant for making me his Midwest Barbie and dressing me up and putting me in a playhouse. But being a Legacy wasn't something I had the option of being indiscreet about. I couldn't just decide it wasn't a big deal and tell everyone. Because it was a big deal. It was dangerous enough that Savannah knew. My mother's best friend had been killed because she'd known our secret, and I hated that now I'd put Savannah at risk. I didn't want to endanger Kalen, too. The fewer people who knew the better. Once again, I considered wiping Gareth's mind.

I thought about our conversation earlier today, he considered me innocuous. I couldn't help but chuckle to myself. My kind was a lot of things, but harmless wasn't one of them. And shifters hated us the most because our magic was the only one that could affect them. Being immune to magic afforded a level of uncontested sangfroid that added to the narcissism often seen in shifters. Most of them were so convinced of their own impermeability that they had god complexes.

"So, what do you think is in there?"

"I'm sure it's not just a stone," I said, bringing my sai up and inching closer to the barn. I leaned in, I heard noise: heavy breathing. Panting? No, snorting? It definitely wasn't human. *Ms. Neal, I am going to give you the ugliest stone ever.*

The door was starting to bend in—she wasn't locking people out, she was locking something in and we were about to release it. I looked back at the porch where we'd parted ways with Ms. Neal and she didn't even have the good manners to look surprised by our findings. Instead her arms curled, hugging her body.

"What's in here?"

"I don't know," she said.

"Is she telling the truth?" I asked Kalen in a low voice.

"Fae, not shapeshifter, remember? I can compel the truth, I can't detect it. I bet you wish your boyfriend was here now."

"Really? *Boyfriend.* The man has threatened to jail me more than once and he's rather vain. Hmm. Being around him is almost like being at work," I teased. I needed to lighten the mood. Kalen looked nervous, and the fact that he hadn't backed out of the job, which we had done in the past, meant there was something in there that he thought was worth the risk. He opened the lock, and we slid back the thick board that secured the door. The sound of thrashing became louder, and I kind of wished Gareth was there. He was a monstrosity of an animal, and what was on the other side of the door was possibly one, too.

Kalen snatched open the door. Orange glowing eyes were the first thing I saw before it charged. I wasn't sure what it was: hellhound? No, they were extinct. A minotaur. He started out on four limbs but shifted to standing. Massive arms the size of tree trunks swung out at me. I dodged him

43

and rolled to my side, jabbing the butt of the sai into his arm. A warning. One that he didn't take. Keeping one arm at his side he stretched out and opened his other hand. Claws extended. He swiped at me, attacking with just one hand while he used the other to hold on to a white and gray ball. Not a stone, definitely not a stone. And I was pretty sure Ms. Neal knew it, too.

I sank the sai into his side and used the other to block his strike. He was just about to hit me with the stone, when Kalen grabbed his arm. As Kalen struggled to keep the hand immobile, I yanked out the sai, sidestepped the mangled-looking minotaur, grabbed the stone from his hand, and started out the barn door. Kalen and I slipped out and slammed the door just moments before he hit it. We secured it with the wood and pressed our backs against it. The barrier seemed as though it was going to hold when we stepped away.

"Great, you have the stone," she said, approaching us slowly. Her attention was split between us and the door that kept buckling as the trapped minotaur rammed against it.

I knew the look Kalen gave her. It usually came right before a tongue-lashing. His eyes had narrowed, his parchment coloring became an odd shade of red, and his jaws were clenched painfully tight. She was going to get more than a tongue-lashing; he was going to excoriate her. It was going to be painful to watch, like a collision where you wondered if there were any survivors. Magic came off him like a storm.

"Stone," he said, his voice cold, hard. "I'll give you a stone, you lying—"

"Ms. Neal, do you know what this is?" I asked, stepping forward to meet her. I pressed my hand lightly into Kalen's chest, giving him just a little nudge back. He retreated, probably just as concerned by his fury as I was. Fae had many magical gifts, but they were strongest at cognitive manipulation. It seemed like an innocuous talent, but affecting someone's mood and mind wasn't by any means harmless. As angry as Kalen was, I wasn't sure what laws he would have broken to retaliate.

"What do you know about this?"

"It's a family heirloom" was all she offered.

"What is it?"

"A Recludo Stone," Kalen supplied.

He made a sound and I looked back; his eyes had widened. I didn't know what a Recludo Stone was, but he obviously did.

"It opens veils—strong ones," he said in a cool, level voice. I could tell he was trying to get a handle on his anger.

"Did she use it?" When he shrugged I turned to ask her, "Can you do magic?"

"No," she said.

None of it made sense. "So your grandfather left you the stone, you went into the barn, and then what happened after that?"

"I activated it by saying 'reveal,' and that thing showed up. It took the stone from me and I ran out and called you all to get the rest of the things." Her voice was low and devoid of any emotions, just matter-of-fact. As if it was just another day of opening portals and releasing half-bull monsters into the world was no big thing. "The Recludo Stone, please," she said, drawing her shoulders back and giving me the same dismissive, haughty look she'd given us earlier.

Kalen, get her. I was ready to sic Kalen on her. No one could give a verbal smackdown like Kalen, and for the first time, I really wanted him to. I'd gain a lot of pleasure watching it. But we didn't have the time.

"I don't care if you say pretty please. This thing is dangerous. You can't perform magic, yet you were able to get this to work."

"Stone," she asserted. "We have an agreement."

Slapping her silly seemed like the next logical thing to do and the palm of my hand was itching to do it so I held the stone tighter and pulled it closer to my side.

"That was our agreement," she said.

"Of course." I reached down, grabbed a few loose rocks off the ground, and then put them in her hand. "Here you go." And then I started toward the SUV.

Hmm. I don't often see that shade of red. She looks like an angry tomato.

"We had an agreement!"

"Well, you didn't see our 'if we get attacked by a minotaur during the job' clause, which voids the contract. Check it, I'm sure it's in there," Kalen coolly offered as he walked past her to catch up to me.

"We need to call the Supernatural Guild," I said, putting my sai in the SUV and taking out my phone. But Kalen had beat me to it and was on the phone with them.

"Your boyfriend and his crew should be here soon."

"He's not my boyfriend!" I snapped.

"Okay, then what are you two calling each other?"

"Nothing—we aren't anything. It's complicated, but we aren't dating."

"Complicated. Hmm. Is that what the kids are calling it," he teased as we leaned against the SUV, grinning at Ms. Neal, who had taken time away from giving us dirty looks to turn around and head for the house.

"What are we going to do with the Recludo Stone?" I asked.

"We can't keep it. It's too dangerous. Anyone can activate it, not just magical beings. I'm not sure what the hell type of supernatural that thing is—maybe a shapeshifter, although I haven't seen one like it before. But it didn't respond to my magic. Your boyfriend's here," he added when three Supernatural Guild officers pulled up, but Gareth wasn't with them.

"Did you and Mr. Complicated have a problem?"

"I don't know." It bothered me that Gareth wasn't with them, and it bothered me even more that I cared.

"What's the problem?" said one of the officers. Definitely a shifter, more than likely a bear given his broad build and thick muscles that wrapped around his body and couldn't be hidden by what the Guild seemed to think was an actual uniform, t-shirt and jeans. His thick beard and square features just added to the bear vibe. His voice was just as coarse as his features as he questioned us. As they passed us, I tried to get a look at the whole group that had arrived. It was still difficult to determine the different supernaturals. Shapeshifters were a little easier; their movements were graceful but aggressive, truly predacious. There were always exceptions, but SG shifters often looked like they were going to get a fine if they dared to smile. Magic engulfed the air, mingled together, and became indecipherable. I didn't know if it was a witch, fae, or mage moving past me.

Kalen inched closer to the barn, and Ms. Neal stepped out only to glare at me a few more times before going back into her home. A bull-monster was trapped in her barn and apparently, she couldn't be bothered to see what was going on. She only troubled herself with having a glaring contest with me whenever the mood struck her.

Eight officers from the SG surrounded the barn, the three shifters in front, and when they opened it, the creature charged out. I looked away just as it seemingly unhinged its jaw to take out a chunk of one of the officers and then went on to devour him. *Shit.*

Kalen and I looked at each other thinking the same thing: that could have been us. And then the monster bull-creature shifted into a massive creature, wings sprouting from his back, teeth elongating and extending past his lower jaw. He pounded toward another officer. His massive body careened into an SG shifter, sending him several hundred yards away and smashing into the side of the house, denting it. The air clouded with magic as the SG officers wielded spell after spell and tossed defensive magic in his path, but nothing stopped him.

I ran to the car, grabbed my sai, and ignored Kalen commanding me to stop. There wasn't any way I could let more people die. How had we dodged this thing? Had he not had the energy to change before devouring the shifter? As I ran around the house, trying to get to the creature from the back without him catching sight of me, I heard shots fired. He stumbled back but only slowed down, not stopping. As he reared up, I jumped on his back, shoving my sai into it. His sudden movement caused me to miss my target—the spine. Howling out in pain, he bucked, trying to throw me off. I held on to the sai embedded in him but wasn't able to stay steady enough to strike again.

Twisting wildly, he leapt and I had just a fraction of a second to jump off, leaving the sai in him as he thrust himself onto his back. I crashed to the ground, landing on my back, gravel biting into my skin. He started to recover, and I rolled over in time to miss one hooved foot that smashed next to me. I didn't get the full brunt of the impact of another one, but he swiped me. I screamed out in pain and kept rolling, to try to miss each thrash of his feet as he attempted to stomp me.

A bear pounded past me and careened into him, enough of an impact to send him back a couple of feet but not to disable him. Moving to my feet fast I waited, and when the bear crashed into him again, he angled enough for me to pull out the sai. They weren't destroyed. Any other weapon probably would have been, but my kind were good at two things:

making great weapons of destruction and committing destruction. They were plunged in him deep and still hadn't stopped him. I wanted to go into the house and pull Ms. Neal out by her hair and make her watch the mess she'd caused.

Weapons in hands, I prepared for an opportunity to move on the thing again. I didn't have a lot of options. This was a creature like no other. If he had been a shifter, he wouldn't have been immune to magic with the sai embedded in him. I waited for the bear, whose fur was matted to his body with blood, to move. But he'd lost the grace and vigor he had once possessed. His movement was slower and lumbering. He wasn't going to last. There wasn't any way I could get to the creature now without the use of magic. *Fuck.* I was going to have to use magic in front of a group of Supernatural Guild agents.

I allowed the magic to unfurl in me, the warmth of it spreading through my body. Once dormant, it now washed over me, making my skin prickle. My fingers extended as the magic wrapped around my arm, inching toward my fingers, and just as I was about to blast the thing with it, a feline moving so fast that the wind that came off him shifted me to the side nearly threw me off-balance. Gareth. The massive animal rounded the bull creature. He lunged at the cave lion, who dodged him and swiftly went behind him, clawing his way up the minotaur's back. Using his claws like knives, he dug into the thing until he was close enough to take a chunk out of his neck, taking out the spine. The monster collapsed to the ground.

Kalen watched wide-eyed with a mixture of interest and disgust as the SG cleaned up the remains of the minotaur and Gareth walked toward him in human form, unapologetic and unashamed of his nudity. He went to his car and grabbed clothes and quickly dressed, using a towel to wipe off some of the blood.

Gareth looked first at me; then Ms. Neal, who had probably only come outside to tell us to keep the noise down; and finally Kalen. Then back at his men, who had started clearing out everything from the barn.

"Do we have everything or is there more?" Gareth asked, his stormy eyes fixed on me.

Kalen hesitated. He wasn't irresponsible, but he planned to give the stone to the Magic Council; they'd pay us well for giving it to them. If the SG confiscated it, we probably wouldn't collect a fee.

Gareth's voice hardened and dropped to a low growl. I thought cats purred. "Mr. Noble, do we have everything?" He'd addressed Kalen by his last name.

There was another beat of silence before Kalen finally spoke. "The Recludo Stone is in the back of the car."

"That's not his," Ms. Neal barked. "It's mine."

Gareth's lips curled into a snarl. "Good. Please arrest her," he told one of the agents. "Mr. Noble and Ms. Michaels, if you two don't want the same fate, it will be wise for you to come to the SG for questioning. I expect to see you two at"—he glanced at the time on the dashboard of his car—"four fifteen."

He stopped and turned, his lips kinked into a smile. "That's four fifteen, Ms. Michaels. Not four sixteen, four seventeen, or any other time you would like to pick to make your defiant little point."

Kitty's in a bad mood.

I considered pointing that out when he crossed his arms, nearly daring a response other than agreement. Under both Kalen's and Gareth's cool stares, I mastered my snarky response and said, "Yes, sir." Or maybe I said, "Yes, jackass." No, it was sir, the jackass part I said in my head.

Kalen hadn't spoken to me since we had gotten in the car. And the silence continued; cold, unforgiving, uncomfortable silence. Which was fine because I was going to need a suitcase for the guilt trip he was going to take me on when he finally did speak. I really didn't need to feel more guilt than I already did about not telling him what I was. The seam of my life seemed to be wearing and as I thought about how close I was to exposing myself to the Supernatural Guild, I inhaled a breath so ragged it made my chest hurt.

As we cruised down the street Kalen went slower than usual, choosing scathing dirty looks over speed. When he finally spoke, his tone was low, gentle, and paper thin. "I've worked with you for a long time," he started. "I consider us friends. But I don't think I really know you. I've always considered you snarky"—then he gave me a once-over —"with a great work ethic and questionable fashion sense. A woman who I absolutely adore. But people who fight like you have a past. I want to know your past."

Damn. Damn. Damn. I swallowed hard. "Guess you haven't seen *The Avengers*, the Black Widow is so kickass. And, come on, *Underworld*, what about Selene? And Elektra?"

He smiled, forced, but at least it helped to lift the heaviness that was getting too hard to carry. "Oh come on, they all had tragic tales."

I knew that. And I figured I was about to hear about each one of them in grueling detail. It wasn't long before I started to regret giving my King of Useless Information an opening to regale me with his long-winded tales while locked in a car. I had a well-practiced distraction plan for the office. I pulled up Neiman Marcus and the season's hot list on my computer, and while he was beguiled by whatever was captivating about cotton-blend shirts, ties, and shoes that pretty much all looked alike, I'd go do some work.

My KUI was winding up to tell me about another superhero franchise just as we pulled up in front of the Supernatural Guild. Before I could get out, he touched my arm. "I'm not that easily distracted. I won't push you, but I want you to know you can trust me."

I would have preferred him to blather on about the evolution of the board game, oddly something he knew a great deal about, than have him take me on a stroll down Guilt Boulevard. Looking into his gentle, entreating eyes made the betrayal feel worse. He deserved the truth—but it was too hard. It had been instilled in me for years that my life and that of others depended on me keeping this secret. I tried to determine which was worse, the harrowing look of sadness or the wilted sorrow that lingered over his words. And things were made worse when I realized we were in front of the SG building. It was a reminder of my last appearance before the Magical Council, and the towering threat that I might find myself in front of them again if they ever discovered who I really was.

"I know I can trust you. I need you to trust that if I could tell you, I would."

He opened his mouth to say something but decided against it. "Okay, fine. Let's go see your boyfriend."

"Really, still?"

"You've seen him naked—he's your boyfriend."

"Okay, by that logic, since I once went through Forest Township and saw the naked butts of three men crossing the street, I should really get their names because they're going to be my boyfriends. And I saw one shifter's happy parts—I guess he's my husband."

"I swear you have to be making this up. I drive through there every day and I don't see anything."

"Why are you driving by there every day? You live in the opposite direction."

"Can't a person have a hobby?" Responding to my look of disgust, he added, "Don't judge me. I'm sightseeing."

"Sightseeing? Is that what they're calling it?" I joked and got out of the car. He quickly followed and moved around the car, blocking my advance. He frowned, giving me another scathing look, his lips contorted into something that was a cross between a frown and a miscreant grin. I'd been able to wipe off some of the blood earlier, but I'd seen better days and hadn't had a chance to look in a mirror.

He tilted his head, the frown deepened, and then he reached up to touch my hair. I blocked his hand. He tried again with the other. I blocked it again. "For someone concerned about being late, you're wasting a lot of time trying to fix me. Stop." Kalen had taken Gareth's command to be on time a little more seriously than I did. To me, it was just a strongly worded suggestion.

It didn't work. He tugged at my shirt until it was straightened to his liking and recuffed the sleeves. I had tolerated it as long as I could. I hated being tugged, poked, and fixed by him. "Stop fixing me. I look fine. We are just going to give a statement, I assure you we don't get points for looking good doing it."

I moved back several feet and glared at the scowl that had become a fixture on his face. "Well, at least you're pretty." And then he spun around and started to walk away.

"You know, there are other people who will give me a job."

"Of course, there has to be a line out the door of employers looking for a smart-mouth, bossy malcontent with an obsession for plaid and Converses. Tell me, where do I sign up for another?" He laughed as he opened the door for me.

53

Beth was sitting to the side reading a book, while Gareth's nephew sat at the reception desk. Once again, he seemed more interested in his phone than anything else. "Who are you here to see?"

"Your uncle," I offered.

Avery looked at Kalen, then me, then back at Kalen. "Just a minute." He made a phone call and then asked us to take a seat. After a few minutes three other people came down with Gareth: Harrah and two men that I didn't recognize. One was dressed casually and the other wore a tailored suit. Gareth was dressed in a simple button-down and slacks, hair clean and not a single sign of ripping apart a bull-monster less than an hour ago. I joked about his office being an apartment but I wondered if he had a shower and changing area in the oversized room.

Gareth spoke in a deep, professional voice as he addressed Kalen. "Mr. Noble, please come with us." Kalen stood. This was more than us giving an official statement. Why was Harrah present? I tried not to panic; Kalen was rather indifferent about it. He stood in silence, and the pleasant smile he'd had on his face didn't waver as he approached them. I knew I was supposed to stay seated and wait but I couldn't. I stood and inched closer to them.

Gareth turned; his blue eyes were hard as they fixed on me. "Ms. Michaels, we will be meeting with you next. Please have a seat." I didn't immediately respond as I tried to read Kalen, a more difficult task than it usually was. Was he concerned, scared, as confused as I was? Maybe if Harrah wasn't involved, I wouldn't have been worried. But this was a woman who'd commanded that someone be killed so that he wasn't alive to undermine the optics of the situation. She would do whatever was necessary to maintain the symbiotic relationship between humans and supernaturals.

I took several deep breaths, but that didn't calm me down

and apparently it was enough to distract Avery from his phone. He nudged Beth and she looked in my direction. I felt the magic coursing through the air, the subtle variations of its existence.

"Don't," I said firmly with enough edge to my tone that she sat up, her eyes narrowing on me before she relaxed back into her position. I didn't want to be calm because it bred complacency. I needed to be alert and aware of what was happening.

Kalen had only been gone ten minutes but it seemed like longer and sitting just wasn't an option. I paced the length of the long room, feeling Avery's eyes on me.

"Who makes you nervous, my uncle or the suit?"

Harrah. But I didn't say it because, like everyone who dealt with her, Avery probably didn't see her as the face of fear.

"The suit," I lied.

One sweeping look let me know he wasn't buying it. Shapeshifters. Lying to them was rather useless. I still didn't believe that they could smell a lie. Really, what would it smell like—god-awful black licorice? But their acute senses made them adept at detecting variations in physiological signs: blood pressure, heart rate, eye blinks, and breath sound. They all changed when a person lied—even in me, and I'd been lying about who I was most of my life.

"You don't have to worry about the suit," he said. Then he returned his attention back to his phone.

"What about your uncle?"

He shrugged, his thumbs dancing over the keys. "It depends if he considers you a danger or not and what side of the law you're on. He's a good guy when he's not trying to teach me a lesson."

"I have a feeling he has to teach you a lot of lessons."

He cocked his head and scowled. "He's known me all my

life, I would think he'd have learned by now. He likes a challenge."

I laughed. His youthful defiance was funny, but the years that Gareth had on Avery made him a worthy adversary. "I don't think you're going to win with your uncle."

"You sound like my mother." He shrugged, his eyes firmly fixed on his phone. "He'll wear down." I'd known his uncle for less time than he had and realized that Gareth had the tenacity of a pit bull. He wasn't likely to wear down anytime soon.

And just as I was about to say something to that effect, a hand snaked behind Avery and snatched the phone out of his hand. "You'll get this back when the workday is over," Gareth said, the suit and Kalen to each side of him.

The same limpid smile was on Kalen's face, as if it was frozen there and he had no other response but to wait for it to be over.

"Ms. Michaels," Gareth said.

"Levy," I offered.

He waved for me to follow, but I couldn't. My attention stayed on Kalen and the suit, who had directed him down the hall.

"Ms. Michaels." Gareth's voice was harder, a direct command that I ignored.

"No." I shifted my weight to get a better look at where they were going.

"Ms. Michaels, your defiance is unacceptable and will not be tolerated," he said in a cold, cutting tone. I glanced in his direction but just couldn't move until I knew Kalen was okay.

"Is he okay?" I said under my breath. *Come on, Kalen, just look at me.* I hadn't moved my eyes from his direction, and just before he followed the suit into the opened office, he looked at me and smiled, a crooked, relaxed smile. Relief came over me quickly and I turned to follow Gareth, who had stood just inches from me, his arms crossed over his chest as he waited.

"Sorry, I just—"

"That's fine." But based on the tone of his voice, everything wasn't fine. The full scope of what my behavior could have led to hit me all at once. Odd things were happening—bull-creatures coming through veils, chaos mages escaping their otherworld prison—and peculiar magic was involved. Did he think I had something to do with it?

Once the elevator closed behind us, I blurted out, "Do you think I had something to do with this?"

He looked up at the top corner of the wall, where I assumed the camera was placed, and remained silent. And the silence continued until we were in his office and he had closed the door.

"No, I don't think you had anything to do with this, but there is a link between you and what has occurred in the past few days. Tell me what happened today."

I told him everything, from the call from Ms. Neal, her persistence about keeping the stone, my initial contact with the minotaur, to how I'd tried to help keep him from attacking more of the SG men. "I'm sorry I couldn't stop him from eating the other one."

His lips pressed into a thin line. Several moments passed before he spoke again. "It wasn't your job to do so. It's one of the hazards of working here. It doesn't happen often." His eyes wavered from mine as he took in a slow breath. I was sure it didn't happen a lot, but once was too often.

"That thing was immune to magic like shapeshifters. What was it?"

"It was a shapeshifter. Similar to how the Legacy are the purest form of magic, it was what shifters are in our basic and purest form. There are very few who can take on larger and different forms, and as you saw, it requires caloric energy to do that." His hands rubbed over his face before he relaxed against his desk.

"Have a seat." I dropped into the chair directly in front of him. He was still rubbing his temple when he finally confided, "I need to figure out what is fact and what is fiction about the Legacy."

I really hoped I could offer more insight, but after finding out about Vertu from Kalen, I didn't feel like I had a firm grasp on it myself.

"Besides the Necro-spears, how many other things were created by the Legacy or the Vertu?"

I wanted to correct him and tell him I hadn't created anything, but that wasn't what he needed to hear. "You think everything is connected."

He nodded. "The Maxwells were locked away for three years, before I even took this position. If they could escape, why did it take so long? Declan"—responding to my confusion, he added, "the shifter I subdued earlier would have escaped again."

Ripping out someone's spine is one way to subdue someone, I guess.

"He was found unable to be contained by the Magical Council and was given the same fate as the Maxwells."

"But the Recludo Stone was only used for Declan," I offered.

"Kalen seems to believe the stone is a remnant of the war," Gareth said.

I didn't feel the same magic on it as mine. It could have been Conner's. But what did he get out of releasing chaos mages and a shifter who had been kicked out of this realm?

Pulled so far into my own thoughts that for a moment I forgot that Gareth was there, I looked up to find him staring at me. "Do you think there's any way Conner is involved?" I asked.

"The interview with Ms. Neal was quite interesting. She wasn't forthcoming at first. We required the assistance of a fae."

I realized why humans didn't ever want to be arrested by the Supernatural Guild. In a human jail when you were questioned, the truth was optional. In the supernatural world, the truth was forced.

He paced for a moment, and when he stopped, his eyes focused on me with intent. "It seems like the objective was to get you there. Apparently she was given the box of things to hand over to you by a gentleman who told her that you would pay her well for it. From what I gathered from my team, most of it is garbage. There were just enough things of value to make it look like a good haul."

That was generally the situation with most of our pickups but Gareth probably didn't know that.

"As much as HF claims to despise supernaturals and all things that are related to them, they seem to be very drawn to many magical artifacts. So after making a deal with this guy she reneged on it after speaking with Daniel, the head of HF. She decided she wanted to keep the stone. Curiosity got the best of her, and as with Pandora and her ubiquitous box, she couldn't manage to have it in her possession without activating it." He made a face. "So she did and Declan showed up. She locked him in and decided to let you and Kalen handle it."

He relaxed some as he recounted the situation, but his ease quickly faltered and he was frowning again. "She gave a different name for the person she dealt with but his description is similar to the one you gave of Conner. Do you think he could be involved in this?"

"He's a sociopath with delusions of grandeur. I wouldn't

59

put anything past him. I just don't see what he would get out of it."

"Can you find him again?"

"I don't know, but I can try."

"And the Necro-spears, can you find them, too? They really shouldn't be in circulation and so easily attainable by the public."

He was right, weapons created by the Legacy and the Vertu could be used by stronger magic wielders who could draw upon the magic within them. He had to be more apprehensive about them; while embedded in his kind, they were some of the few things that could prevent them from shifting as well as nullify their immunity to magic. It was rumored that there were only six, five remaining at large since the Magical Council had confiscated one.

Maybe he considered me to be some type of metal detector for all things Legacy. Finding anything made by my kind was probably easier than finding Conner. I didn't think I'd found him the first time—he'd wanted to be found.

I hated feeling the way I did: helpless and anxious. If this was Conner's doing it clearly wasn't my fault, yet there was a twinge of guilt that it was. I needed to stop him, but as Gareth and I sat in his office wondering how to do that he was probably building his army that thought that the world needed to consist of only the purest form of magic and everyone else should be disposed of.

"Is there anything you need to do this?"

A time machine to go back to the last time I saw Conner and get rid of him.

I had resolved to do what I had to do. I needed to find Conner and stop him. Reasoning wasn't working. If he was behind this, I had no idea what his plans were. Neither I nor Gareth seemed relieved or confident after our conversation. When you knew a person's intentions it made it easier to anticipate their actions, but Conner's behavior didn't have any rhyme or reason. As I left Gareth's office part of me wondered if we had attributed these things to the wrong person. Could it have been someone else?

Kalen was waiting for me in the lobby, studying Avery, and I couldn't tell how he felt about the man bun. But he was relaxed; the placid fake smile that had been plastered on his face earlier was gone and had been replaced by a genuine one.

"Your boyfriend's kind of a jerk at work, isn't he?" Kalen said as we walked to the car.

"Stop calling him my boyfriend, and yes, he's his own special blend of stubbornness and ego. What happened?" I asked, getting in the car after he unlocked it.

"Before or after their little spiel where they told me that if I didn't cooperate things wouldn't go well for me, blah blah blah?"

"Yeah, after that part," I said, laughing. It couldn't have been that bad—he didn't seem very distressed by it as he did a theatrical retelling.

"I told them everything and then Richard, that was the guy in the suit who was born without smile muscles or that's what I suspect since he didn't do it and I'm a delight—"

"So delightful. It's like hugging the sunshine and cuddling with fluffy puppies."

"I'm going to take that as a compliment and not your poor attempt to be witty." He grinned and handed me a check. A check with a lot of zeroes. "Mr. No Smiles gave me this. They will be confiscating everything found and will drop off anything they don't keep in a couple of days."

"What is this, hush money?"

He shrugged. "I signed several confidentiality agreements,

and of course Harrah wanted to mine for memories, but I stopped that real quick. Instead, they gave me the not-so-subtle threat that if I didn't comply with the agreement..." He made a choking noise and sliced his fingers across his throat.

I guessed Gareth didn't need a confidentiality agreement. He'd keep my secret as long as I kept theirs that there was a new brand of malicious magic out there.

It was surprising that Kalen didn't ask more questions about the meeting with Gareth, but I suspected he thought I couldn't tell him anything. I was grateful for it because I hadn't had time to come up with a Kalen-safe version of the story.

CHAPTER 3

Savannah didn't ask a lot of questions but instead looked at my dirty, bloodstained clothes and gave me an "it's been one of those days" looks as I passed her on the way to the shower. I spent several minutes cleaning the blood off my sai before I hopped in. As I stood with the warm water beating over my skin I tried to relax my mind, which was going a million miles a minute. There were too many pieces missing and not enough connections. Why would Conner release the chaos mages? It didn't make sense.

The smell of beef and cheese met me as soon as I opened the bathroom door. *Please don't be some weird vegetable wrap with some peculiar stock to make it smell like beef. Please be cheese —real cheese.*

I rounded the counter, and when I sat at the table, she pushed a bowl of macaroni and cheese with chunks of steak toward me. *Yes.*

Then came the salad. Once I'd pushed the damn tomatoes and cucumbers out of the way I found several pieces of bacon. The lettuce was a problem, because it was every-where. Savannah sat across from me, eating what looked like grass stuffed in a wrap, and on the side were the egg-white muffins she'd been peddling the other morning.

Between big bites out of her grass sandwich, she asked about my day. Frowning, I stopped eating—just thinking about the day made me lose my appetite. I told her everything. I was always torn between the fact that I had irreparably changed Savannah's life and possibly put her in danger and the comfort of having someone that I could be totally honest with. She listened, hanging on to every word, and I paused often trying to eat a forkful of food and let her process it. With each moment, a dark cast of despair washed over her fair skin. Whenever she leaned forward, her blond hair draped over her face, hiding it. I knew she did it on purpose to hide her expression, the fear and dread that she was probably feeling.

I never expected them to go away. She was sitting across from a person whose kind had nearly killed off the world, who possessed magic so strong it had ravaged the country and had taken an army of supernaturals to stop. In a sordid way, I was the face of death. A reminder of a bleak part of our history that had irreparably damaged the world and left a new one in its wake—a reminder who was sitting across from her eating mac and cheese.

"Do you think I'm a witch?"

I really wasn't expecting that to be her next question.

She seemed optimistically hopeful, so I took a long time to answer, giving the appearance that I was carefully considering the question. I had no idea why she thought that. There wasn't anything magical about her except for her ability to be perky before sunrise without the help of caffeine. In my book that made her some kind of wizard.

"Why do you think you might be a witch?"

"The Cleanse revealed that there were a lot of people who

possessed dormant magic. But I don't think mine is dormant. I feel different, like there's something awakening."

"Do you think it's your taste buds trying to escape?" I offered with a sly smile.

"I'm serious, Levy."

There wasn't anything there, but I played along because she needed it. Before, she'd had a casual relationship with the supernatural world, nothing more than her fawning over vampires at a club and her weird obsession with the Master of the city.

"We can find out. There is a witch I know who can help you." It was a futile attempt, but if she needed to get a definite answer, I would help even if the answer was no.

More energetic than usual, she looked at the clock and jumped up. "We should start getting dressed soon."

"Dressed?"

"We're going to Devour tonight, remember? As Lucas's guests."

I moaned inwardly. I didn't want to go to Devour; at least Crimson, previously her favorite vampire bar, was tolerable. But Devour was frequented by older vampires, skilled in the art of seduction, and sometimes their presence was an invitation very hard to decline. It was a hedonistic den of pleasure and sin and humans lined up around the block to be one of the chosen few to get in. Savannah was often besotted by the baby vamps in Crimson; she wouldn't stand a chance in Devour.

I really wanted to just rest and get an early start on tracking down Conner.

"I can go alone. I'll be fine, Lucas will be there," she suggested.

Yeah, of course you'll be fine with the very man who's responsible for siring most of the vamps who populate that haven of choices you'll regret in the morning. I wasn't letting her go within a foot of that place without me. I took my job as vampire blocker quite seriously.

"Of course. Yay, vampire bar. Hot zombies, let's do this." I gave her a little dance of excitement.

"No one thinks you're funny," she said, standing to head for her room.

"That's the second time I've heard that today."

She turned to face me and winked. "And yet you think you are."

The moment we walked into Devour, I turned to Savannah and combed her hair forward, draping the long blond waves over her neck and shoulders. "You're being ridiculous again. They're not rabid animals."

"They're not, but at least make them work for it. Instead you're putting all your goods out on display and decorating to draw attention." I pointed at the black halter she wore and the choker secured around her neck. Adding the formfitting black jeans and three-inch red heels, Savannah looked more in place than I did. She'd made me take off the scarf even after I'd pointed out how well it complemented my peach tank and dark jeans. I didn't fancy walking on stilts so I'd settled on a pair of one-inch heels, which Savannah didn't mind. With our shoe choices, I didn't tower over her as I usually did.

She scanned the room, and it didn't take long before she'd garnered a great deal of one vamp's attention. His dark eyes narrowed and the odd silver ring that circled all vampires' eyes danced in his. He moved with the lissome grace of most vampires, sinuous and seductive. His hair was just as dark as his eyes, and broad winged cheeks and defined rugged features made him the best prospect for a lot of women who were ready to make a host of regrettable decisions. Savannah saw a provocative, smiling man approaching us; I saw a predator with a fork and napkin tucked in his shirt ready to chow down.

He was just feet from us and I was prepared to tell him to go right back where he came from when Lucas appeared from the right. I waved at him, and he smiled. His fair hair was several shades lighter than Savannah's but was an appealing contrast to his dark eyes. Chiseled classically handsome features definitely made him fawn-worthy. He was dressed as usual in a slim-fitting suit that accentuated his sleek and sinewy physique.

He cut his eyes at the approaching vamp, who stopped midstride and turned casually, looking over the crowd of women willing to fall on that sword and take Savannah's place.

She smiled at Lucas and gave him a little wave. I wasn't sure which vamp was the better choice, but at least Lucas was the devil that I knew. He seemed to care about her safety but he was still a vamp—who fed from humans to survive, was capable of having incidents of bloodlust, was strong and fast and hard to defeat when driven to anger. And the Master of the city and a member of the Magic Council. Things that Savannah didn't care about—but I did.

The moment he approached her, he kissed her on the cheek. But there wasn't anything chaste or innocent about it or the embrace that followed. *Seriously, how do you make a cheek kiss dirty?*

"Olivia." He smiled and sidestepped Savannah, and just before he could treat me to one of his inappropriate hugs and the vamp version of a cheek kiss I shoved out my hand to shake his. He chuckled, a dark melodious sound, and took it and pressed it to his lips. Coolness brushed against my hand, and his lips still beveled into a miscreant smile as he pulled away.

My gaze drifted from his over to Savannah, who was clearly in swoon mode. And there wasn't a fainting couch in sight in the modern-chic club. After getting us drinks, Lucas took Savannah by the hand and guided her through the club, stopping to talk to the many guests. Devour was darker than most clubs. Tiny decorative pendant lights gave off just enough illumination to see the details of the deep gray walls and the black, cream, and burgundy leather seating scattered throughout. Small tables were placed along the walls near the entrance and two in each corner. The corners faded into darkness and I could barely see the people cradled into them. One in eyeshot had a vampire feeding. A female vamp wrapped around a man, her face nestled into the curve of his neck. I glanced across the room, and in another corner was a similar scene, but the body part choice was the arm.

I scanned the club and tried to get a visual on Savannah. The last time we'd been at a vamp bar, she'd been attacked, but while she seemed to have moved on, I hadn't. When I reminded her of it, she simply dismissed me with a wave of her hand and said, "They were being controlled by someone. We'll be fine."

The good thing about the bar was that no one seemed to hang around, so I had a perfect view of Savannah, who was just feet away from me. As more people came in, we became more divided by stretches of bodies. And the more people came in, the more I had to keep reassessing the best way to get to Savannah if things went awry, or how we could get to an exit. It wasn't just being in a vamp club that made me think like that. I always did it, and once again I found myself thinking about Kalen's words: behind every good fighter there was a "tragic story."

"Is this how you like to spend your nights, watching Savannah have fun?"

I turned to find Gareth standing next to me; even in the

nearly dark room his light blue eyes seemed bright and enhanced by the cobalt shifter ring that wrapped around his pupils. His lips kinked into a smile.

"Are you stalking me?"

He leaned in, his nose just inches from me before he inhaled. "Remember, I know your scent—I can find you anywhere in the city."

"Right, because telling me that just made this situation *less* creepy," I said, sidestepping him. He moved closer to the bar and ordered a drink.

He took a couple of sips before he directed his attention to me. "Do you want me to leave?" He gave me an assessing look and I wondered if what he saw was appealing as what I saw. I really didn't want to admit that he was handsome— okay, gorgeous, and it would be nice if he pretended he didn't know it for five seconds. The little uptick in his lips took self-righteous arrogance to a different level. I could do without that, too. Once again, I caught myself staring.

"You didn't answer my question. Is this how you usually spend your nights, letting Savannah have all the fun?"

I mumbled as I brought my drink to my mouth, "Apparently I also spend it being followed by a pesky kitten."

He laughed. "I take it you would like to hear me purr."

I frowned. "Are you proud of that one?"

The half-smile remained as he took another sip from his glass. "I have to make do with what you give me to work with."

"The better question is not how I spend my nights but why you are spending it here in a vamp bar. Don't you shifters have a rep to protect? Being here, in a vamp bar, definitely isn't a shifter thing to do."

"I didn't have any pressing plans and when Savannah invited me, I thought it would be fun to see you in a different setting."

"Instead of jail, in front of the Magic Council, or in front of a supercilious Supernatural Guild leader whose go-to line is 'I'm going to arrest you.'" I could feel his eyes on me but I had diverted mine to the room as I looked for Savannah. When our eyes met, mine narrowed into a scope, and fixed on her. *I am going to get you for this.*

With a coy look of innocence, she smiled and waved. Savannah and I had been friends long enough and she knew my "I'm going to kill you" look. She ignored it and turned away from me and continued her conversation with Lucas and the group.

"You don't like your drink?" Gareth asked, looking at my full glass.

"I do, but I like to stay sober." One drink wouldn't bother me, but I didn't like to have my senses dulled around a bunch of vampires, some of whom were ogling me from across the room. A few had already asked for a nibble, and I was sure they weren't talking about hors d'oeuvres, and there were a select few who kept trying to get me to hold contact. That was how they were able to compel you. It was illegal, but they weren't going to let a little thing like that keep them from having a good time in the den of sin.

We both looked in Savannah's direction, watching her with Lucas. They didn't behave like they were people who had met less than a week ago. But most people didn't behave that way with Savannah because she was so personable.

"I'm sure if you are unable to drive home, Lucas will make sure you two are taken care of," he offered in a low voice with a hint of restrained disdain.

"What's the deal with you and Lucas?" I didn't think they hated each other, but there was something strained about their interaction. There was an obvious undertone of the need to be dominant that plagued the interactions between vampires and shifters. Lucas, being the Master of the city, commanded a certain level of consideration and concession from Gareth, and Gareth's position as head of the Supernatural Guild afforded him a level of authority over Lucas that seemed to cause conflict between the two of them.

"I like Lucas just fine," he said after a long drink and several moments of silence. I guessed he needed to numb his lips before the lie passed them.

I didn't have to be able to smell or detect a lie to know that was a big one.

While Gareth's attention was on Lucas, I found my attention on Gareth, taking in his appearance and appreciating it more than I should have. I needed a distraction, and it seemed like he did, too.

"Have you heard anything more about HF?" I asked softly, aware that I was in a room full of people who had exceptional hearing. The music's mesmeric bass tones were loud enough to mask my words if I lowered my voice enough. Clive and several other members of HF had been arrested after I'd stopped them from using the one Necrospear that had been recovered to do another Cleanse. With everything going on, I hadn't had a chance to follow up on what had happened. I knew that they wouldn't stay in SG custody because they were human and the incident between us was considered an act of human-on-human violence, which would be the purview of the human justice system.

Gareth turned slightly and leaned in, his cool drink pressing into my arm because there wasn't much room for it as he had closed any distance I had created between us. When he spoke, his warm breath lightly brushed against my ear.

"He was released on bail a couple of hours ago, but I have someone keeping surveillance on him."

I inhaled the masculine musk and caught the dark hints

of the predator in his eyes. The diametric feeling of being both drawn to and repelled by him bothered me.

I slipped my hand between the little space that he'd left between us and nudged him back.

"We are in public, it's important this conversation remains between us," he admonished, but he moved back just a smidge to scan the room. It was starting to fill with more humans than vampires, nearly two to one. I wondered if that was intentional, to give the vampires a better buffet choice.

"The music's loud enough, and if you can sense me from across the city, I'm pretty sure you can hear me just fine if you give me a couple of inches of space."

His voice dropped, a barely audible drawl. It was so low that I would have missed it if I hadn't read his lips and caught the last part of the sentence. "But can you hear me?"

I pushed a little harder; it was like trying to shove a brick building out of the way. His shirt didn't do much to hide the deep, solid lines of his muscles, and as I pushed into his chest, I could feel what my eyes were focusing on. He immediately tensed under my touch. His attention moved from me, drifted over the room and set on his target—the messy pile of blondish hair sticking up. His nephew and three other people were near the corner. I thought they were all human until one turned to look around the room; the emerald shifter ring, which was always darker than their natural color, had a hint of glow in the dim light.

Avery raised his drink to his uncle and smiled, defiant. *Oh, yes, there is the family resemblance—the stubborn gene. How did I miss it?*

"He can be here," I said. As much as Gareth might not have liked the idea of his nephew hanging out in a vamp bar, he had every right to do so and have the drink that Gareth was eyeing. Supernatural rules were different than human laws. The legal drinking age was eighteen. It looked like

Gareth believed his irritating nephew who'd stolen his car should be locked in his room and on house arrest, as opposed to hanging out in the same bar as him. But when life gave you lemons you made lemonade, or in Gareth's case, you made a pitcher of it and tried to ruin your nephew's fun.

"Excuse me for a moment."

"You're not even trying for the 'greatest uncle award'?" I teased.

In silence, Gareth invited himself over to join Avery and his friends.

I watched as he tipped his glass to his nephew, and after a few minutes they were laughing. I couldn't help but smile; when he wasn't behaving like there was a jackass contest and he wanted to make sure he placed, he was warm and charismatic. I stared—too long—and eventually he caught me. He smiled, enchanting and charming, and I drifted to it, drawn like most to his primal allure. I had to nearly yank my gaze from him.

"And you want me to believe you're not interested?" Savannah said, her pink glossed lips twisted into a combination of a smirk and a frown.

"I never said he wasn't handsome. It's just complicated."

"What's complicated? He's hot—so hot. And you need to have a hookup or something."

"I like to keep things casual, you know that." I didn't intend to do it but I fixed her with a hard look. My life was a little too complex to do anything other than casual and nothing about Gareth seemed casual. He was intense. Very intense.

Savannah was physically next to me, but she was distracted—her full attention was on Lucas.

"You can go back over there, I'm okay."

"Not until you agree to stop being the weird woman at

73

the bar gawking at everyone like you're at a circus and they just brought out the freaks."

"I have better manners than to call them freaks. Besides I'm rather fond of calling them hot zombies and their menagerie of fangirls and boys," I said with a grin. I peered over at Gareth.

"He's really an okay guy ... and seriously—look at him. He's yummy. You can't tell me you're not interested, at least a little." Tilting her head in quiet consideration, she studied him.

He looked over his shoulder with a half-smile and a glint of amusement played at his eyes, and he relaxed more into himself. I leaned into her, lowered my voice until it was barely audible. "He can hear you."

Her smile quickly slipped and her lips pulled into a tight line.

Now look who's gawking at everyone like she has front-row seats to the freak show.

"Are you serious? Even with the music?" she asked in a hushed voice.

"Yeah, even with the music," I said, turning from her to answer, but at that point there wasn't a lot that could be done, and we hadn't said anything that he didn't probably already think about himself.

"And so can Lucas," I added.

Her eyes widened, and then she frowned. He drank blood to survive and had been on the earth longer than her grandparents, and his enhanced hearing was the thing that she took issue with? Savannah was an odd mixed bag that I would never understand. She studied Lucas for a few minutes before directing her attention to Gareth. His lips were still kinked into a miscreant grin, which quickly faded. I felt it probably seconds before he sensed it, the wave of magic that crept into the room.

I erected an *apotrepein*, a wall that would absorb some of the magic, around Savannah and me. They required more magic but were more effective than a ward. I watched the variations of colors of magic that would go unnoticed by most as they coated the air in the room. The same magic from the Square.

Before we could react, a woman grabbed the woman standing next to her, slammed her into the wall, and started to strike her viciously. The vampire who had been feeding from the man earlier and not too long ago kissing him was holding his limp body close to her, her fangs latched on to his neck. Then the shifter with Avery changed into a wolf. He sprang toward the crowd that had erupted into violence. Gareth grabbed him, yanking him back by the scruff of his neck, tossing him back. The wolf soared back several feet, landing on his back. It wasn't Gareth—not SG Gareth. He looked as feral as everyone else. This wasn't the terrible triplets' magic—or not *just* their magic. *Fuck. Conner.*

Savannah started to move, but I grabbed her wrist. "You have to stay next to me."

"We have to stop this," she said. We moved behind the bar, the apotrepein also protecting the bartender, who was crouching down behind the counter and us.

"What the hell's going on?" Savannah asked.

"Chaos mages, the same from earlier, but this isn't just them. They can't control shifters, but Conner can. He has to be involved." I never wanted to hurt anyone more than I did Conner. When I looked over the counter, both Avery and Gareth had shifted. The large cats took up a greater part of the room. As they circled each other, their massive forms knocked anyone who occupied that space out of the way.

Baring their fangs, they slowly stalked each other. Just as they were about to attack, Savannah pitched a Molotov cocktail in their direction. Fire sparked in the middle of the room, and they shuffled back several feet around the small fire that formed. Another flaming bottle hit, and several people retreated to the side.

"You need to find Conner and stop this."

"But if I leave, you won't be protected. I can't do both," I said.

She looked over at the pile of towels behind the bar, a few ratty cloths in the corner, and the fully stocked bar. "I'm good."

I glanced at the bartender, who had joined Savannah in keeping everyone at bay. "Don't worry about him. If he tries to attack me, I'll just clunk him over the head with this." She grabbed another bottle at her side and showed it to me.

He was too busy tossing alcohol bombs to hear her, or had decided not to respond to the woman who had just promised to give him a concussion. I rummaged through the cabinets and drawers looking for weapons. I knew there had to be stakes somewhere for those "break glass in case of emergency" type of situations. I couldn't blame them. I continued to search. They weren't in a glass case but in a closed box, under the counter. I stuffed the two stakes I found into the back of my pants.

Between the small fires throughout the club, people who were beating the crap out of one another, and others trying to get out of the way of the makeshift bombs being lobbed in their direction, I navigated to the entrance. Worried about Savannah and what would happen now that she and the bartender weren't protected by my magic, I looked back in her direction. I didn't see the bartender until I rose to my toes to get a better look. He was laid out on the floor, with broken glass scattered around him. His eyes were closed and he had a very noticeable wound on the side of his head.

"Levy, go. I got this!" she shouted, and she slung another bottle out into the crowd.

As I neared the door, someone grabbed me by the hair and yanked me back. I hit the ground—hard. I rolled to the side and swiped their leg and jabbed my elbow into their throat. If it was a vampire, it would only hurt for a moment. I gripped the stake. I didn't plan on killing them, but I needed to do more to disable them. When the person gurgled for breath, I came to my feet. I didn't have to worry about them. I hoped the Suits, the guys who manned the front door and also seemed to double as Lucas's assistants and bodyguards, weren't out there because disabling them was going to be a little more difficult.

They were outside but too engaged in a bloody fistfight to be concerned about me. I darted around them, the wave of familiar magic wrapped around me like a dense shawl. Two distinct types of magic: mage and an odd version of mine. I closed my eyes for a brief moment to concentrate, isolate where it was coming from, and decide who I needed to stop first. The mages—I had to stop them first.

I ran around the building, through the narrow alleyway, and spotted the terrible trio immediately. I picked up my pace and hauled behind them as fast as I could, clearing the distance between them before surveying the area to make sure there wasn't anyone near. The ambient glow of the moon illuminated the area along with a few distant streetlights. I could see my path and them well enough and all the things that cluttered the alley. The trash bins, shards of glass from a few broken bottles that had missed the containers and landed beside them. I could see most things, yet it was still dark enough that someone wouldn't be able to identify me from a distance.

My magic curled around my arm, inching quickly toward my fingers. A powerful wave of it driven by fear and adrenaline burst forward, crashing into the triplets and sending them careening into the ground. I was on them quickly. Grabbing the thinner male by the shirt, I slammed him into the wall. Stake in hand, I pressed it into his chest, adding enough pressure so he could feel the sharp point.

His lips cocked into a half-smile, giving me and the stake a look of derision. "I'm not a vampire," he said in a deep mocking tone.

"And somehow you think if I plunge this sharp stick into your chest it won't hurt because of that." I pressed harder. He grunted as his eyes flew up past me, to his siblings. I heard their movement behind me. "You touch me and this goes into his chest." I pushed it in a little harder. He winced. "Step back," I ordered.

I glanced over in their direction. They didn't move. If they were working with Conner, they knew who and what I was, which gave me a lot of freedom. I didn't have to pretend to be a mage, witch, or lesser supernatural. I released the mage with one hand, keeping the stake pressed into his heart, and blasted another powerful force of magic into the other two. They crashed into the building across from us and crumpled against it. As they attempted to stand, I quickly swiped my finger across, collapsing their legs under them. They went down with a thud. Then I heard the sound of a gun cocking.

"Let him go," commanded the deep familiar voice. For a moment I contemplated the speed of magic and that of a bullet. I turned to find Clive and three of his companions with guns trained on me. *Great, the Justice League is here.* They were dressed in all black. All they were missing were matching tattoos below the edges of their fitted t-shirts that would signify that they were the Brotherhood of the Cliché. He jerked his chin in the mages' direction. "Get out of here." I heard rustling behind me, probably them trying to get out of there in a hurry.

"Any more destruction they cause will be on you," I reminded him bitterly.

"They won't. We just needed to talk to you."

"Yeah, when I need to talk to people I usually corner them in a dark alley and threaten them with a gun. Meeting at coffeehouses is overrated," I snipped back.

His lips pulled into a taut line, as did the mouths of the other three. The lighting made them appear harsher and more ominous. I took note of their position but I didn't see an advantage. The first time Clive had approached me, the guy he'd had with him wasn't trained—these men were. Their hold was steady, eyes narrowed, and they had the physiques of people who would have not only speed but power in a fight. This meeting apparently wasn't about schmoozing me this time.

"We know what you are."

"So? First of all you will have to prove it and then get people who consider themselves saner than you to believe it. You guys are the weird fundamentalists with the ridiculous name trying to change a world that most people like. Go ahead, tell someone that Legacy exist and that you saw one the other day. You might as well tell them Santa Claus gave you a piggy-back ride. No one will believe you; in fact, they'll see it as another ploy to separate humans from the supernaturals," I said through clenched teeth, speaking with far more confidence than I actually felt. I didn't want to give those who were on the fence any reason to doubt. There was comfort in thinking that every Legacy had died in the war and the Cleanse could never be done again. Everyone needed that comfort.

The other men kept their guns trained on me, but Clive rested his at his side. "Conner sees the big picture—you need to as well." An alliance of people who clearly hated one another, out for one agenda—separation. Conner hated anyone who wasn't a Vertu or Legacy. Humans First hated anyone who wasn't wholly human, and the terrible triplets just seemed to hate—well, peace and order.

As a situational chameleon, Clive had switched into his new role, abandoning the hard-assed representative of Humans First for something friendlier, more charismatic and warm. Clive would be anything he needed to be to get whatever he wanted and I didn't trust him. His voice had lost its commanding edge and when he spoke his voice was soft and entreating. "I don't think it's fair that you have to live like this, Levy," he offered.

That's laying it on pretty thick.

"Magic can be chaotic and dangerous when unchecked," he said pointedly.

"And sending chaos mages throughout the city is *helping* things?"

"No, we are exposing the fragility of this existence. It is only a matter of time before it is more than a planned execution by a chaos mage but actual chaos and unrest. Don't you think the supernaturals will eventually grow tired of the restrictions placed on them, the laws, and the constant monitoring and manipulation to make them seem innocuous? How long do you think that this can go on?"

It was a rhetorical question, although he waited in silence for several minutes. He was assessing how I was responding to his little soliloquy. I wondered how long he'd practiced it —putting the right dark spin on it, pausing for effect, allowing his voice to drop to a low deep rasp as he told me of the draconian world that would come to be.

"We want you on our team. To make things right."

"As flattered as I am to be asked to join your club of misguided misfits, I'm going to give it a hard pass."

Although his partners still had their guns pointed at me, this wasn't going to be violent. I slowly started to back away, not confident enough to turn my back on him but confident enough to position myself for an escape. The man next to Clive nestled his right finger a little tighter on the trigger but Clive ordered him to stand down. Reluctantly he dropped it and so did the others.

I had only gotten a few feet away when he said, "I know you have delusions of stopping it. You won't."

"I was pretty good at stopping you the last time. And I will make sure I do it this time and each time you and Conner or anyone else you align yourself with give it a try. I have more at stake than your Utopian world where people like me don't exist. I assure you, like the last time, I will win —you're just playing Humans First mercenary, or whatever GI Joe fantasy you have in your head. I'm playing for my life."

The anger made its way to his eyes. His lips twisted into a snarl. His tone was hard and sharp. "I assure you, sweetheart, I'm not playing anything. You won *one* battle, don't think you have a handle on this. I'm giving you a chance to walk out of this alive in a better situation than you will be when we are finished. We have four Necro-spears—" He stopped abruptly, and I realized his anger had gotten the best of him and he'd disclosed something he shouldn't have. But he was too rehearsed and confident to make it seem that way. "We do. What do you think happens to you when we do it?"

I stopped midstep and sucked in a ragged breath, my chest too tight to take in any more. If he had four, and the Magical Council had one, then there was another one out there somewhere. He only needed someone strong and as misguided and thirsty for power as he was to help him. His little speech probably wasn't as practiced as I thought but had become polished by being given so many times that he knew how it needed to be delivered to get people to comply.

Conner had had three Legacy before, and Clive might have helped him find more.

Fear was something I hated to feel. It made me impulsive and reactionary. It was the worst way to handle things. It took a few moments for me to master it, control it, and think of this rationally. But rationality was far from my reach—I wanted to kill a lot of people, starting with Conner and the rest of his band of misguided minions. I'd always considered myself better than this, but at that moment, I didn't want to be better. I wanted violence, the very thing that had changed my life and the world and made me a lifelong fugitive who had to hide and could never have a normal life. This jerk was treating me with the same casualness that one used when deciding what shoes to wear. People were going to die. Lots of people.

"When would you like to meet?" I asked with quiet resolve.

"David, our founder, has wanted to meet you for a while. Meet us at our office, at seven tomorrow." The arrogance of his success just made the vengeful thoughts in my head easier to accept.

By the time I'd returned to the club, I hadn't calmed down enough to get past deciding which way was best to kill Conner and how many ass kickings I planned on giving HF before they met the same fate. My hands were shaking with anger when I walked through the club's doors. Several Supernatural Guild cars were present, along with an ambulance from the Isles, the hospital more often used by humans who were injured as a result of a supernatural occurrence than by supernaturals. Witches and mages could heal themselves with spells and magic. It took a lot to injure vampires and shifters, and they often healed so fast that medical attention was rarely necessary. I wasn't sure what I'd expected; after all, Savannah had tried to control the violence by fighting with fire and it looked like she'd succeeded but hadn't burned the place down completely. Pools of blood covered the floor, shattered bottles all around. Significant parts of the floor and walls were scorched. The previously fully stocked bar had only a half a shelf of liquor.

Savannah sidled in next to me, looking at her fingers, which were bandaged. "How bad is it?" I asked. When she winced once as she pressed them to each other, I had my answer. Scanning the area, I looked for Lucas.

When I didn't see him, I asked, "Where's Lucas?"

She shrugged. "I kind of lost touch with him once things got really out of control." I caught a glimpse of Gareth off in the corner, talking to Harrah. Her face flushed as she period-ically looked over the destroyed club. Stress and anger competed for expression on her face. But she softened some as she examined Gareth's arm. I could see the angry red burns from across the room. Her face and body surrendered to her smile and she relaxed a little, or relaxed as much as one could knowing she was responsible for fixing the situa-tion and spinning it into something palatable. She waved in Savannah's direction and then gave her a nod of thanks.

"What's that all about?" I asked, referring to her fingers again.

"I got this trying to stop Gareth and the other lion from ripping each other apart."

"That was his nephew. It would have devastated him if he'd hurt him."

"I figured that much. I hope they aren't as stubborn in human form as they are in animal. Nothing really worked. I had to get between them and hold them off."

"You did what?" I snapped.

"It was only for a minute. Just a few moments later every-thing stopped. Everybody was calm and the shifters had reverted back to human form."

"Savannah, you can't—"

"I know, I know. Save the lecture, I realize how stupid it was. Adrenaline just took over. Maybe I'm a fire witch or mage."

I didn't know which I wanted to do: hug her and be glad she was alive, or strangle her for behaving so irrationally. But she seemed so calm that it helped me to grab a little for myself. Knowing Savannah, she was probably too busy fixating on her new life as a fire witch or mage, which was *so* not a thing, but I had a feeling she had given herself over to the idea of being a fire-y Wonder Woman with the outfit and all. *Please don't let her start looking for lassos.*

I stared at her as she looked around the room with an odd kind of pride. *Yep, tomorrow we are probably going shopping for outfits and lassos.*

CHAPTER 4

I waited patiently for Savannah, who was still riding high on her discovery that she might be a fire witch or mage, to go to sleep. I just didn't have it in me to tell her that they absolutely without a doubt were *not* a thing. She considered finding Conner and the Necro-spears *our* job, but it wasn't. I'd put her in enough danger, I wasn't going to get her more involved than she already was. Humans First had four of the spears and I needed to find them. I doubted I would be lucky enough that they stored them in their offices, but if David was as controlling and fanatical as Clive seemed to be, they would be close. With any luck I would find Conner, too—if he hadn't put up a ward to prevent me. Maybe his arrogance had made him careless or maybe he wanted me to find him. Ready to present me with a rousing speech about how I should join Team Demagogue.

With my sai secured to my back in their sheath, I slipped into my pit cave—my magic sanctuary. Initially I had abandoned it because both Lucas and Gareth knew about it, but I didn't have many options of where I could do magic and not be discovered. It had to be a place where a lot of various magic had been performed to mask mine to the point it was indistinguishable. There weren't many that fit the bill and still gave me the privacy I liked. I felt safer swathed in darkness, with the only light being that of the small flashlight I carried. And the dirt that kicked up each time I moved and the strong earthy smell of the hardened dirt walls that surrounded me were oddly comforting.

Once I closed the cover, silence. The noise of the world disappeared, making it easier to concentrate. This was my nirvana. Safety. My magical home where I didn't have to hide behind the mask of being human.

"I thought you would have been here earlier," said Gareth, emerging from the darkness. With smooth, agile movements, he approached me in silence.

Responding to the voice before recognizing it, I dropped the flashlight and readied my sai. He continued to advance closer, allowing the point of the sai to press lightly against his chest. From the small illumination given off by the discarded flashlight, I could see his raised brow and the little smile.

"Do you plan on putting those away?"

"I don't know. Do you plan to stop stalking me? Because it's really creepy and weird."

"I don't stalk you, I know how you think and I told you—I know your scent."

I lowered the twins and then sheathed them. "Are you telling me that before you said that, a little voice in your head didn't speak up and say, 'This is something I should never say out loud'?"

"I make you uncomfortable?" he asked softly.

I didn't want to give him the satisfaction of an answer. He made me uncomfortable because I hated that when he was near me, I looked at him too long, watched him too carefully, revisited the time he had kissed me too often, and had much too vivid flashes of his body, which I'd seen far too many times. I tried to convince myself that it was him—he ignited some kind of primal longing in most people, and it wasn't unique to just me.

"I can track most people as long as they don't use magic to block it."

"You wouldn't happen to know which spell it is, would you?" I asked. His light chuckle reverberated off the walls, a deep, throaty sound that made me smile.

"If you are so ready to get rid of me, then why don't you hurry up and try to track down Conner?"

He was right, he knew how I thought. I picked up the flashlight and handed it to him and then knelt down before taking out the knife that I had secured at my ankle. My fingers ran over the loose dirt to create a large circle. I used the knife to cut my finger and spill blood into the circle and then rested back on my heels. My magic, which was used so infrequently, required a little coaxing. Often forced into dormancy it unfolded in waves, and I could feel the warmth of it wrap around me. I looked up at Gareth, wondering if he could see the various hues that unraveled and entwined, representing the various types of magic I possessed. They coiled together and floated over the circle. A large map appeared, an area with about a hundred-mile-radius from my position. All the intricate parts of the city were displayed, and there it was, a silver glow that pulsed over it. Not like before, when it had popped up and quickly disappeared. He wasn't using magic to block me anymore, but instead extending an invitation to where he was.

"Is that where he is?"

I nodded. "But I don't know if it's just him or more. If they were in other areas of the city, there would be more flecks of light. Instead it's just in one spot, and it's more than a fleck of light. It's wider, longer, indicating that there are more than just Conner." I didn't know how many more. Before, he'd only had three, but in the past few days had he recruited more?

I smothered the magic and watched as it recoiled back to me, but Gareth was still staring at the spot intensely, and when he spoke his voice was edged, lower. "I don't know how people deal with being so vulnerable to magic."

The confidence and arrogance slipped for a moment and I saw a person worried—concerned about magic, a victim of it. I knew it had to bother him. Someone had snatched away his volitions and not only forced him into changing but controlled and incited enough anger and violence in him that he'd almost injured his nephew. I wasn't the only person who wanted to kick Conner's ass. The belief that magic could be evil probably lurked in the minds of everyone who'd been in Devour, and for the moment Gareth seemed to be consumed by that thought as well.

"It's not all bad," I said softly. I held the knife and magic wrapped around it. It drifted slowly from me to him, and he plucked it from the air. I made the dirt kick up small pebbles and then moved around the dirt rhythmically as I created a small vortex. He watched it with amused interest and as it died down his attention moved to me.

My life had been spent seeing and knowing about the darker side of magic. I guessed most people's were. They only knew of vampires compelling people to become their food, or fae using cognitive manipulation or changing their appearance for nefarious purposes. And mages and witches casting spells and curses. Besides the love spells, the escape spells—*effugium*—and witch weed, there was a lot of ugliness to their magic, too. Although curses were technically illegal, they managed to find loopholes.

The dancing dirt vortex had completely died by the time Gareth inched his way into my private space. He was close.

Really close, and when I spoke, our lips brushed lightly. "See, magic's not that bad."

"Not bad at all," he whispered. He leaned in and kissed me. He didn't move when he finished. Instead he kept his lips gently against mine. A few moments passed before he kissed me again, more commanding, hungry, urging a response that I freely gave in to. His hands pressed into my lower back as he pulled me closer. The kiss became more fervent as he walked me back until I was pressed against the dirt wall of the pit cave. His fingers roved slowly over me and I clawed at his shirt, a fistful of it enclosed in my hand as I urged him closer to me. His beeping phone forced us to pull away. He was panting softly as he turned on the speaker.

It was someone from the SG, telling him that they had a visual on the Maxwells. He held my gaze for a moment, and I could still feel the warmth of his lips on mine. I didn't think I would ever have a reason to thank the terrible triplets, but this was one. I couldn't have anything with Gareth. There was a fragility to our interaction that would only make things worse. He was the head of the SG, and on the Magic Council, his responsibilities were to maintain the tenebrous alliance between humans and to protect and govern the supernaturals. I was a threat to both groups, and I wasn't absolutely confident that, if he ever considered me an immediate one, he wouldn't deal with me as he would any threat.

We hurried out of the cave and I was halfway to my car when he called my name. "Don't confront him without me," he ordered.

That was what I had decided to do even while in the cave. I wanted to bring unspeakable pain to Conner, but there was a part of me that hoped he could be reasoned with. My position as his potential—albeit unwilling—consort might work to my advantage. It would definitely be hard to be reasonable while watching Conner and Gareth see who got the trophy for being the most narcissistic, arrogant alpha-hole. I didn't have the time.

I shook my head.

His voice became low and commanding.

Oh, there he is. Here I thought he might have turned over a new leaf.

"Ms. Michaels, this matter needs to be handled more strategically. You will stand down and let it be handled by us."

I just didn't have it in me to argue with him. If I used all my patience and diplomacy with him, what was I going to use with Conner? My well was quite shallow in dealing with these matters. Nope, I just couldn't adult with him today. I just couldn't.

"Mr. Reynolds"—*two can play this game*—"which would you prefer: for me to tell you I'm not going and go anyway, or for me to tell you the truth—I'm going."

Having a cardiac event wasn't either of the options, yet that was what he seemed to have chosen. His eyes narrowed to slits until all I could see was just a hint of his icy blue eyes and the indigo shifter ring that glowed around it. His lips pulled taut into a frown that was cemented on his face. I slowly walked backward to my car, not feeling fully confident he wouldn't grab me and take me with him. After a few more seconds, he got into his car and sped off.

CHAPTER 5

*T*he large stretch of trees that surrounded the area where the locator spell had led me made it difficult to negotiate around it. I could feel the magic and its strange draw. It was so similar to mine. It overshadowed everything—oak, flowers, dirt—surrounding it all and draping over the air. The stronger the magic became, the more my heart started to pound.

I'd gone over my rousing spiel a hundred times, making all the points that would work on anyone, but I wasn't dealing with *anyone*—I was dealing with the self-proclaimed liberator of our race. A person who felt that he could restore us to what we once were—magical royalty. But his memory was very short, because in order to claim the position, he was going to have to do the very thing that made people loathe us. The Cleanse was our downfall, after which we were reduced to nothing more than the hunted and the loathed. And our name became synonymous with great wards, mass murder, and draconian magic.

Sai in hand, I approached the area, slowly trying to find the veil, which I found I didn't need to do—the translucent barrier rippled, then bulged out, creating an opening for me. As soon as I planted my other foot on the new soil it snapped closed.

Deeper into the foreign territory, I looked around. This was their new home, nothing like the first one I'd seen—fallow land, bare trees, and small unimpressive houses. This was very different, created for a long stay. Lush green neatly manicured grass extended throughout the massive space. Flowering trees were interwoven between the oaks and poplars. Redolence of the exotic plants that my mother had spoken of lingered in the air. A small pond to my right had decorative flowers scattered around it and neatly placed stones in earth tones of brown, blue, and green. Each home was impressive, palatial: decorative pillars at the entrances, trimmed bushes that surrounded them, and flowers that led to the front doors. Instead of three homes as he'd had before, there were nine. I assumed he had at least nine Legacy or Vertu that had joined him. This was going to be harder than I'd thought.

Conner waited for me, several feet away. After several roving looks over me and my weapons, he dismissed both. I was dressed in a t-shirt and jeans that were just one rough fight or stain away from being tossed in the garbage; I was very underdressed compared to Conner. He wore his customary light shirt, this time a pastel green, with complementary tan slacks.

His broad features and narrow aquiline nose contributed to his aristocratic features. His haughtiness and air of arrogance were so poorly veiled he might as well have held up a sign telling the world he thought he was better than them. Even the sword, worn at his hip, was held in an ostentatious ornate sheath.

Touching his weapon, he gave my sai another look. "Here I thought my invitation would be met with less violence than before. But I wouldn't expect anything less from my consort. Please put up your weapons. I invited you here to talk, and although I enjoy seeing my warrior consort in action, this isn't the time."

This again. Apparently my trying to kill him the last few times we'd encountered each other was his version of foreplay and the beginning of some sordid mating ritual. He'd claimed me as his partner and wanted to use me as a broodmare to create what he considered magical royal children. I guessed we dreamed differently, because my only goal was to stop him by any means necessary even if it meant killing him.

I sheathed my weapons; this didn't have to be violent. But as he stood wrapped in his brand of insolence, punching the haughty look off his face was looking a little more appealing than diplomacy.

"I'm so glad you accepted my invitation."

"Which one: the chaos, bloodshed, and violence in the Square, or the chaos, bloodshed, and violence at Devour? Please put your rabid mages back in their cages where they belong."

With slow, measured steps, he approached in silence until he was just inches from me. "Well, Anya, that is up to you. You want them caged, then you stay here. That is my offer. If not, there are two more wards I will break, and before long the humans will be begging for me to put a stop to the chaos."

"This isn't a win for you. Do you think anything that can be done will overshadow the fact that our forebearers killed a huge part of the world's population? This small tantrum you are throwing is just proving you can't be trusted. You think the humans will forget that if it weren't for their alliance with the supernaturals they wouldn't have won? Together they kicked our asses. Make no mistake about it:

93

they will weather this little storm you put out, and in the end you will be no better off."

"You're so pessimistic."

There wasn't going to be any diplomacy with him. I wasn't going to change his mind, and out of my peripheral vision I saw the new addition to his plan. There were eight homes, but twelve people now surrounded me. Most of them younger, close to my age, and four older people who I assumed had been there for the first Cleanse. I looked out at the small group of people with persimmon red hair, the mark of our people now synonymous with betrayal.

I turned to the group. "He's going to get us all killed." Then I addressed the older ones. "You were there, do you really want to go through this again? It's been over thirty years. I believe we can work things out, stop hiding. Perhaps discuss it with the Magic Council and have normal lives. But if you all try this again and fail—then ..."

I was met with various looks of disinterest. "That's what you want—not us. We want the life we had before and we will get one even better," one of the older recruits responded.

Damn. For a moment I did feel like a unicorn—different from my own kind. But I couldn't believe that we were all like this. I realized that the only way to stop the body was to take off the head. I grabbed my sai in one swift move and lunged at Conner, grazing his side with the tip of one and then puncturing through his arm. I made a quarter spin in the opposite direction and embedded the other sai deep in him. I dropped my remaining sai, snatched his sword out of the sheath, and was about to angle it in an arc to strike when I was hit hard. What felt like a lightning bolt that exploded in me threw me back and sent me smashing into a tree. I choked on a gasp of pain when my rib cracked. Another jolt of magic seized my body, singeing like hellfire. Magic was so interwoven in us and our bodies that when I launched the same ball of magic back at the advancing woman, I felt it in my ribs.

Fighting through the pain, I lobbed another one at the others. There wasn't any way I was going to win against twelve Legacy and Vertu. A ball of magic rested in one of their hands, ready to be expelled in my direction. I sucked in a breath, closed my eyes, and prepared for the pain—nothing. Standing between them and me was Conner. He raised his hand. "That's enough."

I rolled to my side, propped myself up with my arms, and surveyed the area. As they stepped back, a slender woman stepped back a little farther, but sparks of magic, in hazy colors of teal, yellow, and peach, flicked from her fingers, not as easily extinguished as the others', which led me to believe that she had more power than control. But the rest seemed skilled in their execution of magic. I wondered if they were as skilled with doing spells, which was where I fell short. My parents knew that spells could always be traced back to the creator, so they'd taught me only the ones that I needed to survive. Magic was often defensive in nature, and although it could be traced it was a lot harder to follow than offensive action. Most just felt the magic that lingered in the air, coated their tongues, or singed their noses, but all magic had a fingerprint that could ultimately be linked back to the user. If the supernatural had been exposed to the purveyor of the magic, then they could identify it.

Conner's shirt was as it had been before I'd attacked him, crisp and clean, without any signs that I had attempted to behead him. He knelt next to me and reached out to touch me; I knocked his hand away, and when he attempted to touch me a second time, I did it again. Distracted by his unwanted touch, I went to block him again at his third attempt. His other arm swiped the arm that was propping my body up and I collapsed to the ground. He hovered over me, his hand running over the crown of my head, over the top and down the length of the ponytail. And when he spoke, his voice was a genteel whisper with a melodic cadence that might cause a weaker mind to forget he was batshit crazy.

"They will protect me because I've earned their loyalty. What do I need to do to earn yours?"

"You can't work with Humans First. They can't be trusted. People like them should not have access to our magic," I said, my cadence and tone matching his. I wasn't sure who I wanted to have the Necro-spears the least: HF or Conner. I had to pick the lesser of two evils, but they both were pretty high on the scale of bad choices. Conner had a larger plan, so he wouldn't behave irrationally; I wasn't that confident about HF.

"For you, done." He stood and extended his hand to help me up, and everyone around him watched with interest. I took it. I hated every second of being reduced to a distressed damsel who needed the narcissistic knight to assist her. But I also didn't want to fight twelve Legacy and Vertu.

The easy smile remained on his lips as he stepped back. I watched him and the others closely waiting on their response as I took a couple of steps away from him to pick up my discarded sai. His smile didn't waver as I picked them up.

"I'm leaving."

"As you should."

What is his deal? I preferred my demagogues to be blathering nutjobs who couldn't shut up about their plans for world domination. The charismatic, calm, attractive gentleman before me definitely wasn't what I needed. But he was what his cause needed. The twelve people ready to destroy the world for him were a testament to the effectiveness of his charisma. I didn't have a chance of talking them out of following him. And I'd probably just helped his cause.

I'd attacked, and he was going to let me walk out alive and unscathed. He'd stopped them from retaliating. Looking over their longing gazes that they kept on him, I realized he'd won them over and I'd just made lifelong enemies.

By the time I'd backed myself up to the opening, I'd centered my magic and readied myself to use it, including preparing for the pain in my body. Adrenaline had long worn off; my body ached and every breath caused a shrill pain from my broken ribs. But I didn't need magic: the veil formed a thin opening, just enough for me to squeeze through, and I was nearly out when someone gave me a magical nudge—hard. I turned to get a quick glance at the woman who hadn't been able to quickly extinguish her magic, standing just a few inches from Conner, glaring at me just as the veil started to close. He might have chosen me as his consort but I had a feeling she wanted the honor. I would have gladly resigned from the position.

I hobbled away, the pains in my ribs and shoulder so intense they were making me nauseous. Nearly twenty feet from my car, I rested back against one of the trees. I had healed cuts and bruises before with my magic but I'd never used it to heal broken bones. But I needed to do something—the pain was getting harder to deal with. The air was clean, I didn't feel a hint of magic in the air despite being just ten feet from a veil that held enough powerful beings to destroy one-fourth of the country.

And then the reality dawned on me—they could. It was estimated that there had been only eighty-nine who had done the global Cleanse. What if Conner changed strategies and went that route? Or would he stick with his initial goal and do small ones all over the country? With the addition of twelve more Legacy, four Necro-spears, and mages who were willing to betray their kind for a chance at more power, how much damage could he do?

Waiting just made things worse—the pain and the speculation—I needed to get to the pit cave, where the wards and location would hide my use of magic. I couldn't afford to be careless.

The moment I pushed myself from the tree, I saw the last thing I needed—Gareth—coming around the corner. Nearly five feet away from me, he stopped abruptly. His brow furrowed as he continued to stare at me. His head tilted slightly and then the bevel of his frown deepened.

I looked down at my shirt and jeans. They were dirty but the evidence of me attacking Conner was gone. That was something else I needed to learn—how to retrieve my blood. It left a sour taste in my mouth that the one person who could teach me how to defeat someone like Conner—was Conner.

"Your hair," he finally said.

For heaven's sake, if you say something about my hair being a mess I'm going to give you a piece of my mind.

"It's red. Real red."

I ran my fingers over it and brought the end of my ponytail into view. It *was* red, our odd trademark persimmon color. I stared at it for a long time. I'd never actually seen my natural color. As long as I could remember, I'd had dark brown hair. As a child, I'd thought it was my natural color; as an adult, my four-week regimen of coloring it made sure that I would never see it.

Gareth quickly noticed my pained movement and came closer. "You're hurt."

"Not really, just my shoulder, and I might have a few broken ribs."

"And *that's* not really hurt?" he asked incredulously.

"Just a little nick."

He pressed his hand against my ribs, and I gasped. "I'm taking you to the Isles."

"No. I can fix it. I'm fine."

His voice dropped, cold and commanding. The same one he used when he started calling me by my last name and spouting his orders. "You have two options, Ms. Michaels: either I take you to the Isles, or to the hospital. Which do you choose?"

"The write-in option—go home and fix it myself. I'm not under your command, I don't have to pick your options."

Uh-oh, kitty's mad again.

And he was. Eyes that were usually blue and crystal bright had darkened like a storm before a torrential rain. "If you were under my command, I'd try my best to keep you from getting hurt. I'd like to think I'm a better person, who wouldn't throw you over my shoulder and make you go to a hospital. You're making it real hard to be a better person."

I'd like to see you try. And then you can tell me how the twins feel. But the way I felt, I didn't think I was going to be a good adversary.

"Ms. Michaels, choose."

Levy, play nice. You can do this. But I didn't trust myself not to tell him where to stick his choices and when he was done, there were a few other places he could stick them again. But through all his shapeshifter machismo, he was just trying to help. Whether I liked it or not, I needed Gareth and the Supernatural Guild.

"I'd rather not go to either. I can fix the ribs and the shoulder." I looked around. "I just don't want to do magic here. Please, I need to go to the pit cave."

He considered it for a moment and then nodded. "I should drive."

In his car, I had a chance to look at my hair in the mirror. It was red—really red. It was very distinctive and so reviled that people who had hair similar to it often changed it for fear of being mistaken for a Legacy. Conner was trying to out me. What if it had been someone else other than Gareth who'd found me—what would have happened?

Gareth looked at my hair once more and seemed to be struck into a concerned silence.

I wasn't sure if him driving was better or not. At least if I drove, I would have something to distract me from the pain. I rested back against the soft leather seat after finding a position that didn't cause me too much pain. "Did you get to the Maxwells?"

He shook his head. "We just need one because their power is divided among the three of them. Take one and you effectively restrict their power. They were gone by the time we got there, leaving just a trail of violence and injured bodies as evidence of their presence." He sighed. "I don't know how they got out of each ward. We separated them."

"They didn't get out, Conner let them out."

"Why the hell would he do something like that?"

"Because he is working with HF, whose only goal is to make the world fear supernaturals. What's a better way than to have a supernatural do a spell to cause humans to hurt each other? Soon you'll have people thinking the Cleanse wasn't such a bad thing because it got rid of the *bad and terrible* supernaturals. In the end, the Legacy and Vertu come out looking like heroes."

"Conner's very strong. The human justice system collects fingerprints; we collect blood. We had theirs and the best mages on our team couldn't track them. We've been reduced to tracking their activity and there isn't a pattern to it." His lips twisted to the side as he became distracted by his thoughts.

"You have their scent, can't you track it?"

"Not if they are blocking it with magic."

"About that, do you know what spell they're using? If so, can you get a copy?"

"The lady doth protest too much. As I said before, our mouth always says one thing, but the body betrays us each time. I can hear your breathing increase, and the uptick of your heartbeat is undeniable. You don't dislike being around me as much as you claim."

"I'm in a lot of pain right now, so that explains the heart rate, and I think I have allergies."

He chuckled. "Of course, that's what it is."

In an effort to ignore the furtive glances, I looked out the window and realized we had passed the pit cave and were inching down the street to his home. "Why are we going to your house? I said I needed the cave. Do you ever listen to anyone or do you just do whatever the hell you want?" I really wanted to blame the coarse edge of my voice on pain but it was more than that. I was angry.

He considered the question for a moment as we drove down the long street leading to his home, past stretches of land with dense groves of trees that obscured almost everything. There appeared to be only four homes on his street, and the distance between them couldn't really justify using the word *neighbor*. Maybe *street mate* was more apropos. "Not when I have something better suited."

"Stalking me to a club, tracking my scent, and taking me to your house against my request sounds like the behavior of a sociopath. You're the head of the Supernatural Guild."

He shrugged as he pulled into his garage. "Yeah, that sounds about right." He quickly got out of the car and came to my side to open the door. I didn't move.

With the door open, he stood and waited. Seconds quickly became a minute as we tried to outstubborn each other. But this was a fight I had to win. Gareth wasn't going to bulldoze me into giving in.

"I guess your injuries aren't that painful—you don't seem to be in a rush to fix them."

I turned to face him, my eyes fastened on him, shooting him the full force of my anger. My teeth were clenched together so tightly that my jaw started to ache. "I deal with pain just fine." *Now I'm going to deal with you.* "Take me where I asked."

He sighed heavily and knelt down. "I have a room you can use—it's safe. The nearest person to my home is nearly seventy yards away. Here you will not have to work in the cold or climb into a cave, which seems like it probably would hurt pretty damn bad with the shape you're in. And I heard your stomach rumble twice—I have food. Satisfied?"

Damn. His idea is better. I packed up my indignation and shame at being unnecessarily obstinate into a little bag of humility and got out of the car. I started to reach for my sai, but Gareth grabbed them.

"I guess I should make sure you don't try to stab me with them," he said with a grin. "You seem to respond to acts of hospitality differently than most women—perhaps you're broken."

You really don't make it easy, do you?

Gareth took me through the house, and I followed him down the hallway to stairs that spiraled into a basement. Some would have called it a man cave: a large-screen TV covered a great deal of wall, a dark comfortable-looking sofa placed in front of it, a leather recliner on the side. And like his office, it was set up like a small apartment, with a refrigerator and kitchen area. In the corner were a foosball table and several games. Like the main house, the walls were a neutral tan, a contrast to the mahogany tables and cocoa-colored furniture. I stopped and considered the area—it didn't seem like him, and it was neat, unused. I doubted he came down here often, and I doubted that he used the room.

"My nephew uses this area more than I do," he offered and tugged on my arm to get me to follow.

Exiting through another door, we descended farther; the walls narrowed and changed from drywall to cement. The walls were cooler, and the lights he turned on didn't offer any more illumination than the flashlight I'd used in the cave. I stayed close; he led me into the "room," and calling it that seemed too tame of a word. *Bunker*, maybe? *Bomb shelter*, possibly? We were underground, deep underground, and I experienced the odd comfort that I felt in my cave. We went through two thick doors into a smaller room. His little hideaway was nice living quarters. Much nicer than my apartment. And it was warm, a lot better than being outside, where it hadn't quite warmed up, or gotten as warm as I expected with the fall temperatures in the Midwest.

"Expecting an apocalypse?" I asked, slowly turning to take in the room.

He barely committed to the light smile, but it remained as he shrugged. "You can never be too sure. Strange things happen, don't they?"

I didn't answer, but I wondered if the strange things that he referred to were the Cleanse. Would this protect him? I didn't know. I didn't feel wards, and even sigils on the walls wouldn't help him because he couldn't perform magic.

He moved farther back, giving me space. "Do you need anything?"

I shook my head, and when he moved back toward the stairs, I expected him to leave. He didn't. With a gentle smile on his lips, he crossed his arms and waited patiently. "I'd like to watch."

"I'm sure you've seen a healing spell done by a witch or a mage," I offered.

"Of course, but I haven't seen one done by *you*. I'm curious."

I took several steps back as he leaned against the wall, his eyes fastened on me with acute interest. I tried to ignore his attention. This was the first time I'd ever done magic around anyone other than my parents and Savannah. It felt odd with an audience.

After a few minutes of uncomfortable silence, I turned my back to him, aware that his interest probably didn't falter. And the magic started as it always did. Even though I'd used it just hours ago, it was so used to being ignored and unused that it came in from its latent state. I'd started using it more in the past two weeks than I had in years and it wasn't as foreign to me as it once was. It unfurled in me, gently coursing through me, the warmth spreading slowly as it encircled my limbs. The various colors that represented the unique origins of my magic emerged separately and then slowly wrapped around one another until it became something uniquely its own. Our magic. Legacy magic.

The painful throbbing in my shoulder was reduced to a dull ache. I inhaled a breath. Before, it had been ragged and painful; now it was just a slight annoyance. I slowly relaxed into the magic and let it course through me again, repairing the damage of the day. And when it was done, as it always did, it seemed to recoil and became a compact little bag stored away for the times I needed it. A travel bag just for emergencies. Emergencies that I was experiencing too often. Emergencies that were going to get worse if I didn't stop Conner.

By the time I turned around, Gareth was close to me and our eyes locked. He hesitated for a moment and then reached out and touched a strand of my hair, slowly twirling it around his fingers. The warmth of his body beat lightly against me. The light flicker of his shapeshifter ring, gentle but with hints of danger, held my gaze. We were close, too close, and I debated between the prevailing contradiction of interest that made me want to stay close and aversion that made me want to move as far away as possible.

"Not what I expected at all," he said softly.

"What did you expect?"

"Just something different. Anya Kismet." He said my name in a low, strained whisper. It was different from the way he'd said it in his office, as if it had meaning to him.

"How did you know my name?" I asked again.

Gareth gave a deviant smile that made the shifter ring sparkle against the light. "I told you, you told me."

I had a hard time believing I'd ever told him such a thing. I had been Olivia Michaels the majority of my life. The moment I had taken on that identity, my parents had drilled it into me that Olivia was who I was. I couldn't imagine I would be so careless to let something like that slip out. I was Anya Kismet because that was my origin; that was who I would have been if things were different. Anya Kismet was who I was supposed to be. Gareth shouldn't have had the information. No one had that information except—

"What did you do before you were with the Supernatural Guild?" I asked, taking a few steps back and watching him with a new caution, becoming more aware of my surroundings. It was in fact the place he had built to protect himself. And it was equipped to do just that. Swords were affixed to the wall: a katana, a saber, and a jian. The katana was at the bottom, not my sai, but easy to use if I needed. A fridge on the other side—nothing I could use there. A large safe to the right, which I was sure had firearms in it. On a shelf there were herbs, tannin, various salts and liquids, all things that you'd find in a magic shop and that I'd seen at the house where we'd met. At the bottom of the shelf he had several little amulets that the witches sold. People loved them, but they weren't much for protection, providing just a small little burst of magic, like a firecracker that couldn't injure unless it was close and near sensitive skin.

"I was head of the Shifter Council," he said.

"For only four years." It was information Kalen was very enthusiastic about giving. The moment I'd asked him to give me more details about Gareth, I'd quickly realized he had a dossier on the Magic Council and the Fae, Witch, Mage, and Shapeshifter Councils as well. It wouldn't have been Kalen's if it hadn't been at least a quarter full of useless information. I didn't think anyone was going to consider tidbits like someone's favorite restaurant or the drink they ordered at the restaurant he saw them at useful at any point in their life.

The discord between us became palpable. It wasn't like anything we'd had before.

His tongue glided over his lips, moistening them, and I prepared for a lie. When he opened his mouth again, only a deep sigh came out. "I don't want to lie to you."

"You mean *again*," I offered.

"I didn't lie the first time. I asked if your name was Anya Kismet and you confirmed it."

"Okay, but how did you know to ask me that?" He was too close and easily closed any space I put between us. I wasn't going to move; I had magic and a katana on the wall, just a quick step away.

The peculiar dance of me keeping my distance from him and him closing it continued. Then he took several steps back from me until he was near the stairway, the only exit. I scanned the room again to make sure.

He slid teeth over his lips. He wasn't going to tell me the truth. People did that when they were going to lie, and they didn't take this long to tell the truth. "For a year I was with the Guardians of Order."

It was a name I knew but never used. Adrenaline kicked my heart into overdrive, a sharp breath caught in my chest, and protective magic came alive in me. It pulsed and wrapped around my fingers, lively colors ready to be released and bring about an unspeakable amount of pain. "A Tracker?"

He nodded, and just as I raised my hand to lob a ball of magic in his direction, he quickly made a half-turn and pointed an odd-looking gun at me. It was a cross between a 9mm and an automatic crossbow. "Don't. I am not going to hurt you. I knew you were going to react like this, which is why I didn't want to tell you."

"I'm sorry you thought I would react defensively after finding out that your job was to track down and kill my kind. How presumptuous of you to feel that way." I rolled my eyes away from him, assessing the situation. Magic versus bullet or whatever was in the pseudo-gun.

"It's not a bullet; it's a dart made of iridium, and it will not kill you but it will hurt like hell upon impact. Based on the results of testing at the Guild, high-level mages lost their ability to perform magic for fifteen minutes. We didn't realize iridium works on them as well. Because you're so strong, I've estimated you'll be indisposed for less than six minutes. That will give me enough time to disable you. To your right behind the sofa there's a set of cuffs thick enough to keep you from doing magic. I'm sure I can have you locked in them before the six minutes are up. Don't test me."

I considered the whole thing. Six minutes. I could get to the katana before then, and without access to magic, that was the only weapon I had. I was adequate with a sword, good enough to fight someone who wasn't skilled, but that was it. And I wasn't sure that he wasn't skilled.

"You can go for the sword, but the way it is positioned, you will have to use your left hand—you're right-hand domi-nant. I'll get to the other one and have the advantage before you will," he said, moving closer. "You're good with the sai, you would be a threat to me if you had them. You don't. I'm excellent with a sword—don't test me. Again, I would have you subdued and in cuffs before the six minutes."

I had to give it to him—when it came to confidence and egotism, he was a gold contender.

"Olivia, I've had six opportunities to kill you if I wanted to."

"That's very specific. The kind of information a psycho would know." I should have just stayed still to prevent any chance of being shot but I felt trapped, and with a Tracker nonetheless. My fight or flight reflexes were in a heightened state—set for survival—and I couldn't temper them.

He chuckled. "Really, *I'm* the psycho. You walked down here, looked for every possible exit. FYI: there's another on the right around the corner. Then you set your eyes on the sword and kept yourself strategically positioned close to it. I think the whole pot-kettle thing is in play." The corners of his lips lifted into a smile.

After a few moments of uncomfortable silence that was riddled with distrust and tension, I let my arms relax at my sides. "Talk."

He watched me for a few moments, intensely. "You aren't going to attack, are you?"

It really depended on what he had to say, but I knew that wasn't going to work. I shook my head, and it took him a few minutes before he brought the gun down. He moved aside and waved me toward the stairs. I had to play nice because he had valuable information I needed. He could give me the inner workings of the clandestine group and maybe even help me find more Legacy before Conner could get to them and persuade them to join him.

Once upstairs, he holstered the odd gun behind him.

"You can put it up, you won't need it," I said.

"Truce?"

"Truce."

He winked. "Good, I think we should play nice."

He returned with a binder in his hand, which was pretty much what I'd expected. For years, I'd assumed the clandestine group that hunted and assassinated us probably didn't operate in large high-tech rooms, with computers, large screens, and a database of information. Nope, they were probably just a group of people in a dingy basement, looking at binders, scrolls, and paper scraps of information.

Gareth dropped the binder in front of me and then went over to a coffee station and made us cappuccino and a plate of pastries: mini muffins, cinnamon rolls, and Danish and an assortment of berries. "Your house manager?" I teased, looking at the ready-prepared food.

He made a face and then nodded. He said that she ran the house for him, but "house manager" seemed like a nanny.

I grabbed a muffin and started to flip through the pages; it was far more extensive than I'd expected. I didn't know if it listed every Legacy, and it didn't differentiate between them and the Vertu, but everything else was very detailed. Name, age, place of birth, place of death, and how: Tracker, natural causes, or in the war. I scanned each page, looking for Conner. I didn't see him but I saw my mother's and dad's names, the day they were killed. And mine—the day I died. I jumped up without thinking, and the jolt flew from my fingers and Gareth crashed into the wall, plaster crumbling around his body. I shouldn't have been using magic in the open, I knew it and tried so hard not to. I wasn't sure how far the aura of it traveled or if someone driving down the street would get a sense of it and know it was mine. Anger had driven out all logic, and the only thing I wanted to do was hurt him.

He'd lied to me, and all the anger I felt about my parents' deaths, having to hide most of my life, changing my name, hair, and overall identity had built to something that I couldn't handle.

"It's not what you think," he said as he folded into the floor. It was all just white noise drowned out by the anger. As he recovered and came to his feet, something hit the wall. I looked. It was only seconds of distraction, and I quickly realized Gareth had tossed something in my direction. When I turned back to face him, he tossed the small speaker next to him at me. I took my attention off of him, just for a second, to flick my finger and send it in another direction; he lunged at me. We crashed to the ground. I screeched as something pierced my skin. Instead of the blazing heat of magic that had consumed me, my body cooled. I called magic—nothing. Again—nothing. Moments later I felt metal clasped around my skin. My arms were cuffed in front of me.

I could feel the heat of my anger rising off me; warmth nicked at the bridge of my nose and my cheeks as it always did when my ire had reached a point where I couldn't control it. I pulled Gareth to me and slammed into him again. Panting, he moved back, wiping the blood from his lips. I wasn't aware that I'd punched him. Several feet away, he rested his head back against the wall and glared at me, the shapeshifter ring seeming to glow. I felt like I was in the presence of a cave lion rather than a man. His head still pressed back against the wall, he closed his eyes, his breathing starting to slow. When he spoke, his voice was a rough, cool whisper.

"You didn't let me finish."

"That information is recent. Less than three weeks ago, someone came after me and I implanted that memory so they would think I was dead. The only way you would have that information is if you were in contact with them recently," I hissed. The thought of it made me angry all over again.

The cuffs were tight and dug into my skin each time I yanked on them.

"Ms. Michaels, you are going to hurt yourself."

"Don't 'Ms. Michaels' me! You lied to me. You asked me to trust you, but how can I?"

"I didn't lie." He moved closer and took a seat on the floor a few inches from me. "I was part of the Guardians, that's true. I failed my first assignment. It wasn't something I could do—they killed Legacy. Period. Regardless of age, family, whether the person posed a threat or not. We watched them day in and day out looking for a perfect time to strike—that's what we are trained to do. But you're not like the books make you out to be. You're no more dangerous than a mage —if you don't want to be. I couldn't go along with killing someone because they *might* be a danger or *might* have participated in the Cleanse. People like to forget that there was a small group who resisted and fought it. I couldn't do it."

He slid closer and examined the cuffs on my arms. He hesitated before he leaned forward and examined the skin around them. "You're going to bruise your arms if you don't stop trying to get out of the cuffs."

"You can take them off," I suggested, extending my arms. I tried the coy thing again: gentle doe eyes, pouty lips, and soft limpid voice, and even half-assing it made me nauseated.

"Aw, how cute are you? Innocent puppy eyes and every-thing. Is that a pout? You're pulling out all the stops, aren't you? Truly bringing your A game. If you hadn't just given me this"—he pointed to his quickly healing split lip, which was still stained with blood and swollen—"a minute ago, I could halfway believe you."

"Truce."

"We tried that, remember?" He shifted back on his heels. *This isn't going to be good, and it's going to taste horrible coming out.* "I'm sorry, I overreacted." I had. He was right. He'd had every opportunity to kill me, and if he didn't want to do it, he could have reported me to the Magical Council and tasked them with making my life—or whatever was left of it—a living hell.

The sharp edges to his features had softened and the deep frown faded into just a straight line.

"How did you get the new information?"

"I'm going to have to ask you to trust me on this because I can't tell you right now," he entreated.

I extended my cuffed arms out again, and he considered it for a long time. "Ms. Michaels"—his rumbled warning—"if you attack me again, I will have you arrested and charged. Period. Puppy dog eyes or lovely smile or cute little simper will not save your ass. You will sit behind bars until I'm satisfied you've learned your lesson. Are we clear?"

I nodded and he unlocked my manacles. "You know that threat is going to lose its effect if you keep using it."

Shut up, Levy. And I snapped my mouth shut when he pulled back his lips; if he were in animal form, I would have been looking at fangs. Gently taking my arms, he examined the marks on them. They didn't look as bad as they felt. I'd rubbed the skin raw, but that was my own doing by struggling.

I took a moment before I actually moved, the contained magic releasing with force and spiraling around in me. I needed to get some semblance of control over it. I studied Gareth and then the room, counting the few seconds it took for him to get the upper hand. It wasn't that I ever forgot that he was a predator—if I did, the lissome predaciousness of his movements was a reminder. But he'd been able to distract me, grab the cuffs from wherever they were hidden, and disable me before I could strike. Twice I'd won against Trackers, but would I if it were Gareth sent for me? I pushed down the uneasiness that started to rise, but the thought had created an uncomfortable silence that Gareth quickly noticed. I didn't want to talk about it right now. He was about to speak when I stood and moved to the table. He took a seat next to me. "I don't see Conner's name."

"Yeah, and they are quite thorough, I can't believe that they don't know him."

That was suspicious. How had Conner been able to stay under the radar this long? I didn't want to be impressed with the magical Napoleon with the dream of world domination, but he'd managed to do something I couldn't. It scared and impressed me. And now he'd increased his army from three to twelve people in a matter of days. He was better than Trackers at finding Legacy.

"I don't get Conner," Gareth said, slouching back in his chair, his hands clasped behind his head.

"What do you mean?"

"You think he released the Maxwells and Declan. Ms. Neal was given the Recludo Stone by someone who fits Conner's description."

"And he's allied with HF," I offered and went on to tell him about them approaching me.

"I get the Maxwells—if you want chaos and destruction, you employ them. They'd do it for the hell of it and wouldn't charge a thing." He leaned forward and touched a strand of my oddly colored hair that had pulled away from the ponytail, allowing it to slowly fall from his fingers.

"And Declan definitely caused a lot of chaos and destruction, too. Is Conner really doing all this to out you? It damn near worked. If I hadn't gotten there in time at Ms. Neal's, how would you have handled Declan?"

"I had the situation under control."

He dismissed the idea with a deep chortle before saying, "Yeah, it seemed to be pretty controlled when I got there. If you were reduced to using magic in public on a shapeshifter, everyone would have known what you are. Either she would have reported it or Kalen would have. It's citizen obligation. Technically you are all fugitives as far as the supernatural world is concerned."

I knew that, but hearing it come from him somehow made it seem worse. Would Kalen have reported me? He followed the rules of the Magic Council and the state laws regarding supernaturals. He'd mentioned on more than one occasion that the only good that had come from the Cleanse was the regulation of magic. And it was his belief in the rules that compounded the many reasons I was reluctant to tell him. Did he care more about the rules, justice, and the laws than about me?

"What happens if I'm reported?" Trackers' rules were easy —they killed us—but what would the Magic Council do? If my only crime was being a Legacy, could they really sentence me to death?

"Just don't get reported," he said softly. Well, I had my answer.

We went through the binder, and he made copies of the list of Legacy and their nearest known locations. It lessened the risk of me looking for them because I wouldn't have to use a locating spell to do so. The less use of magic, the better. But I still didn't know the names of the twelve who were now on Team Conner. Time was of the essence and tracking people who had already been found and recruited by Conner made the task more difficult.

CHAPTER 6

*A*lthough I'd come through the door of our apartment the night before bruised, tattered, and with an oversized baseball cap over my head, Savannah completely accepted my appearance once I gave her the explanation that I'd been with Gareth. Apparently in her mind, my interaction with Gareth could simply be reduced to an unexplained night of unbridled violence ending with me sporting a blue baseball cap. Or maybe she cared less about that than finding out about her potential of being a fire mage or witch—I still hadn't had the heart to tell her it simply wasn't a thing. She was insistent that I call the witch I'd mentioned who might be able to help her uncover her "gifts."

Blu's voice was oddly bright and enthusiastic for a person who was getting a call at eight o'clock on Saturday morning. I was still cranky from having to get up early to dye my hair back before Savannah or anyone else could see it. Savannah knew what I was, but the hair wasn't me.

Blu listened as I told her that my roommate suspected that she was either a witch or mage. I left out most of the things that had gone on at the club. "Why does she feel that she might be a witch?"

Because she's mistaken her taste buds needing a sugar fix as magic vibes or whatever. "I know this might sound odd, but she seems to have a weird connection with things—namely fire." It really felt like I was telling her my roommate was a pyromaniac.

Blu seemed oddly at ease with it. "Well, it's not unheard of for mages and witches to have a connection. Earth witches can draw from the earth for their spells and have been known to be influential in helping farmers with their crops and using the rain. So have mages, but their abilities are a little stronger. They can't make fire, rain, snow, and the like but have been able to influence the weather to their advantage." Blu might have become Kalen's newest crush for her fashion sense, but she had definitely earned favor with me by not calling my friend a raging nutjob. Only I had that pleasure.

"Are her parents witches or mages?"

"Nope."

"Has she attempted any spells?"

"That's why I'm calling you. Is there any way you can check it out and see?"

"It would be my pleasure."

Three hours later, we were driving to meet Blu at the same home where I'd met her before with Gareth. I kept shooting a look at Savannah's multicolored satchel that she'd packed for our "quest." Her word, not mine. She didn't consider our ride to the other side of town to confirm she was the quirkiest of quirky, nothing more than a human who might be a fire aficionado, or in some circles a pyromaniac, whose taste buds hated her, a simple day trip. Nope, she'd decided to call it a "quest," and she'd packed for it: flashlight, fruit, granola, and quinoa and bean salad. I didn't mind telling her that if we got lost on the "quest" I was more likely to eat her than the crap she'd brought. At least *I* thought it was funny.

Dampening her hopes wasn't something I wanted to do, but I wanted her to be realistic about what might happen —nothing.

"About this—"

"Quest," she offered with a faint smile.

"Okay, Frodo," I said, rolling my eyes as she cut her eyes at me, probably recounting the hours of her life lost because I'd made her watch *The Fellowship of the Ring* with me. "This could be absolutely nothing. From what I've heard, you were impressive, but it could be that you were just brave in a crisis —or maybe you're a pyromaniac, but that's a topic for another day."

"Or I could be a witch and be able to help you more with Conner."

And there it was. Over the past weeks, her life and involvement in the supernatural world had changed. She'd harassed a grumpy cave lion who was not only the head of the Supernatural Guild but on the Magic Council just to get me out of the Haven, been attacked by a vampire, been kidnapped by a psychopathic mage, and been befriended by the Vampire Master of the city, and to top off the cornucopia of bizarre she was dealing with, her roommate was a Legacy. I got it—I would want some kind of power, too, but desire and hope wouldn't make it a reality.

"I just don't want you to be disappointed."

She gave me a faint smile. "I won't be. What's being done about Conner?"

"I don't know. The only thing I can find comfort in is that he will not do the Cleanse anytime soon, but he's still doing enough damage without it. Between releasing the Maxwells, the chaos at the Square, the shifter at the Neal house, and the incident at Devour, no matter how good Harrah is, she can't cover it all up."

I tried to hide the concern in my voice, but that was a task in itself. Things were a mess, and I still couldn't stop thinking about Gareth being an ex-Tracker. He was right, it wasn't something he could have just told me, and he could have continued to lie about it. However, he still had ties to them. How? Did he have a friend on the inside, and even if he did, how could he be friends with someone who was nothing more than an assassin? What drew him to that? But I pushed aside the thoughts. I would have to deal with them later. I had a *quest* I needed to carry out.

Blu introduced herself to Savannah using the same rehearsed line she'd used on me, explaining that her name was Blu without an *E*. And blaming the odd spelling on her jazz enthusiast parents whose artistic nature couldn't allow them to be so pedestrian and just spell it the typical way. They needed her to be unique.

We followed her farther into the house. "I want you to relax. If you are able to do magic, I will guide you and it will be easy. Okay."

But Savannah couldn't relax, she was hyper by nature. And I knew she wouldn't be able to relax, because in her mind, her life was about to change. And mine was, too, because for the next few days I would have to deal with woefully deflated Savannah, whose dreams had been crushed. While Blu set things up, Savannah perused the many books on the shelves and fixated on the herbs, candles, and various sigils and symbols on the walls. She seemed more tense and hopeful than ever, and a part of me wanted there to be something, too. For her to be able to protect herself with more than a knife, which she was getting better at using; protest gear; and a handful of legal terms that I was sure weren't right.

When Blu called her to the table, she offered her *herba terrae* to get her to relax, and Savannah was about to take it— or I assumed she was, because it took her a while to decline it.

"Can she try without that, please?"

Blu nodded and started. I split my attention between watching them start with simple spells and looking at the many books on the shelves. Most of them were in English, but several were in Latin. I started to go through them, trying to commit some of the spells to memory. I was sure these were books I wouldn't find in a magic shop and that probably had spells in them that my parents hadn't taught me. Wards, location spells, memory manipulations, and defensive magic were the only arrows I had in my quiver to protect me. Conner could teleport; could Legacy do that as well, or was it exclusive to Vertu? He also had skills of animancy. Although I didn't like the idea of controlling someone against their will, it seemed like a good tool to possess if I were ever confronted by a misbehaving shapeshifter.

Blu continued working with Savannah, for nearly forty-five minutes, failed spell after failed spell. She even assisted with one, igniting the *herba terrae*. The herbs that were gathered in an oddly shaped container illuminated orange, red, and silver, Blu clasped her hand with Savannah's, and the colors brightened. Vibrant movement occurred inside the container and smoke swirled around it until thick puffs choked from it. Blu quickly dropped Savannah's hand and the colors died down, muted to nearly nonexistent.

"Hmm." Was that the only thing she would offer? Her brows pulled together as her lips twisted into a moue.

"What?" Savannah asked, concerned. I waited for Blu to

gather her thoughts, which seemed to be taking an awfully long time.

"I will need to take some time to consult with my mother and a couple of people in my coven. I don't think you're a witch or mage, but there is something." At first I thought she was just offering something to placate our fire enthusiast, but she wasn't. A combination of confusion, interest, and concern melded and settled over her forced smile. "I think she's an *ignesco*. Very rare, which is why I need to discuss it with others. If she is, she can't do magic herself but can assist others during spells to make them stronger."

Blu was more anxious than she'd ever been and kindly invited us to leave. "Are you interested in that book? You're welcome to borrow it."

Yes. "Some of it is quite interesting. It's our history and a few basic spells." I grabbed a couple more. "Do you mind if I borrow these as well? I'll bring them back in a couple of days. I'm just interested in them."

She looked at the books, took two of the four I'd taken off the shelves, and agreed. I was happy with what I had. A spell was a spell, but how it responded was contingent on the wielder's magic. A witch could erect a ward, just as a mage could, but he strengthened it. What a ward could block was based on whether it was done by a mage, witch, or even a Legacy.

Savannah and I both left Blu's a lot happier than we'd arrived.

The unknown number had come up on my phone for the third time when I finally answered it. It was Clive. I didn't expect him to hold me to my commitment of meeting with them. I'd figured by now Conner had taken the Necro-spears and HF would be too preoccupied with trying to get them back from him to be concerned about meeting with me. Then I realized Conner was probably all talk. I recalled his assertion when I'd told him Humans First shouldn't have the Necro-spears. "Done"—*yeah, right.* The ironclad deal he had with Clive and Humans First was most likely better than my "no way in hell" offer.

Conner had left me no other choice. If he wasn't going to get the Necro-spears, then I had to meet with HF, if only to retrieve them myself. That was my sole intention as I walked into the small tan brick building and glanced into the only office in the place. It was empty. Instead of going in, I went across the hall to the training room. A large window that covered a little over half the wall gave a perfect view into it. One person was in there, working a heavy bag. A large mat covered most of the floor, and far off in the corners were free weights, a few pieces of cardio equipment, benches, and a large cooler. They had several training dummies crowded in the nearest corner. On each wall was their mission statement and a reminder that their sole purpose was to inflict their help on other people who didn't have a problem with supernaturals. A constant presence, a chastising organization to ridicule those who openly accepted and actually liked supernaturals.

"Do you like it?" Clive's voice came from behind me. I turned and took several steps back from him. A smile flicked at his lips. He liked the idea that I was afraid of him, and everything in me wanted to dispel that myth, but him thinking that I was afraid of him worked in my favor. He wouldn't be as guarded and reactive. I kept my hand on one of my sai for a while longer. I wasn't afraid of him, but I didn't trust him at all. He focused on my hand that remained on the sai. He chuckled. "We're all friends here, there's no need for that," he offered.

"Hmm, we definitely have a different definition of friend-ship. I generally like my friends alive. But that's just my silly preference, I guess," I shot back.

The smile, genteel and welcoming, was firmly planted on his face. "I don't want you dead, Levy. I actually like you. Perhaps if you were the face of magic, then it would be more palatable for me."

Is he flirting? Based on the crooked smile that he had given me, I guessed he was. But all I saw was a wolf baring his fangs, who would gut me the minute he thought he could.

He turned and started toward the office that was across from the gym, and when I didn't follow him, his brow rose in confusion. I went after him into the room, and sitting behind a large executive desk was Daniel, the founder of HF. I remembered seeing him at the auction where Kalen and I had acquired the first Necro-spear. Now he had four, and I was curious as to how he'd acquired them.

Unlike Clive, who was dressed in their traditional clichéd outfit of fitted black t-shirt and jeans and a wry half-cocked smile that sealed the badass spy guy look, Daniel wore a neatly pressed black dress shirt and slacks. He wore a busi-ness look on his face that mirrored his clothing. Deep, expressive dark brown eyes revealed that this was nothing more than a meeting and he wasn't even going to bother himself with giving me a smile, which I suspected he gave sparingly. The chilling look coursed its way to his eyes, where it remained. He sat upright in his chair, and every-thing from the cool, intrigued look, the thin rigid line that his lips formed, and the way he clasped his hands in front of him telegraphed that this was a business meeting. Plain and simple. He had one objective, and if I didn't comply, then he had no use for me.

"Ms. Olivia Michaels, please have a seat." His voice was soft, lighter than I would have expected from him, but firm.

"You can call me Levy," I offered, although I doubted he would.

"I'll remember that." He waited for me to get seated. But I couldn't get comfortable until Clive wasn't behind me. I didn't think he was above stabbing me in the back, metaphorically or literally.

"Clive and the Justice League said you wanted to talk to me about purchasing the Necro-spears. What do you want for them?" I asked.

That pulled a laugh from him, dark and ominous. "Clive said you were quite … let's just say witty to keep it cordial. Ms. Michaels, you are aware of why we are having this meeting. Conner is a good person, someone I can definitely get on board with, but he seems to be reluctant to go forward, and you seem to be the reason. I wanted to meet with you to see if we can discuss matters and come to an agreement so that we can move this forward in a timely manner."

I couldn't help but choke out a laugh; I wasn't being condescending or snarky or dismissive. I was flabbergasted by the casual way he was discussing killing off a large portion of the world's population—as if he was asking if I wanted to get an extended warranty with purchase.

"I'm sorry; shouldn't we be discussing this over a large quantity of alcohol so we can at least have an excuse for discussing something so reprehensible with a straight face?"

His eyes flew in Clive's direction and narrowed on him as if he'd been given bad intel. Did he think I was going to be agreeable to doing the Cleanse over, and all I needed was a good talking-to?

But the Necro-spears were in the building—close. I could feel the presence of familiar magic in the area. The aura of its existence. The good fortune of it made me overlook their arrogance. I scanned the room again making sure there weren't any attached areas where others could be hiding.

A desk was the only thing between me and Daniel, and he moved and carried himself like he was more than just a stone-faced man with expressive hard eyes.

"Ms. Michaels, there are only two sides of this situation: you are either with us or against us," he said in a breezy tone that held a hint of a threat.

I scoffed. "That's the same threat Clive made. You know, the whole 'you are either with us or against us spiel' is ineffective. Unless you have a cat you plan on pulling from under your desk and stroking while you cackle like a madman, you can just screw off."

"Ms. Michaels." His tone was even cooler than before, the edge gone as he came to his feet. "Don't be fooled, we want the same things. You are just too stubborn to accept it. This is going to happen; the question is whether you will be a victim or a survivor."

They had the Necro-spears, and the crux of it was they couldn't be trusted. While Conner was the same diabolical crazy as they were, he seemed to have a plan. I was sure Daniel couldn't care less if anyone with magic was left in the world. Conner, despite how selfish and self-serving he was, wanted to preserve the Legacy and Vertu—and, for some odder reason, me.

"Show me the spears and then we can talk about it further."

Daniel's mouth twisted in derision and his eyes turned cold and deadly as they narrowed on me. "Ms. Michaels, I do believe your perception of your bargaining power is distorted. Your options are limited. If we go to the Council and inform them of your existence, what do you think will happen?" His voice was grating.

"I'm not sure. Why don't you tell them that you think I'm a Legacy and the reason you're telling them is because I won't help you do the Cleanse. I'm sure I won't be the one coming out looking bad in that scenario. But first you have to convince them of that. Remember, I went before them and walked away with them none the wiser. I know exactly what my bargaining power is."

His jaws clenched so tight, if they were glass they would have shattered. It seemed like he had to unhinge them just to speak. The moments of silence drifted to minutes, his eyes narrowed again, and I was sure he contemplated several times how he would deliver my death. I thought about how I would disable and subdue them and get to the Necro-spears. I didn't plan to kill them; there was a part of me that really wanted to, but being misguided twits didn't warrant a death sentence.

At a single nod from Daniel, Clive lunged for me. I jerked his arm and quickly maneuvered, placing myself at an angle and hip-tossing him to the ground. I snatched my sai out of my sheath and pressed one at his throat, near the carotid, and the other I left pointed in Daniel's direction, warning him off any further movements.

"Give me the Necro-spears. Now." Daniel hesitated and looked down at Clive's sneering face and the blade pressed lightly into his neck. I pressed it hard enough to let him know that I wasn't playing and was willing to use it. I didn't want to—I didn't kill. That had been my mantra for so many years, and the only time I'd violated it was when I'd finally found the Trackers who killed my family. They'd deserved to die, but not this misguided, delusional fool. He deserved to be smacked a bunch of times and given a time-out until he decided that genocide was wrong. The problem was, his beliefs were so heavily ingrained in him that he'd romanticized the Utopic magicless world—a well-deserved ass kicking might not be enough.

Clive screwed his eyes shut for a few moments, and when he opened them they were devoid of emotion, empty, as if he had resigned himself to a fate of death. "Don't give her anything. Either she is with us or against us."

"What is wrong with you!" I snapped. "You aren't on the right side. I'm not on the right side, but it's by default. I was born into a group of people who attempted to ruin the world and I have to live my life differently because of it. I've had to run from people and live in fear that I would be found out, and you are trying to repeat history. Don't be a fool." But I had given up on Clive. His face was fixed in consternation and there was no reasoning with him. "You give me the Necro-spears—I will find a way to destroy them. This will be just a misguided attempt and you can go back to your 'humans are special snowflakes' rallies. Buy shirts, I don't care. But if the Legacy failed before, when there were more and the strongest of their kind doing the spell, do you think you will succeed using the bottom-feeders and those willing to betray their kind for power?"

Daniel bit down on his bottom lip. I had his full attention. *Good, you just seem like a sociopath, you might not actually be one.* "The Cleanse had several benefits—it secured an alliance between the humans and the supernaturals. The strongest supernaturals exist now, and there are only a few of us. Conner has given you false hope. You might kill a few supernaturals with smaller versions of the Cleanse as you attempted to do with Jonathan. But—"

Daniel dropped to the floor, his head twisted at an odd angle, and Conner stood next to the collapsed body. "Well, he turned out to be quite useless. You nearly had him. Persuasive, a good fighter, and beautiful. I've chosen well."

Clive made a choked gargling noise, and then silence. Next to him was the woman who gave me the final shove through the veil; she dropped the knife she'd used on him next to his body, which was slowly having the life drained from it. Death wasn't coming fast enough, because her hand illuminated and magic commanded the room. So did the stench of death as he convulsed for a moment and then stopped moving.

Close, I plunged the sai in her direction, striking air. I turned to face Conner and she was next to him. A pulsating ball of magic danced in her hand and anger flickered in her eyes.

"Evelyn, don't." Keeping his eyes on me, he opened his hand and the ball vanished from hers and reappeared in his. A show to demonstrate his strength and skill with magic that I was no match for. I was a novice on so many levels and I couldn't help but wonder how I compared in regards to the others. Was he training them to be as skilled as he was, or was he this skilled because he was stronger than me—than the Legacy?

He frowned. Playing with the coiled magic, twisting it around his fingers, unwinding the various forms of it, only to force it into submission until he entwined it again, moving it effortlessly from one hand to the other. Master of magic would have been impressive if it wasn't wrapped in the package of a crazy megalomaniac. "We do not attack our own, no matter how foolish they are being. Please, go retrieve the spears for me while Anya and I speak."

Bile rose in me as I watched how dismissive he was of Daniel's body as he negotiated around it as if it was inconsequential, and Evelyn scurried off to carry out his orders. What had he said to them to warrant such loyalty and easy acceptance of his commands?

His magic was a thick blanket smothering the air. I had chosen not to use mine because there were people on the streets, some human and some supernatural. I just saw the various shadows that passed by the partially closed blinds. Conner no longer seemed to care about hiding behind the cloak of secrecy, which made things worse. He was gearing up for a war and must have felt confident he could win.

I wasn't going to allow him to casually dismiss murder victims, even if they were members of HF who considered my kind and other supernaturals reprehensible. I was better than that. My grip tightened around the sai, my attention acutely fixed on him, looking for that moment that only a narcissist like him would have when he was vulnerable because he assumed his presence was enough to disarm anyone. He didn't present that moment and threw the magic that he'd been playing with like a kitten with a ball of yarn. I blocked it, but it wasn't enough to stop the powerful bolt that hit my field of magic. I stumbled back and the fraction of a second was all he needed. He had taken that advantage that I'd been looking for myself and had pinned me, arms stretched out with my sai, to the wall.

He made a clicking noise with his tongue as he paced the floor. "You are making this quite difficult for me, Anya." He spoke in a low, soothing tone. "I don't want to treat my consort this way. It's beneath me. It's beneath us."

He's having a delusion-fest and invited just himself to the party.

"I need to tell you this in no uncertain terms, I will *never* be with you. I'm not sure why you feel the need to choose me when you have a woman who actually is allied with you. I loathe you and I don't really know you, but getting to know you will probably amplify this. And if you think you will force me into this—go ahead. It will be the shortest relation-ship you'll ever have because you won't be able to trust me. I'll be plotting your death while you are filling out a wedding registry. You'll have to drag me down the aisle of whatever dumb-ass, unnecessarily elaborate, and I'm pretty sure tacky celebration you hold to celebrate our union. And I'll be trying to poison anything I think you might eat and I won't care if it kills our guests, too, because they probably deserve your same fate. Your consort will be the very person who has denied you and will continue to do so, making it a hobby to make your life a living hell."

He smiled as though I had just sung him a love song, or recited a lovely poem as a tribute to him or something. *Is this what narcissism on magic looks like?*

Evelyn returned, her face flushed with anger, and it was obvious she had heard my threat, or at least parts of it.

"You asked me to do this for you. I did. Anya, I will earn your loyalty or *you* will earn my wrath. It is time for you to choose. I cannot waste more time appealing to your naiveté and cynicism." He sighed, and his mood and features darkened—I glimpsed what I was truly dealing with. It came in an innocuous-looking package of pastel shirts, slacks, and an amalgam of aristocratic and broad features, but he was in fact a monster who saw murder as just a necessary inconvenience. A chill ran down my spine, obviously his desired effect, because he smiled and nodded in my direction. Then he and Evelyn disappeared. I dropped to the floor alone with Clive's and Daniel's bodies.

It took me a minute to regain my composure. I didn't know what to do. Should I call Gareth? The police? Leave the scene? How many people had seen me come in? If someone had seen me, could they identify me? The few minutes I thought I took ended up being nearly fifteen, after I stared out the window, trying to remember the faces of the many people passing by. It wouldn't help, because I didn't know who had seen me, too. Finally, I called Gareth. He answered on the first ring.

"I need your help," I said, trying to keep my voice level. But if I was asking for his help, he knew it had to be bad.

"Now? Can it wait a few minutes? We've had another incident in the park."

"Clive and Daniel are dead, and I'm pretty sure people are going to think I did it."

"Where are you?"

"At the Humans First office."

There was a long, uncomfortable silence. It was so long that I thought the call had been dropped. "Gareth?"

"I'm here." He sighed. He cursed—a lot. "Did you use magic in there?"

"Yeah."

Another string of curse words. He seemed to know a great deal of them and put them together in ways I hadn't thought of. I was particularly fond of *clusterfuck*, which I thought summed things up quite well.

"I'll be there in a few minutes."

Gareth arrived about fifteen minutes later and found me in the gym, where I had been drilling punches and kicks into the heavy bag. It hadn't made me feel any better. I needed to clear my head, and usually a run was what really helped. Hitting the bag made me wish I had the chance to land the same strikes on Conner, but the guilt was getting the best of me. If I hadn't told Conner that HF shouldn't have the Necro-spears, would they be dead?

"What happened?" Gareth's voice was a lot gentler than the stringent look on his face. He looked like he'd had a day similar to mine, maybe even worse. I explained everything— the unedited version—and he listened, periodically looking in the room, as though he'd had his fill of seeing dead bodies.

"So he has four Necro-spears, twelve Legacy ... Vertu or whatever ... and ..." His voice drifted off.

"And what?"

"And he helped three other mages escape from the Haven

today, the triplets are having their way with the city, and I suspect he is doing all of this to distract us."

"They can't do a global Cleanse," I pointed out.

"No, but they can destroy enough of us for it to hurt." He blew out a hard breath before washing his hands over his face. "I can't cover this up, Olivia."

Fuck. Why am I Olivia now? This was bad. No Levy. Even Ms. Michaels was tolerable, because that meant he was in "head of Supernatural Guild" mode and got a jerk-in-charge pass. This was ... different.

"What do we do now?"

"You're going to have to come out and expose who you are and let the Magic Council know that you exist, and apparently in great numbers. We need a lot more people involved."

"No."

"Olivia."

"No. Don't 'Olivia' me! You know what will happen. I might as well find a Tracker and let him do the job. Maybe you'll get points if you do it!" I knew I was being irrational, but everything was happening too fast. Come out—now. Did I get to prepare a speech, defend why I got to live when I was of the same kind who not only had done the Cleanse before but wanted to do it again?

I tried to calm myself by taking several breaths, but it didn't help. Panic and fear came over me hard and I didn't like feeling that way. Gareth's appearance softened, and so did his voice. "There aren't a lot of options. At least with you out and the rest, I'm not fighting a ghost or what seems like a ghost. We'll have help, I can actively get the SG involved." He paused. His voice lowered. "Maybe even the Guardians of Order."

Whatever else he had said was to my back because I walked out the door, ignoring him calling my name. I was at a slow run by the time I got to my car. I drove aimlessly for nearly an hour and then I found myself in the middle of the crowded forest, feeling the subtle hints of Conner's magic lingering in the air as I traipsed through the thicket in the direction where I'd encountered him and his group of followers. I was just a few feet from where the veil had been the last time when I stopped. Fear and panic cause people to make foolish mistakes, and I was making one now. I couldn't beat them the last time, and being pissed off wasn't going to suddenly improve my magical skills. I needed to learn. I had only gotten through half of the spells in the books that Blu had loaned me and hadn't practiced them. I had to practice, improve my skills, and freaking learn how to disappear the way Conner and Evelyn did—or at least try. I wasn't sure if that was a Vertu trick or if I possessed it, too. It continued to be one of the things I wondered about. It seemed as if it was a valuable skill to possess.

I stopped in the middle of the woods and went back to my car and after a few more minutes of mindless traveling, ignoring Gareth's five calls, I sat on the ground in the pit cave, using the flashlight from my phone to read the spells in one of the books. Most of them I knew: wards, locating spells, object displacement. There were some elemental ones that I wanted to try but calling forth fire in a cave wasn't the smartest thing to do.

A few minutes later I was playing with a ball of magic in the same manner that Conner had. It was concentrated power used to displace objects or people but I found it soothing as it bounced around in my hand, folding and unfolding at my will. Separating into a string of colors, each one representing a magical entity. I never learned which one was which, but I doubted it was of any importance. Our power came from them melding together to become something that was uniquely our magic. Its origin before it had been changed and diluted and possessed by others.

"That's quite impressive." Gareth's voice traveled out of the darkness from the other end of the cave. The only thing I could see was the flicks of illumination from the shifter circle around his pupils. They all had it; his seemed darker than most, entrancing. But I supposed that was the appeal of the predator. Seduced by the unique eyes and sinewy and lithe movements and drawn to the predacious nature, you found yourself too mesmerized to protect yourself. I wasn't going to fall for it. I came to my feet, the ball of magic beating at a steady pace, thumping like a heartbeat, the kaleidoscope of colors dangerously deceptive about its danger.

I palmed it, holding it securely to me, making a promise to find some way to secure the other entrance to the cave so that it couldn't be used.

"Talk."

"You're not going to convince me to do it."

"I didn't think I could. I have no intention of you coming out on the losing end of this, Levy. I don't ask this lightly. What do you have to lose?"

"My life. The world sees us as monsters."

"They see *them* as monsters—Conner and his allies. He's going to keep causing problems and things are going to get worse. He's not even hiding anymore—he's overconfident and the face of the Legacy now."

"Don't make this a political or PR thing—"

"I'm not. You come out, others will, too. You get to them before he does and make sure he's not able to recruit more people. You'll have the SG behind you, and the Magic Council."

"For someone who claims he's not here to convince me to come out, that little spiel begs otherwise."

His lips cocked into a crooked smile. "Levy, I don't think

anyone believes they can get you to do something you don't want to do."

He waited patiently and I busied myself with the magic I'd been playing with.

"Okay, but I need to talk to Kalen first. I'll meet with them tomorrow."

He nodded slowly and started backing out. "Hey, can you have that exit closed?" I asked as he disappeared into the darkness of the cave. "I keep getting unwanted visitors."

His laughter traveled and reverberated off the walls of the cave.

"Is that a yes or a no?"

"I'll see what I can do, Ms. Michaels."

I hated when he called me that—but that was likely the point.

CHAPTER 7

*T*he next morning I sat at the desk Kalen and I shared, with his coffee, pastries, and my information bomb waiting for him. I should have been late and waited until he had asked for coffee, because he wouldn't have seemed so suspicious when I handed them to him.

"What did you do?" he asked, looking around the room.

"I always bring you coffee and pastries," I scoffed back. He took a sip, keeping a cautious eye on me as he went into the next room and pulled out several boxes. He must have gotten them over the weekend, because I didn't remember them being there.

Most people didn't rummage through boxes of other people's discards and junk in a custom suit. Kalen didn't really think about ruining clothes because he'd always had money, and it hadn't come from Kalen's Collectibles—in the antiques and glorified junk-collecting business, there were very little opportunities to make money. We were lucky that through some of his connections we had a chance to acquire magical objects from auctions and somehow had become the city's acquisitions specialists, retrieving those objects that had been lost or misplaced and those only rumored to exist.

I plopped down on the floor next to him and started sorting through the boxes. His suspicion made things tense. Usually we chatted the whole time through the process, with him for the most part making sure he maintained his status as King of Useless Information. Once in a while some of it was interesting, but generally, I fixed a plaintive fake smile on my face and just nodded.

It seemed harder coming out to him than to Savannah, and I wasn't sure why. I considered Kalen a friend, too, but while Savannah might have lost some people during the Cleanse, Kalen had lost many, devastating his family. I bore the guilt as though I had been directly responsible. I opened my mouth to speak, but what I wanted to say didn't come out. "Blu thinks Savannah is an ignesco."

"Really?"

"What does it mean? Is she a witch?"

"No one actually knows what they are. I suspect they are pixies, some say witches, and others think mages. There are so few that no one has ever really studied them. Hmm, how did you all come to this realization?"

"It wasn't an *us* thing so much as Savannah thinking it while we were at Devour."

"Devour? You've been holding out on me, girl." He grinned. "Usually your life is boring; now you're hanging out at Devour and being seen by everyone in the city with"—then he stopped and did dramatic air quotes—"'Mr. Not My Boyfriend' Gareth. I thought when I saw that photo it might be you, but since your life hasn't proven to be that interesting, I assumed it was a look-alike or something. You know how they say that everyone has a twin, I figured it was yours. After all, she didn't have on plaid and Converses. In fact, the woman was quite lovely, with gorgeous hair."

Once again, my messy ponytail was treated to one of his looks before he delivered the same scrutiny to the jeans and yellow and blue plaid shirt. Then, for good measure, he looked back to my hair again.

"I guess I have to be a hot shifter for you to even bother," he teased.

I shrugged off his jabs at my clothing as I usually did. "How did you get a picture of me at Devour?"

His eyes sparked with excitement and he pulled out his phone and flashed the screen at me, and there I was leaning into Gareth as he whispered something into my ear. "Apparently you're the woman to hate," he joked.

I didn't think me in something other than my typical attire, in a club, with a drink in my hand, leaning into Gareth was exciting, but apparently it was the gift that kept on giving. *I guess I can mark him off my Christmas list.*

"Why would anyone care that I was talking to Gareth?" I asked, redirecting my attention to a box and pulling out a hat that piqued my interest.

"Nope"—he snatched it from me and tossed it into the corner—"I already have to deal with the ponytail, you don't get a hat. Women hate you because of Gareth. People pay attention to him." Once again, he gave me a weird smile, like a host on a morning show right before they barraged the guest with a slew of personal and invasive questions. Kalen enjoyed his gossip moment and it seemed like he was gearing up for one.

"You were in one of the hottest and most exclusive clubs in the city, with Gareth—what's going on?"

"Can't be too exclusive—I got in without a problem." I shrugged. I didn't want this to be the big deal that he was about to make it into.

"Could it have anything to do with this?"

Again I had a picture pushed in my face. This time it was

Savannah, and she did look awfully cozy with Lucas in the picture. But based on what the picture of Gareth and I looked like and what had actually happened, I quickly dismissed it. Even with his hand wrapped around her waist and his face so close to hers it looked like they were about to kiss. Kalen might have been enthralled by this, but I wasn't. It was a reminder that things were spiraling fast from what I had once known, not more than three weeks ago. I needed to get back on track, but I couldn't imagine anything was going to happen over the next few days to make that possible.

I lived in the shadows, a private life that worked, and now people were taking photos of me. And I was somehow hanging out with Master of the city and shapeshifters who were popular for reasons I had no idea of.

"I get why people care about Lucas. The whole Master of the city, owns the hottest vamp club in the city—it's not like he's hiding from the attention. He seems to need it as much as he needs blood, but why the hell do people care about Gareth? I didn't think his title of Mr. Arrogant had a following."

Kalen blew out an exasperated breath before rolling his eyes away from me.

I don't need that from you.

"His mother."

"Yeah, the cable/mall lady." *Whoa, that's a different color. You don't see that shade of red except on strawberries.* My KUI had gone on and on about her so much, I'd Googled her: I was aware of her past career as a designer, which is why Kalen adored her. As a teenager, she'd modeled and had a very short-lived career in music. And then she'd eventually taken over the family business. I wouldn't have called her a socialite, but most people knew her. After seeing a dozen or so pictures of her, I knew who she was, but I couldn't turn down a chance to see the appalled look on Kalen's face at my crass summary. Sometimes it was the little things that made the days better.

I was just about to confess, when someone knocked at the door. Before we could answer, blond hair with hints of silver poked in. When he saw me, he came in. Behind him was another man, both of them in police uniforms.

"Does an Olivia Michaels work here?" one asked, looking at me as Kalen approached them.

I didn't respond, but instead came to my feet, taking several steps back, my nails biting into my skin as I balled my hands tight. Inching back a few more steps, I angled myself so that I had a direct shot to the back door.

"May I ask what you want with her?" Kalen requested in a firm but professional voice.

"Does she work here? That was the question," snarled the other guy, his hand resting on the gun holstered at his side. So much adrenaline pumped through me, triggering full-on fight or flight mode; fighting an officer wasn't the wisest thing to do.

"I'm Olivia Michaels." I nearly yelled it because I didn't want it to sound as small as I felt.

Both of their eyes fixed on me, cold and hard. The blond approached first, pulling out handcuffs.

"Stop!" Kalen barked through clenched teeth. "What are you doing?"

The blond's partner shifted over to block Kalen from advancing, and when he stepped forward more, he shoved him. Kalen's teeth clenched as if he had to force back his words. He moved back with several forced lumbering steps.

"She has the right to know why she's being arrested." It was a benefit of human law—they had rules that were strictly enforced, and as far as the police and Kalen knew, I was human and protected by them. They read me my rights.

Everything slowly droned out, and they continued to put

the cuffs on me and tell me that I was being arrested for Clive's and Daniel's murders.

He guided me out the door, his partner still standing in front of Kalen, who wore a look of anger and confusion. The moment I was out the door, the officer grabbed the chain of the cuffs and pulled me into him, his voice deep and thunderous.

"You may have killed our founder, but you will not destroy Humans First."

It was early, and with the exception of our neighbor, a witch, who opened several hours after us, the bookstore, and the small café just a few doors down, the rest of the area was all residential and no other activity was going on in the neighborhood. Most people had left for work, which was a good thing so the neighbors didn't see this. Humans—I could get away from them. My mind cycled through all the spells I'd memorized from the book Blu had loaned me, and there wasn't one that could remove cuffs. Obviously they weren't privy to the same information as Clive, because they'd put me in regular steel handcuffs without sigils or iridium—I still had access to magic. But did I want them to know what I was and that I possessed magic? That would make it worse, and they still had guns. The other officer had his trained on me, just waiting for a reason.

Fuck.

They shoved me into the backseat. I expected them to call someone to tell them they'd apprehended me or something of the sort, as they had done when I was arrested before. But they didn't. They started to pull off when an SG sedan darted out in front of them, blocking them; a blue SUV boxed them in from the rear. As soon as the SUV drove up, the door opened and Gareth got out, walked to the driver's side of the car, and tapped on the window.

When the officer let down the car window, Gareth had a

forced smile on his face, as if he was trying not to expose fangs. As he looked at them with a stern gaze, his voice was low and brusque. "Hello, Officers, I suppose you didn't get the memo."

"We got the memo. But this is in our jurisdiction. We handle human laws, and although our captain seems to ask how high whenever you say jump, that is not how things are going to go here. You all may have let her get away with murder before; we will not."

Gareth's smile quickly turned into a frown as he realized diplomacy wasn't going to work with these officers. "She was released because she wasn't guilty. I do think it's a conflict of interest for you to deal with this case as a member of Humans First, don't you, Nick? And since I gave your commanding officer enough evidence to prove she didn't do it, this is an unlawful arrest and I want her released."

"And what is that evidence? I would like to see it."

"And you are welcome to. I strongly advise you go to your commanding officer and ask him to let you review it. That's more than appropriate. Release her."

They were slow to move.

"I only plan to ask you once before this becomes a problem. You don't want to be one of my problems." And this time, Gareth did bare his teeth and gave them a glimpse of the predator that lurked behind the shifter ring. The blond still hadn't moved, but his partner jumped out of the car and opened the door for me. He was more gentle as he removed the cuffs with Gareth standing over him.

When he got back in the car, the blond said, "I hope you are right about this preponderance of evidence you have that exonerates her. Because I'd hate to be you if you're wrong."

"Thank you."

"No problem."

141

Once the officers had left, I asked, "What evidence do you have to prove that I didn't do it?"

His lips kinked into a half-smile and then he chuckled. "Not a goddamn thing. I don't think I have any favors left; I've used them all on this request. I think we need to meet with the Council sooner rather than later."

I looked at the door where Kalen was standing watching us. "Okay. But give me a few minutes." And I jogged up to the house and guided Kalen into it.

"We need to talk," I said in a low, grave voice.

He nodded slowly and took a seat in the sitting room, dropping into a chair and relaxing back as he waited for me to talk. This conversation wasn't happening anywhere near the way I had anticipated and practiced. And it wasn't something you just blurted out.

"You're in trouble, aren't you?" he asked.

"More than you can imagine." I started to pace, which only made him more nervous. "Remember when we came to you to find out more information about the Legacy and Vertu?"

His expression immediately changed. He tensed and sat up taller. "Yes. Why, have you found one?"

I nodded. Leaning forward, he rested his arms on his elbows, genuine concern marking his face. Perhaps assuming that they existed and having eyewitness accounts of their existence were two different things. He was content to know that the boogeyman existed but didn't want to know that there was the potential of it being up close and personal. The spark of anger that flittered along his mouth and eyes wasn't going to make this less painful. Legacy made him uneasy, and rightfully so—we made everyone uneasy.

"When we retrieved the Necro-spear, there was one involved. He was trying to do the Cleanse again."

The anger quickly devolved into fear and it was getting

harder and harder to tell him about me. "I witnessed him kill two members of Humans First—the founder and an associate."

His eyes narrowed. "How did you do that?"

Bits and pieces of the story weren't going to suffice, so I told him everything. At first I started slow, but then the more nervous I became, the faster I spoke and Kalen had to stop and ask questions. But the biggest one that I had to prepare myself for was, "How did you get involved? Why does Conner want you?"

My admission was barely audible, and he looked as though he wished he'd heard me wrong. His complexion went pallid, and for a long time there was a tense silence— something that never existed between us. I waited for something that was normal and comfortable. Long stretches of time passed as I waited for him to make a joke or say something inappropriate or colorful, make light of it the way that Savannah had.

He looked out the window at Gareth, who was leaning against the SUV, waiting for me.

"I know I should have told you long ago. I really thought I could—"

"You don't want to keep Gareth waiting much longer. He seems to be getting impatient."

I glanced out the door and surprisingly, he didn't look impatient. He was assessing the area, scanning cars that drove by and people, and his emotions tightly wound. I assumed that he didn't enjoy the level of diplomacy that he'd had to extend to the officers.

Kalen kept his attention outdoors on Gareth, dismissing me.

"With everything that's going on, I can't continue to stay hidden, so Gareth thinks it's a good idea to let the Council know so that he can openly use the SG to assist."

"Mm-hmm."

He still hadn't bothered to shift his eyes in my direction. I was talking to the side of his face, focusing on how sharp his jawline was when he clenched his teeth.

"Okay, well, we will talk later," I said softly. Again, nothing. He barely moved his head into the nod.

I thought the fresh air would be a little sobering, but it wasn't. The world looked different, scarier, more dangerous, and I felt like I wasn't going to be dealing with just Trackers anymore but also with people who might feel like Kalen, happy to suspect I existed but okay with me staying hidden and being just folklore.

It was déjà vu, except this time I wasn't on trial for my life—or was I? The same people who had been present to judge me before were there to hear my story. The only exception was a new mage who had taken Jonathan's place, and I assumed that included him looking down his nose at anyone who stood before them, the same way Jonathan had done. The same sigils were on the wall, which I speculated weren't activated because they too would have had to be really strong to stop me. But I was sure they owned a pair if not several pairs of the shackles that Gareth had placed on me. I wondered if they had the iridium-laced dart that he'd threatened to shoot me with. The two guards at the front door and six behind me looked like they could handle themselves in a fight. I sensed strong magic, but there was so much of it in the room, I didn't know who it was coming from.

Lucas didn't look any more interested in being there than he had before. He did offer me a small smile, and if he was curious at all about my presence, he didn't show it. Could he already know? How? I knew Savannah would never betray my trust, but had he influenced her? It was rumored that vampires could read a person's mind while feeding from them. If it was true, it probably wasn't information the donor willingly provided. I was sure they didn't tell their meal for the night, "Hey, I can read your thoughts, so keep it interesting so I don't get bored while I'm chomping on your neck."

Gareth was the first to speak, probably because he'd called the meeting. "I thank you all for attending this meeting on such short notice on something that most of you may think isn't any concern of the Council, but I can assure you that it is. Ms. Michaels, please, speak."

I hadn't prepared a speech or anything, and the one that I hadn't gotten to use on Kalen was probably a little too familiar and riddled with silly inside jokes that would only make me seem weird. But maybe it was better for them to consider me weird than dangerous.

"There's a man by the name of Conner, a Vertu who is trying to do another Cleanse."

With the exception of Harrah, who seemed unfazed by the information, which was why she was so good at her job, they all seemed shocked and fearful. She remained calm and collected at all times. Even if she was telling you that we were on the edge of an apocalypse, her gentle, demure countenance made it seem that things weren't so bad. World coming to an end? Big deal, look at those doe eyes—she doesn't look worried, why should we? Lucas looked like he had second thoughts about the nap he appeared to be ready to take. He leaned into the desk, interested for the first time since I'd started talking.

"Vertu are like Legacy but stronger."

The revelation was punctuated by silence. Strain and concern covered their faces as they waited for me to continue. I informed them about how Conner had convinced

Jonathan to betray the mages and the Council and help him by using the Necro-spear that possessed our magic. And that he now had the four that had originally been in the possession of Humans First. I recapped everything, leaving out the part about me telling Conner that HF shouldn't have the spears. The guilt of my culpability lingered. I was having a hard time shrugging it off.

"If we have others who are willing to betray us, then we could be facing another Cleanse," Harrah speculated, and for the first time her face demonstrated something other than just passive nonchalance. It was stricken with worry. She was most likely considering how she was going to spin the story. She steepled her fingers, her cool eyes on me. It was the first time I'd ever considered how strong she had to be in order to be on the Council and given the role that she had. To what extent had she manipulated the world, people's minds, and emotions to maintain the alliance between the supernaturals and humans?

"Ms. Michaels, one question remains—how have you become privy to such information?" She asked the very question that, based on their faces, they had all been thinking.

Memories of Kalen's reaction resurfaced. I could have very well made up something and walked away and stayed behind my wards, impervious to magic—let this be their problem. But it wasn't *their* problem. It was *our* problem because it affected me as well as other people. I would have forever been the person who let this happen, and then there were Kalen and Savannah. Even Gareth, Blu, and my neighbors were people I worried about. And the people whose faces I knew, and although they were just associates, I didn't want them dead. Who I wanted dead was Conner and all the dumb-asses who fell for the charismatic "only the purist magic should exist" BS.

"Because he tried to recruit me."

"You're a Vertu or Legacy?" Harrah asked.

"Legacy."

She directed her attention to Gareth. "You said that she didn't possess magic. We released her based on the fact that she didn't possess magic. Were you incorrect, or compromised by your libido? Your outside relationship with Ms. Michaels hasn't gone unnoticed, nor has the position you've put the Magic Council and the Supernatural Guild in by your association."

Gareth chewed his words and then held them before he spoke. Based on the way he looked at her, I had a feeling he needed to tame and smooth off the rough edges before he said them.

"Neither. I decided to withhold that information because you all seemed to care only about someone, anyone, paying for three murders, not about finding the person who actually committed them. That is my decision and I stand behind it. My libido has nothing to do with it. The reason she is here is because she wants to stop him as much as we do. I'll be more than happy to continue to address any concerns you may have about my relationship with Ms. Michaels later, but as far as this meeting is concerned it is irrelevant."

I wasn't sure why he needed to discuss it later. *There isn't one. See, I did it in two seconds. No muss, no fuss. Easy-peasy.*

"What happens now? Do we warn people?" the new mage asked, taking a moment from looking down his hooked nose at me. At first it had been the casual disdain that most people were probably treated with. Now it was disgust. I had limited experience with mages, but their brand of superiority complex seemed to be uniquely theirs. No wonder Conner had been able to get Jonathan to betray his kind for the chance for more power. I wondered how many of them realized that the Cleanse was meant for them mostly, to rid anyone of magic that rivaled the Legacy even on a smaller scale.

"We will do no such thing!" Harrah snapped. "This needs to be contained quietly and as quickly as possible." Once again, her attention landed on Gareth. "What are your plans?"

Gareth directed his attention to the new mage. "You will need to discuss this with the Mage Council, and I need a list of who you consider the strongest mages. Conner may approach them—to make them either allies or victims who cannot use their magic against him. They need to know that we are aware of this and are watching them to prevent this from happening."

Don't forget to add an asterisk by the ones with questionable ethics.

I looked at Harrah: she felt the need not to warn people, but they needed to be told. "Discretion isn't going to help, and when people start dying, what will the optics look like then?" Harrah always seemed to care about how situations "looked." I understood why she cared about the peaceful coexistence between supernaturals and humans, but the lengths she went to in order to maintain it made it hard to like and trust her.

She inhaled a deep breath and held it before speaking, and then she cut her eyes at me before addressing anyone. "Discretion is always important, but there is a need to warn others to be careful."

Gareth came to his feet. "I will keep you all posted on what else is needed. We have to find the Maxwells, who are destroying the city, and at this rate, Humans First will have more members despite their loss. And that's Conner's point. The chaos is a distraction and the best way to recruit others. The humans will hate us and eventually turn." He looked up at the mage. "Especially some of the mages."

Moments later, Gareth was at my side, guiding me out the door. I questioned whether we were going to be allowed to leave since it took a long time before the guards stepped aside.

Gareth remained quiet for most of the drive and seemed content to do so. "That was painless," I admitted. I wasn't sure what I'd expected.

His response was simply a frown.

"Are you upset that they didn't form a mob and try to attack?"

"I never expected such a thing, nor would I have allowed that to happen, but they were more accepting than I expected."

"Do you think they suspected it?" I wasn't sure how I felt about that. All these years, I'd lived in fear of being found out when it seemed like I probably could have just come out and said, "Hey, I'm a Legacy, but I don't have any plans to try to destroy the supernaturals. I'm Legacy-light, no plans for world domination. Cool."

Gareth inhaled a long, ragged breath before washing his hands over his face. His cool, controlled demeanor dropped for just a moment before it reasserted itself.

"We need to get Conner, today."

If only it were that simple. He now had twelve other Legacy, and I was positive that the two of us weren't enough.

"How many high-level mages do you have at the SG?" I asked.

"Thirteen."

That definitely wasn't enough. "Conner isn't likely to do a global Cleanse anytime soon, he needs more people." I sounded more confident than I felt. A small one wouldn't work for him. He wanted to make sure he succeeded where our ancestors had failed, so he would be recruiting more. And we needed to get to the others before he did. But were there enough to do it? Conner now had the Necro-spears, and he could use the magic from them to make his attempt stronger—unlike HF, who didn't have magical resources to do anything other than a small one. It would be bad, but not as devastating as the global Cleanse that Conner wanted. I needed to make sure his numbers didn't increase.

I thought back to the dossier that Gareth had shown me. If Conner was missing from it, how many more were? Were there other Vertu using their magical ability to stay under the radar of the Trackers?

Gareth's phone rang. "What do you need, Avery?" When the person spoke, Gareth frowned. "Sam? Where's Avery?"

I couldn't make out what the person was saying but the moment he hung up, Gareth turned the car around. "Sam said Avery's freaking out in a store and has three people cornered and will not let them leave. And there's a bunch of fighting. The witches are involved, too."

He took the next exit and minutes later we were driving down Coven Row, where most of the witches had shops and other businesses.

"Why is he there on a Sunday?"

"Why do you think? Why do college students hang out there?"

We knew it wasn't for the food or the various candle stores, or places where they could get charms and amulets or have various spells performed. They frequented Coven Row for the *herba terrae*, the earth plant that made the witches most of their money.

"Unless Conner or a Legacy is there, he can't be controlled," I said.

That didn't seem to bring him any comfort, because there

was a pretty good chance that someone from Camp Conner was there.

It wasn't long before we hit the string of shops whose unique colors identified what type of goods and services they offered. Delicate pinks and lacy curtains and lovely flowers and plants snaked around the doors and windows of all the shops where love spells were performed. Darkened windows and maroon or midnight walls indicated where you could go if you wanted to get a look at your past life or journey to experience a future one.

Sam was right; there was magic, a great deal of it, consuming the air. People crashed into windows. More bodies expelling shallow breaths lay in the middle of the street. There were broken windows and small flames that were starting to smother out. This wasn't anyone's doing but the triplets'. *Please let it be them that Avery has cornered.*

A tall, lanky redhead stood in the street, waving his hand wildly to signal us. My sai in hand, I followed Gareth to the store. Avery had two of the mages, the woman and the broader man, cornered. He padded in front of them, his lips pulled back. His large mass was intimidating and had the benefit of being immune to their magic.

I knew if they were there, the other was somewhere close. "You have things here?" I asked. Gareth nodded. There was too much magic to try to follow it. I stopped and scanned the area. The buildings were clustered together; there weren't many hiding places, and he would be close trying to get to his siblings. I went through each store next to the building and came up empty. Within ten minutes I had cleared several more buildings. The next alleyway I entered from the opposite direction gave me access to the back of the buildings. If I were him, that was what I would have done—try and use a back way to get them out. He saw me before I saw him and started to rush down the alley. I hit him hard with a blast of magic and rammed him into the wall. He slid to the ground, and I hit him again. I wasn't in the mood to be nice and lobbed one more into him.

He was a lot more resilient than he looked, and he stood, shoving me back with his magic. He tried again, and the field I'd erected blocked it. His fingers spread, his lips moved as he attempted to cast a spell to remove it. Nothing. Again he tried, and once again he failed. He pulled his lips back in a snarl and charged at it. It sent him crashing back into the wall. *He's definitely not the brains of the trio.* My field wavered and then it crashed. I felt a sharp thrust in the middle of my back and was thrown against the wall. I pushed back quickly, sai in hand, to find Evelyn standing just a few feet from me. Magic wrapped around her hand, nearly consuming it. I wasn't sure if she was stronger than me or a Vertu, but she damn sure had a better command of her magic than I did. With confidence, she walked toward me, an illumination of light shielding her from anything I could launch her way.

"You can leave," she informed the terrible triplet.

I pointed a sai at him and aimed it at his heart, roiling magic around it until it was concentrated at the end. His eyes widened in fear as he looked at the furled magic, strong and ready to do damage at my command.

"I would be very careful who you chose to listen to, me or her," she cautioned, dismissing me with a light roll of her eyes and a turn of her lip.

Misguided nothing. This woman was a total and utter ass. I doubted Conner had needed to do more than show up, and she was Team Conner and ready to destroy the world.

With a quick turn, I blasted the magic at her shield, shattering it. Sparks of differently colored destroyed magic scattered around her. I charged her and swiped her foot, dropping the sai. I snaked behind her and wrapped my legs around her. I locked her close to me and pressed my fingers against her carotid. It would be really hard for her to do anything more than fight to stay conscious. Can't do magic if you're unconscious, no matter how strong you are.

She panted under my pressure, her fingers clawing at me, trying to get me to release. She managed a few words. "The cats are going to kill each other." And her lips moved, slowly, I assumed casting a spell. Seconds later I heard the "cats'" distinctive roars before a booming sound erupted and then the sound of breaking glass filled the air. People screamed. Roars reverberated off of the walls, nearly dominating the thunderous sound of bodies crashing into things. Panic—I didn't have to be a shapeshifter to know it and feel it.

I released her, shoving her off me and waving one hand. Using magic I pushed her into the wall. I picked one of the sai up with the other. "Make them stop."

She shook her head; I smacked her into the wall. I was ready to do it until she was disoriented enough for the spell to stop, but that wasn't really how it worked. A spell could be stopped if the person who did it, stopped it. Or they died. And as much as my hand was itching to do it, I couldn't kill Evelyn. I needed to get over that though, because in the end that was what it might come to—me killing my kind. Bile crept up and I pushed it down. They'd made the choice. Even knowing what would happen and that there was an alternative—they'd made their choice. Gripping the sai harder, I drove it toward her chest and it hit the brick wall. She was gone.

The roars of the lions continued. I ran toward the sound and the only way I could tell who was who was by the very negligible difference in size, but it didn't matter—one was about to strike the other with a paw. The SG was there, several with tranq guns trying to get a shot, and I wasn't sure they were going to get it. Gareth's eyes were ignited with a primal fury that only seemed to care about survival and destruction.

His claws landed on his nephew, cutting into his side. Avery moved back and exposed his neck as he looked at the fresh cut. Gareth reared back, about to lunge, and I pushed enough magic into him that he careened back and smashed into a car, denting it. Avery charged at the shaken lion, and I gave him a magical shove. I ran to get in front of them, using more magic than I knew I had available, ignoring the gawkers and their realization that I was using magic on shapeshifters. It was getting harder and harder to keep them from each other.

"Do you plan on taking the shot or just chilling like these two aren't ready to tear each other apart? Let me help you out with the answer. *Please take the shot!*"

And they did, but one wasn't enough to take them down. Three shots later, Gareth and nephew were out on the ground in the middle of a city that looked like it had just been the site of a battle. The only comfort I had was that two chaos mages had been apprehended and each one placed in separate cars. I had been so focused on them that it was too late to react to the approaching SG officers, who had me surrounded. Six. Two with guns and the rest with magic that they were ready to hurl, and by the looks of the brightly colored masses, I didn't know which was going to be worse.

The magic tapped at me, then it flitted around me, testing. It pushed harder, and the intrusion into my thoughts was subtle at first—submission. A gentle entreaty for me to stand down. When I didn't, the magic coaxed me harder to comply. It seemed almost innocuous in its intent for a second. I paused, relaxing into it before I put up an apotrepein. *Damn fae.* In the sea of faces of the members of SG, magic inundated the air. I couldn't distinguish any one unless they were using defensive magic or I saw them do a spell. If they changed their appearance or affected my mood or mind, I knew it was coming from fae.

I didn't have another battle in me, especially against a department of supernaturals.

"You are going to come with us," one of the mages said. I recognized him from the Guild. Brown hair cut so short waves clung to his scalp, tightly hewn features belied by his ever-present light smile. Now there wasn't a smile, and his molten hazel eyes fixed on me. Standing a little over six eight, he was already an imposing man. I didn't move but carefully watched the sparks of magic that played at his fingers, merging together into thick, brightly lit bands and then contorting and bending into a ball. It was an unnecessary display of magic used to exhibit his power and control of it.

"I'm not going anywhere with you." I started to go for my sai. They had a lot of perks, but deflecting bullets wasn't one of them, and I wasn't sure magic would do it, either. It would take care of the shifter I caught in my peripheral vision. His broad, sturdy build, sinewy muscles wrapped around his arms, and predator's glint as he stalked into position reminded me of a wolf. A wolf that didn't need a pack. I gripped the sai tighter. I didn't want to hurt anyone, and exposing myself like this wasn't the best way. I scanned the area again, noting the people who were positioning themselves around me. I took a defensive stance and held the sai ready to strike.

"Call Harrah," I ordered. I wasn't sure if that would help, but with Gareth out, she was the next best thing.

The shifter lunged; a bolt of magic shot through the sai directly into his chest, sending him back several feet. A look of shock and emblazoned anger reflected back at me. The shifter ring glowed around his pupils, and his lips pulled back into a snarl. I quickly erected a barrier. When the mage released his coiled magic, it wavered at the impact; a rainbow of colors ignited and were slowly absorbed and disappeared into the barrier.

"Call Harrah!" I demanded again. The standoff was escalating fast as more of the team moved in, closing the distance between us. I had a feeling this was going to get violent, and I wasn't sure I was going to come out on the other side uninjured or on amicable terms with the Supernatural Guild. The last thing I needed was to be on questionable terms with them.

"No need," said a firm voice from a distance. Harrah. Good. Chaos and violence had broken out and she was there to spin the hell out of it until everyone thought it was as benign as a bunch of rambunctious teenagers who'd gotten too rowdy, or a party that had gotten out of hand.

"She's free to leave. Please get Gareth and Avery to the Isles. Things will be explained to you by Gareth and myself later." Then she turned to me. "You are free to leave. Thank you for your assistance, Ms. Michaels." And she gave me an obligatory smile, the same one she gave to a reporter or other people who challenged anything she said. It was better than a shut-the-hell-up scowl, and she probably had a stop-being-a-troublemaker stare in her arsenal of looks that she had to shelve to protect the alliance.

CHAPTER 8

Savannah's smile was unusually broad. Even after an eight-hour day at work, she was always smiles and sunshine. Usually it was contagious, but there wasn't anything she could do to brighten up this day. Confessing to Kalen and the Magic Council that I was a Legacy; nearly being arrested for Clive's and Daniel's murders; fighting with Evelyn, one of the triplets, and the SG; and breaking up a fight between two cave lions had placed this one on my list of the top three bad days. It topped the afternoon I'd had to wade through sewage, and was only surpassed by the times Trackers had tried to kill me.

Her gaze slowly roved over me, then she frowned. "I guess the big reveal didn't go as planned."

"It went fine, it was all the crap that happened afterward. After I have a shower, food, and a nap I will tell you every moment of it in excruciating detail." The way she liked it. Savannah liked details—very explicit details. What color was the car that he crashed into? Did she slice the right or the left arm? The person who was going to shoot you, was it a man or woman? What type of gun?

"It looks like someone got their ass kicked."

I shrugged. "Honestly, I feel like it was me."

"Well, this should make your day." She stepped aside to reveal two very large bouquets of flowers.

One was a bundle of flowers so exotic that I had no idea what they were, and her name was on the card. My name was on the lilies.

She inhaled each one and then handed me my card. "Jake and Terry brought them by just a few minutes ago."

"Who are Jake and Terry?"

She rolled her eyes and sighed. "You call them the Suits and I have no idea why."

"Isn't the better question, why don't you? Why are we learning the names of the mean guys who guard the door at Devour and look like they are more comfortable with violence than the average person?"

"Says the woman who has a section of her closet named 'somebody's getting their ass kicked.'"

"You named it that, remember, when you decided my room was a danger zone and organized it," I pointed out, looking at the card. It was in Lucas's beautiful handwriting. Handwritten notes seemed to be something he was adamant about retaining from the old world. To me they were a reminder that he'd lived during a time that both Savannah and I knew about because of our history classes and the History Channel.

"How lovely are they?"

I really tried to be as excited about them as Savannah was. This was her thing, not mine. I smelled them, played with the delicate petals, and then smelled hers. Her arrangement was more extravagant than mine.

"I wonder what they're for. My card simply reads, 'I hope this brightens your day.'" She inhaled them again. It was similar to my note. I glanced over at Savannah. *That's what swooning looks like.* It was so fitting on Savannah.

"I think they are consolatory flowers. Mine are 'My apologies that you're a Legacy; must suck for you.' And yours are probably 'My sweet, dear, lovely vampire kittle, your roommate is a Legacy—you probably can do better. I'll start looking for a roommate for my lovely little petal.'"

She scoffed and rolled her eyes. "You're so pessimistic. He probably assumed you had a bad day and mine are just obligatory."

"Well, we see who he likes the best," I teased.

"Of course he likes me better. Every time you go near him you try to wear a turtleneck and give him a strange look each time he touches you. He probably isn't used to such poor manners."

I forgot I lived with the manners police.

"We have to call and thank him." She grabbed her phone.

"No, we don't. Who said that? That is not a rule, and you can't make me believe it is one."

She shook her head. "I know you weren't raised by wolves, but sometimes I have to remind myself of it," she said, smiling. "It's the polite thing to do. Maybe we should visit him, invite him to dinner."

"You mean show up with our necks exposed, maybe rub a little bacon on them, and offer ourselves to him because that's dinner for him. Have you forgotten?"

"How can I? You remind me of it every chance you get. Come on, Levy, it's the polite thing to do, and before you even suggest it, I will not send him a text. You don't send the Master of the city a text. It's tacky."

"Are you sure? You won't know until you try it. If you want, put a smiley face emoji, I don't care, add a couple of hearts, too."

"I will not."

I shrugged; she was going to do what she wanted, and because it was Lucas, it would be a call and we were going to have dinner. I was sure my presence was optional. "Do what you want. I'm sending him a text later, and I'm wearing a turtleneck to dinner."

"No and no. I will not hear of it."

"Whatever you say, Mom."

She inhaled the flowers again before she stepped away from them. Her lips twisted into a moue and then a deep frown etched itself on her face and remained.

"The Witch, Fae, and Mage Councils contacted me today," she informed me grimly. What Blu had discovered must have gotten out. I wasn't sure how I felt about Blu disclosing it. Was it something that they needed to know? I thought she was just going to consult with other people, not discuss it with councils. It wasn't like Savannah was dangerous—she had no magical ability. She was a booster. I could see how that could be dangerous with the wrong person, but most likely there weren't people scouring the area to find an amplifier for their magic.

"What should I do?" she asked.

Don't go. That was the advice I wanted to give because it seemed like the soundest thing to do. But would there be consequences for her not doing it? "I don't know."

"Maybe we should ask Gareth?"

I shook my head. He was probably still dealing with a tranquilizer hangover. He was also part of the magical community and I wasn't sure how biased his advice would be. I couldn't call the person I trusted the most and part of me wondered if he would even answer when I finally could and he saw the number. I frowned at the thought.

"Let's just wait and see." It wasn't the best advice, but it was all I could think of at the time. I had limited knowledge of the individual Councils other than they served to regulate the different sects and often worked with the human government to determine magic rules and what was considered acceptable and unacceptable practice. But like any governing body, they could be your best ally and your most ruthless adversary. I didn't want them to ever be Savannah's adversary, but did she really need an alliance?

I excused myself to my bedroom and called Blu. She'd started this mess. Her voice was just as lively and gentle as usual and remained that way even though mine was harsh and cold. "Why did you tell them about Savannah?"

There was a long pause. Maybe she was trying to determine the situation and I wasn't helping things by being so brusque with my tone. I softened it. I liked Blu and didn't suspect she was doing something intentional to hurt Savannah.

"I thought it would be better for her to choose which group she will be governed by," she offered.

"Why does she need to be governed by anyone?" I said, easing it to a softer tone. My anger had been misdirected. I wasn't angry with Blu, just the situation. I'd been dealing with situations all day. I didn't want another one. "She's not dangerous. She doesn't even have any magic!"

"True, but she is strong and can be a danger. I don't think she is or will ever choose to be but keep in mind that she has the ability to enhance the magic of anyone she touches. You saw what she did at the house. Imagine what will happen if she is used by the wrong person. High-level mages are nearly invincible, and Savannah could make the magic of any regular mage that of a high-level mage. In the wrong hands that can be a problem."

Stilted silence persisted. After a long moment I decided to get her opinion on who Savannah should talk to, although I knew who she would recommend.

"Who should she meet with?"

Blu didn't answer immediately. And when she finally answered, her tone was crisp, even, and low. "She should meet with them all, and when they make their little pitch about the advantages of forming an alliance"—she dropped her voice even lower, I could barely hear—"she should pick the Shapeshifter Council. They can never exploit her, and if she is ever in need of protection, they would be the best ones because of their immunity to magic."

"Not the witches?" I was sure she would rally for the witches.

"As I stated, she should pick the shapeshifters. Am I right in assuming they are the only ones that haven't contacted her?"

"Yes."

"Tell her to choose the shapeshifters." With that she hung up the phone.

I slouched onto the bed. I really needed to take a shower and then get some sleep. Before taking the position with the Supernatural Guild, Gareth had been head of the Shifter Council, but I wasn't sure if we should talk to them or go directly to the current head. Too many things were going on in my brain; I needed to shower and rest to sort them out.

The nap came first because I didn't have it in me to stand up once I was comfortable on the bed. The shower wasn't as relaxing as I thought it would be and didn't help relieve my aching muscles or perk me up. Nor could I turn off my racing thoughts. Magic was like any muscle, it needed to be trained. I needed to learn to teleport and hone my animancer abilities, although they weren't things I wanted to use. Erasing memories was a violation and against the law. Manipulating them was, too, but the rules were different for the Magical Council and Supernatural Guild because it was the only way they could maintain a strong alliance with the humans.

I felt the weight of the situation heavily on my shoulders. The more I encountered other Legacy and Vertu, the more I realized I needed to learn about magic. The benefit of being out now was that I could learn; but from who? Possibly Kalen, if he ever decided to speak to me again. Thinking about the fact that he might never speak to me again made a pain shoot through me. I assumed when he was ready to talk, we would. I'd decided not to go in to work the next day.

If Kalen did decide to talk to me, I wasn't sure how much help he could offer. Fae could do cognitive and manipulative magic, similar to what Conner had done when he'd changed my hair back to my natural color. And it was something Kalen used often to change my clothes and hair. Magical manipulation was a good party trick, but it wasn't effective defensive magic. I could already manipulate memories, as I'd done with the shifter Tracker who'd come after me, and wipe memories.

Maybe Blu could teach me more about spells. Savannah could help with her ability to enhance them. And then what? That was the real question.

I shook off everything. I needed to give my mind a break. Maybe Savannah was right—dinner with Lucas might not be a bad thing. I wouldn't mind going to Devour; after all, whenever I was there, I was too busy watching my neck, declining offers for "a drink"—like they were fooling someone with that offer—and trying not to be seduced by hot zombies, or vampires as they preferred to be called. It was a distraction, and a lot of alcohol wasn't a bad idea, either. I'd decided to tell Savannah to agree to see Lucas, although I was sure she already had.

Finding Gareth pacing the floor in my bedroom when I

stepped out of the bathroom to get dressed wasn't what I expected. I pulled the towel around me tighter. I'd seen him naked more times than anyone who wasn't sleeping with him should have. It didn't bother him, but nudity didn't bother most shapeshifters. It was something humans had to get used to. Most didn't mind since it was hard to find many shifters that physically weren't worth a second, third, or maybe a fourth look.

He grinned as I tightened the towel around me again and ran my hand through my damp hair. I wished I had at least attempted to comb it.

"Savannah let me in," he offered, addressing my curiosity.

"Back here? In my room?"

He nodded, his eyes slowly traveling the length of me. I felt the heat on my cheeks. *Don't you dare blush*, I threatened myself. Ugh, this was a long, bad day.

Savannah popped her head in. "Hey, Levy, Gareth's here." Then she waved at him.

"Thanks, I never would have guessed with him standing in my room and all. Top-notch observations, Detective."

She simpered, "I thought so, too. I'm heading out."

I didn't have to ask—she had on makeup, her hair was curled and flowing, and I just got a hint of the pink shimmering top she had on. I wasn't going to be able to stop it. There was definitely something going on with Savannah and Lucas. Dating? Did vampires date? I knew they didn't have problems with casual encounters, and I'd blocked many vamps' attempts to seduce Savannah into a one-night stand. It had to be hard for them to engage in the art of seduction with me just a few inches away, scoffing, laughing, and pointing out the lack of originality in their prose, all the while scowling at them.

"I need to get dressed," I told him.

He nodded and leaned against a wall.

"Unless you have cash to toss at me while I do it, get out," I said.

He shrugged. "I think I have cash." He reached into his pocket, pulled money from his wallet, and held it between his fingers. "Do I get to stay?"

"It was a joke."

"Are you proud of that one?" he said, throwing my own line in response to his purring joke of a few days ago back at me.

"Very. I just need a minute."

"It's not like you have something I haven't seen before."

"Good for you. Your congratulatory card is in the mail. You've seen naked women. Hooray. You don't get to see this one."

He grinned and I could have sworn he said, "Yet."

We'll see about that.

He plopped in the chair and gave me a long, roving look as he clasped his hands behind his head and relaxed back in the chair. "Ms. Michaels, I've seen women in various stages of undress and a lot of naked women"—the gentle bevel remained firmly planted on his lips—"and I've managed to control myself. I assure you I can do so with you." Taunting smile was replaced with smirk. "Or are you implying"—his placid blue eyes moved over me and settled on my hands, which clutched the towel tighter—"that you are so beguiling I won't be able to control myself? Now who's the arrogant one?"

Without commenting, I went to my dresser and grabbed some clothes and underwear and went into the bathroom to dress. Gareth was standing and looking over the books on my shelf when I finally finished. "Hmm, you have a lot of thrillers, mysteries, and espionage novels. Not a single romance."

"There's romance in the thrillers."

165

"Ah, I see, is that the way to your heart? A man has to put you in danger—or is it fighting that gets you going? Is it the adrenaline rush of possibly winning at hand-to-hand?"

"*Possibly?*" I teased. "But most men aren't feeling particularly sexy after they get their ass handed to them by a woman."

"Is that right? I wouldn't know. I've never had my ass handed to me."

"*Really.*" My brow rose as I hoped he recalled the time at his house. It seemed to have slipped his mind. "How quickly you have forgotten the incident at your house," I reminded him.

He grinned, approaching me with slow, lissome steps, his eyes glittering with amusement. "I do believe you were the one cuffed and on the floor, or am I not remembering correctly? And I do believe I did it in less than five minutes."

I could feel the warmth of his body, just inches from me. Shapeshifters always ran hot—I thought so, or maybe it was just Gareth. "You cheated."

"Did I?" His breath wisped lightly against my lips and I became very aware of him, the defined muscles that molded around his body and brushed against mine. And his lips, soft and commanding. For a brief moment, I closed my eyes, trying to push all the sinful thoughts out of my mind. It was primal—not real. It was just igniting an unfathomable craving. It had to be some weird type of shifter magic. I didn't believe for a moment the attraction was real, but on some level I wanted to.

His fingers ran along my arm until they came to the crease of my wrist. And then he cuffed his hand around them. "I had cuffs and you had magic. I was faster."

The magic sparked inside me, slow at first. Gradually rising along my arm before lacing around it. A small splash of vibrant colors twirled and contorted into a tight ball of magic that rested on the tips of my fingers.

He looked at it, and for a moment his eyes were shadowed with concern and possibly a brief memory of being controlled by magic similar to mine. It was a colorful, vibrant reminder that there was magic that he didn't have immunity to. The wispy smile on his lips faltered for a moment. The concern and aversion slipped as he released my wrist. His finger coursed down my hand until it was close to the magic, but he held my gaze. I pulled away, long enough for his finger to brush along the side of the ball. The turgid muscles of his arm contracted and then relaxed. He moved closer, leaving nothing between us. I smothered the magic, but the spark remained, and he felt it as well as our lips connected. His pressed harder against mine, entreating a response that I willingly gave. His hand released mine and traveled over my hip before it slid under my shirt, his finger tracing along the curves of my waist before drawing me to him.

Then he slipped my shirt over my head and tossed it on the floor. In one swift move, he did the same to his, and then we were skin on skin. My fingers explored the muscles that wrapped around his torso. Pulling me closer to him, he kissed me again, hungrily. A raw, heated sensuality that I hadn't experienced before ignited, and then he started to tug at my leggings. I helped him, barely moving my lips from his, my fingers entwined in his hair as I attempted to wiggle out of the leggings.

Breathless and panting, he pulled them off of me and then pressed his hard body against mine. His lips pressed harder, hungrily caressing mine as his hand plaintively glided over the intimate parts of my body. He nestled in closer to me, his fingers digging into my thighs as my legs curled around his waist. His arousal pressed against me. He started to walk me back toward the bed when my senses reasserted themselves. *This can't happen. Not with Gareth.* I unraveled my legs from him and eased them to the floor, reluctant to put any distance between him as his soft lips brushed lightly against mine.

Reluctantly I put a few feet between us. Breathing heavily, he approached again, his eyes holding mine, leveling the defenses I'd put up. I inhaled a ragged breath and pulled my eyes from his and tried to slip out the door past him, but he took hold of my arm.

"We really should figure out what to do next about Conner." My breath still came at a rapid pace.

He stared at me for a few minutes, his eyes narrowed and assessing. After a few moments, he released me and picked up his shirt, following me out of the room. *Please put your shirt on.*

His shirt was still in his hand as we made our way into the living room. *Please put your shirt on.*

His brow furrowed with confusion as he slipped his shirt over his head. I wanted to give him a reason but I didn't have one that he would understand. He was Gareth, the head of the Supernatural Guild, a member of the Magic Council, and an ex-member of the Guardians of Order—he was complicated and overwhelming. He was the very last thing I needed, because I had my fill of complicated, and my life right now was a lot to handle.

"How's Avery?" I asked once he'd taken a seat on the opposite end of the sofa.

"Shaken more than anything." An immunity to magic gave them a level of confidence and cockiness regarding it, and I was sure it was difficult dealing with having it used on him. Causing him to hurt his nephew was probably the worst of it.

I tried to distract myself with anything other than

looking at him, and he noticed, smiling at every attempt. "Have you spoken to Harrah?"

He nodded. "And everyone else once the panic died down. They'd just seen a unicorn in action, they were concerned."

"I'm sure they were more concerned when I told them more existed. Many more."

He breathed out. "I don't know."

"At least you have the Maxwells, or at least two of them, so there shouldn't be any random fights breaking out around the city."

"Yeah, but if Conner got them out, then what's to stop him from doing it again?"

I had nothing to offer. "How do we stop him from doing it now?"

"We have more manpower that we can continue to use guarding them."

There was some comfort in that. Not the excessive need to guard them, but the fact that they hadn't killed them.

"It was a consideration," he said.

"What?"

"What do you think? You're not as elusive as you would like to believe."

"Now you not only can determine when someone is lying, have weird super-hearing, and can locate someone anywhere in the city, but you've added reading thoughts to your creepy invasive superpowers, too?" I asked, surprised.

"No, but I can figure yours out. You are very strategic and realize that is the best option. With everything that they've done over the past few days, it would be warranted, but I wonder if Conner will try to retrieve them."

"And if he does?" I asked.

He shrugged and relaxed back on the sofa, but there was a hauntingly menacing look about him. There wasn't any doubt that he would do anything to stop Conner.

"I need to get more proficient with my magic," I admitted. "They're able to do things that I'm not."

"From my understanding, you were quite impressive today. Some even described it as *scary*, and I think *threat* and *danger* were thrown around, too."

"I kept you from ripping your nephew apart while they gawked at me while I did it. How am I a danger? Them being dumbstruck was the real danger." He was just repeating what was said to him, but I couldn't help but be offended by it. Conner was a danger. Evelyn was a danger, but I wasn't. I was okay with being considered innocuous, because people who were considered a threat were treated as one.

"Where do you feel that you fail?" he asked.

"I just need to learn more spells and do some of the things that Evelyn can do—"

His brow rose. "Like control shifters?"

"No, transport."

He frowned but remained quiet. No one else could transport; that was something only Legacy and Vertu could do. But I could be shown how to do better magic. Stronger spells and other things.

Gareth stayed for longer than I expected, especially since the conversation had continued and we hadn't come to a resolution.

CHAPTER 9

I didn't bother to set my alarm, positive that I wasn't going to hear from Kalen for a while. After checking my phone five times and not seeing a message from him, I gave in to the reality that he probably wasn't going to call. I should have been working on alternative employment plans, but I just didn't want to think about it. Telling my potential employer that I'd lost my last job because I'd admitted to my previous employer what I really was would surely be the best way of being asked to leave without an invitation to return. But I hadn't just lost an employer, I'd lost a friend. I was still in my pajamas when Kalen texted me to ask whether I was coming to work.

It didn't take me long to get dressed, and just forty-five minutes after the call, I was walking into the office. I didn't bother to get coffee, something I was supposed to get every morning. At this time of the day he would have been working on his third cup.

He greeted me with a wry smile, one that took a great deal of effort. "I screwed that one up, didn't I?" Then he picked up a hat off the desk. "Peace offering," he said, handing me the one that he'd taken from me two days ago and forbidden me from wearing. I could smell the chemicals coming from it; he must have had it cleaned.

I put it on my head and tapped the top until it came down too far, covering most of my head. He frowned. In one sweeping look, he took in my black fitted jeans, white Converses, and striped button-down shirt with the sleeves cuffed midforearm, along with the hat.

He shook his head. "You don't even try, do you?"

"I used to, but what would you do with your time if you didn't spend it commenting on my clothes and making poorly veiled insults about my ponytail or bun?"

He laughed. It seemed we weren't going to discuss the elephant in the room, the obvious thing that we were ignoring. I was trying to read him, but I couldn't. Was he in an active state of denial, or had he accepted it? Did he have questions but was too afraid to ask? Was he incapable of dealing with the reality? I cursed under my breath. I had no idea how to handle the situation.

We didn't handle it; instead we went into the storage room and started sorting more boxes. For an hour, we did it in silence while he cataloged things, deciding what was junk and what wasn't. Someone from the SG had dropped off some items confiscated from Ms. Neal. Most of it was junk. Anything that was magical or could be used for magic had most likely been confiscated.

"How long have you known?" he finally asked. His back was to me and he was packing things away.

"I've always known. It's not really something you accidentally discover."

"And your parents?" he asked in a stiff voice. Was he making small talk, or was this one of the few things he just didn't know?

"Have you heard of the Guardians of Order?"

"Yes, they're similar to Humans First, just a lot more fanatical and violent, right?"

"I never considered them similar until now. HF seems to be human-exclusive; all supernaturals are enemies to them, and the only reason they even considered dealing with Conner was because of his agenda. The Guardians of Order's only enemies seem to be us."

He nodded slowly and turned. The dour look eventually slipped away after several minutes of silence. "What happens to you now?"

"We have to stop Conner. If I can't, then I don't think I will be viewed any more favorably than Legacy were in the past. People don't hate us because we possess magic, they hate us because of the type of magic we possess. Well, I think shifters hate us. Not being immune to our magic really gets their panties in a twist."

"Of course it does, it totally dispels their god-among-men complex. You all reduce them to just some regular schmoes like the rest of us who can be taken down with magic."

Then he went back to working. Occasionally I caught him looking in my direction with a blank look on his face. After several hours, I'd gotten used to the silence and figured that was going to be the way things would be between us from now on. Tension-riddled silence and furtive glances. I couldn't help but wonder what he was thinking about. He frowned at the hat, which had moved a little lower on my head.

Quietly I sat on the sofa, tablet in hand, cataloguing the items we had. "That's going to be a thing, isn't it?" he teased as he perched on the arm of the other end of the sofa. The slim-cut suit made him look thinner than usual, and the crisp white shirt didn't do much for his fair complexion. I hadn't noticed the slips in his ordinarily impeccable clothing choices until he was next to me. I studied him as he studied me. Deep in thought, his eyes narrowed and cast a dark look over his face.

"Okay, if you're going to wear the hat, then ..." His finger twitched and I knew he was about to do his magic mojo.

"You change anything and tomorrow I wear the plaid flannel shirt you forbade me to wear and the *hair*."

He gasped, recalling the day that I'd decided to wear two pigtails. It was a bad hair day and, apparently, one that would live in infamy to him. We hadn't gotten a lot of work done because I'd spent half of the day dodging magic he'd lobbed my way trying to change it, or him physically cornering me and trying to.

"If you're not a five-year-old girl, you are forbidden to wear pigtails," he reminded me with a broad grin and shuddered at the thought of it again. But he'd relaxed into himself and a smile emerged. As he shifted position, the color of my shirt changed to a light blue, complementing the hat that I'd grown fond of.

"Keep it up, I'll turn you into a frog."

He stopped laughing, his head tilted to the side as he considered it. "Can you?"

Good question. But I shook my head with confidence. I didn't know, but of all the magical gifts to have, I didn't think changing people into green amphibians was brag-worthy.

I shrugged. "I can do the same things fae, mages, and witches can do. I think I'm supposed to be able to transport, but I haven't figured out a lot of things yet," I admitted and then I told him about how my parents had restricted magic, only teaching me things that they felt I would need to protect myself. He seemed to gain a little relief by knowing that I didn't have full access to magic. Perhaps he assumed that others had been raised the same way. It wasn't the truth. The Legacy that I had encountered had magic that had been trained and cultivated, making them a force—a menace.

"I can help you if you like."

"With what?"

"Improving your magic. You of all people would never abuse it. But with Conner around, you need to be able to protect yourself." Even though he hadn't said it, Kalen and I had been friends long enough that I knew it was about more than just protecting myself. It was also about making sure Conner didn't do more harm.

"I've been reading some of the spell books that Blu loaned me."

Part of me wanted to ask her for help, but I had come out to the Council and the SG, not the rest of the supernatural community, and I wasn't in a hurry to do so. Blu seemed to adhere to the full disclosure rules among the supernaturals. If she knew, then I was sure others would find out. The heavy feeling that always accompanied me thinking about Savannah as an ignesco reemerged, and I felt the muscles of my back and arms tighten. Stress. Fear. Apprehension. They were all there, and it bothered me that Savannah was feeling them, too.

I decided to be honest with Kalen about everything. "Savannah's an ignesco." I kept my voice level, trying not to let any of the concerns I had filter into my voice. Kalen attempted to remain expressionless as I delivered more news, turning his world upside down. But his emotions were expressed in his eyes, and I could see the fear, concern, and apprehension as he waited for more big reveals. I didn't blame him; things had changed, and neither one of us was naïve enough to have the luxury of denial that things were going to be different.

"Blu reported it. I'm not sure why. I suspect she was obligated to do so." Irritation colored my words. Even if she had to, it still bothered me. "Savannah's been contacted by the Mage, Fae, and Witch Councils."

175

Kalen sucked in a sharp breath and held it before releasing it. "What is she going to do?" he asked in a level voice, missing any inflection that would clue me in to what he was thinking.

Shrugging, I folded my legs underneath me trying to find a more comfortable position or do anything that might cause me to relax. I wanted to focus solely on Savannah's situation, but I had to deal with Conner and his legion of misguided degenerates.

Holding out on telling him Blu's advice, I waited to get his opinion. He took a long time to consider and I was appreciative of this. When he spoke, he chose his words carefully. "The Councils have their benefits." He took time with each word, which was a true indicator that he had doubts and reservations about the situation. "When you are a specific supernatural, it is expected that they will have your best interests at heart, and that can be invaluable. While the Supernatural Guild is over all the supernaturals in regards to order, a specific Council has on many occasions been allowed to exact punishment instead of the SG. That has its benefits and has worked out well for the most part. The Councils play a major role in establishing the laws of each sect and try not to restrict any of us too much. We are our magic, and overrestricted people have a tendency to rebel. These things are all great qualities and benefits of the Councils. But they are made up of the most powerful of our kind, and those people are not immune to being seduced by power or the acquisition of more. If Blu saw fit to inform the others of Savannah, I suspect that she's strong and has the potential to be used. A request from a Council is rarely denied, and from my understanding they aren't made often or without cause—but 'cause' is subjective. How many times will there be 'cause' to call upon her talents? Can you imagine how strong a high-level mage or fae would be with Savannah's help?"

He stopped, probably trying to find the right words to say that Savannah wouldn't be safe with any of them and there was a chance of her being used to do some bad things.

"What about the Shapeshifter Council? It seems like she will have to be under a Council, why not them?"

Kalen's eyes flashed when he grinned. "You are brilliant." Palpable relief overcame his face. "What a splendid idea. They can't use magic, and they are so territorial that no one would dare approach Savannah without checking with them. That's unlikely because people would rather hug a porcupine than deal with them."

I was so close to taking credit for the idea, but my conscience wouldn't allow me to. "It wasn't my idea. It was Blu's."

He slowly nodded his head, and a different smile flourished over his features with a hint of admiration. "Fashion sense and common sense, she's quite the package, isn't she? And she's not hard on the eyes, either."

"Should I be jealous that you don't swoon over me like that?"

"If you ever manage to walk through the door without cosplaying a trucker I will."

"'Cosplaying a trucker'? Now you're just making things up. That's not a thing and it can't be one just because you think it should be."

He brushed off my comment with a wave of his hand and stood. Then he shot a sly smile in my direction as he walked toward the kitchen. "Perhaps you should call Gareth and have him set it up."

"Or I can Google them and have Savannah call them. I'm sure if everyone else is buzzing about it then they probably know about it, too. Besides, Gareth isn't part of the Council anymore. Remember?"

"I didn't forget, but do you think for one moment that Gareth would concede so easily without having anything to do with them? I think just Googling them, cold-calling and just showing up on their steps with your perky adorable friend is a mistake. I do believe the shifters will be more accommodating if the idea is suggested by the head of the Supernatural Guild, as opposed to the cute blonde with a basket full of flourless pancakes or some other tasteless concoction and her obstinate brunette friend dressed in trucker cosplay and a weird hat."

"It's still *not* a thing. It's not going to catch on," I chided back, tapping the brim of my hat. If he rolled his eyes any harder he was going to give himself a headache.

An air of apprehension still remained between us, but it wasn't nearly as thick or obvious as before, and as the day went by we'd settled into our normalcy. It was what I'd needed. Finding a solution that Kalen agreed with had removed a lot of my stress and left me focusing on Conner and crew.

CHAPTER 10

I hadn't heard from Gareth for nearly three days and I wasn't sure if that was a good thing or bad. My calls and text messages went unanswered, and I had no idea what was going on regarding Conner. The last time we'd spoken, Gareth had suggested that he wanted to imprison Conner and his group of followers. I was ready for whatever plan he had to do so. Lock them up and throw away the key. But I knew it wasn't going to be easy no matter how much I wanted it. Wards had to be broken and veils ripped open; he had people to do it, but he needed one more —Savannah. She agreed without hesitation. I was the last holdout, looking for every option available to ensure that she didn't get involved. It took a long hour of deliberation before I reluctantly agreed.

The next day, as we walked through the area where I'd encountered Conner and the others, I looked over my shoulder at the small army of supernaturals behind me: eight high-level mages and fourteen witches, eight fae and nearly thirty shapeshifters, and it still didn't seem like enough. We were only going to do a reverse ward. Instead of blocking people from coming in, we were going to block them from coming out. It had worked with the chaos mages, and now it had to work with the Legacy and Vertu, or so everyone optimistically believed. I didn't—I had my doubts, because Conner had proven to be more cunning than I had given him credit for and more ruthless than I could have imagined. He wanted the Cleanse to happen again and was okay with it being a zero-sum game. That made him very dangerous.

Savannah standing next to me with her goddamn "quest bag" just made it worse. But at least she also had enough weapons strapped to her that she should be able to protect herself. I ignored the gnawing images of her dropping them constantly when we practiced. She wasn't an expert by the time we'd finished, but she'd substantially improved. I had Gareth's word that keeping her safe would be the number-one priority. I knew, however, that if it came to stopping the supernatural crew bent on destruction or saving Savannah, her protection would be an afterthought, so I had to make it my priority. As far as I was concerned, they were equally important.

Why couldn't she just be a barely acceptable ignesco? I would have given anything for her to be just a run-of-the-mill pyromaniac. Not someone that they needed. Not someone who was about to put her life in danger. No matter how I tried to talk her out of it, she felt obligated to help. I understood, I just didn't want it to be the way it was.

As we neared, I kept going over the spells. When I stopped feeling the ward near, so did everyone else.

"If they come out, take the shot as soon as possible. At best, we have six minutes." Although after letting Gareth try the iridium dart on me, I thought six minutes was being generous. After two minutes I was able to do magic, but not at full strength. At six minutes I was in full form. Each shot had to be perfectly done because a second one wasn't an option. My body had adapted and formed a barrier to prevent it from happening again. The cuffs had to be iridium and fairly large, often too heavy for use by anyone other than a shifter. They were no good at all if those carrying them couldn't get close enough to Conner and the others to put them on. I'd like to think Gareth was a lucky lion that day when he got a pair on me; I doubted the others would be.

Inches away, a powerful force of magic like a tornado thrashed over us. Hard currents of magic hit. Two bodies flew past us, crashing across the field. I stabbed one of my sai into the ground and held on to it and grabbed Savannah's shirt, holding her close to me as the blast of magic continued. It stopped for just a moment. We were surrounded by Conner's followers. The magic wafting off them drowned the air. Before they could deliver another wind of it, shots were fired. Not in sync, but it was enough time. I pulled out the sai and released Savannah. A wolf soared past me, capturing one of Conner's people by the throat; it was a clean and quick ending. In a few minutes, we had the advantage and we used it. The sound of bodies falling, bones crunching, and screams were the only hints that the shapeshifters were prevailing. But it was only a matter of time.

Before I had time to assess the situation, a blade swiped at me. I stopped it with the moto of the sai. Evelyn used the other blade in her hand and stabbed at me, catching me on my side, and then pulled it out. Pain seared through me. I swallowed the groan, refusing to give her the satisfaction of hearing it. She made another attempt at a drive; I blocked it with the edge of one sai and thrust the other into her gut. She stumbled back; I pulled it out and did it again. I had to use the other one to block her hand. I couldn't allow her to touch it and heal herself. By the fourth time the blade of my sai had met her flesh, she was bleeding uncontrollably. She wasn't going to heal.

I looked away. The desperation of her trying to fight for a life she couldn't save pulled at my guilt. I had to feel something—I wasn't a sociopath—even though this was a necessary evil. She'd made a choice—the wrong one—and this was the consequence. She made a feeble attempt at using magic. It sparked at her fingers; the colors flared and then waned as she did.

One down, but I couldn't assess the situation to see how many more to go. With the one the wolf had taken down, Evelyn, and the other Legacy I'd taken out, I knew of three killed out of Conner's twelve.

Time was up, and the magic was back with a mighty vengeance. It hit hard, and I felt like I'd been slammed into a brick wall. I put up a field, covering me and whoever managed to be behind me. It was the first time I was able to see the damage. Five followers were gone, but I didn't see Conner. I did a sweep over the bodies lying around and didn't see him. I didn't see Gareth, either. A sharp breath caught in my throat, but I didn't have time to think about it. I had to finish this.

"I'm going to drop it, you can't do magic through it," I informed the four mages and two witches behind me. I counted to three and it dropped. I moved out of the way of the exchange of magic. The plans we had were down the drain. This wasn't going to end with us containing them in the little world they had created for themselves. It was going to end with them being casualties of their ideology and warped Utopian view.

Magic continued to dominate the air. I rushed to the right as the SG attempted to hold the remaining members of Team Conner off. I needed just a moment and it would be over; the magic started as a small circle, growing larger until it was a whipping force, a cyclone that crashed through the area. A powerful force that I was barely able to control, it moved, ravaging through the air, ripping up trees and leaving nothing but shredded bark in its path. My head pounded, sweat dripped along my temples as I attempted to control it, and directing it was like trying to corral an unruly, temperamental child. It was chaotic and poorly directed and powerful.

I needed the power but control as well, and when I felt Savannah's fingers slipping through mine, the control grew. It was still a rebellious force, a summation of magic that had been subdued and ignored and was now fully able to be expressed. It sucked the other Legacy up, whipping them violently through the air. At first it moved in a choreographed dance, and then it became chaotic, the top moving independent of the rest. It grew wider and bigger, pulling from the magic of the engulfed Legacy it spun. Their screams of distress were drowned out by the whipping sounds. I concentrated, and it took everything out of me. Fatigue started to set in, but I couldn't stop, and so I fought through it. I made it—I controlled it. It came to a manageable calm, and I moved it closer to the opening of the veil, where it spat them out and pushed them through with force. I collapsed the whirlwind, which was easier than giving it a controlled release. Then I ran to the veil and closed it.

My lips were moving fervently, trying to erect the reverse ward to enclose them, and I heard the others from whoever was left from the SG join me. When the last words fell from my lips, a powerful magical lock crackled in the air. I wasn't sure if it would hold them or for how long, but they were contained. The remaining seven could spend the rest of their lives stewing over their failure.

I nearly collapsed to the ground but forced myself to stay

standing in order to look over the area. We had losses, but so did they. I called Gareth's name, but he didn't immediately respond. Several feet away, he started toward me, his clothes disheveled like the others'.

"That was a hell of spell you cast. We weren't prepared for it."

When he was closer I admitted, "Neither was I."

"So, you just winged that?" he asked, surprised.

"No, I planned it, but it was harder to wrangle than I expected. Let's just be honest, this didn't go the way we expected at all."

He made an attempt at a laugh, but it was just a gruff chuckle, and I knew it had to be. Some had died. But it was over.

"We kicked ass," Savannah said, jogging to keep pace with me after Gareth had left my side and was talking to his team. Several vans were lined up, I assumed to take away the bodies. I hadn't seen Conner. Had he been swept up in the cyclone?

I needed to see a body. I needed to see *his* body, because I wasn't convinced that he was with the others.

"What's wrong?" Savannah asked.

"I didn't see Conner."

She shrugged. I'd forgotten that I was the only one who had seen him and most people were too busy trying to survive to care. There had only been twelve the whole time. He was never there. Was he still behind the veil, having sent them out there to fight and possibly die while he stayed behind, protected? If he was behind, he was in the veil and unable to leave as well. But if he wasn't …

Gareth's brow furrowed as he noticed the look on my face. Just before I could speak, I was snatched away.

Damn.

I looked around the dank environment reminiscent of

the very first place Conner had taken me away to. But this one was totally barren—no trees, homes, exotic flowers. Nothing beautiful or reflective of what seemed important to him.

"You're a coward," I said, moving away from him, ripping my sai from the sheath and holding them as I assumed a defensive stance.

The insult rolled off of him with ease. He stepped away from me, his sword casually placed in his hands.

"Not a coward, a strategist. You have proven to be worthy of the adoration I've bestowed on you. But I wouldn't expect anything less from my consort."

Irritation flared and I sighed my displeasure. "Must we take a trip down delusional lane each time we meet?"

He bared his teeth in a forced smile. "We will take this trip as long as it is needed."

I didn't want to exchange banter or try to compromise with him. How did you compromise with a person whose only goal was to kill off all supernaturals and possibly humans that had supernatural traits? A pang went through my chest—Savannah. It was as though he had directly threatened her. I felt no less vengeful than if he had taken out his sword and attempted to injure her. It started with a prick, and then magic rose through the fatigue, strong waves difficult to contain for the moment I needed to before I expelled it. It exploded from me and hit him hard in the chest. I lunged forward, and one sai neared his midsection but ended up embedded in the ground. I left it there and turned in time to catch him as soon as he popped up behind me. I caught his side with the other. He groaned, twisted, and then grabbed me by the throat and pulled me back hard against him. His slim, sinewy body was harder than it looked. His fingers pressed against the carotid, his breath a warm beat against my ear as he spoke.

"I really enjoy moments like this. Each time I see you, I know I've chosen well."

He was the only person in attendance at his delusional party. If getting his ass kicked did it for him, I was happy to oblige. "Good, you are going to absolutely love me after this." I brought my heels down on his feet. He wailed at the impact. Trained since I was five to fight and survive, I was reduced to something that some would consider crass and unskilled. I didn't care. I hit him in the groin and he buckled to his knees. They always do. I turned and shoved a sai toward his neck, just inches from making the strike—the kill. I'd left the belief that he could be handled amicably behind me. I could have been the most talented orator and skilled persuader on earth and I wouldn't have been able to convince him of anything.

He slipped away, and when I looked up he was nearly twenty feet from me. He glared at me with chilling stern eyes. Perhaps he was starting to see in me what I'd seen in him from the first time we'd met—an enemy. We were bound by the DNA we shared, but we had no more in common than what could be seen through a microscope.

"You disappoint me; I thought you would eventually come around."

"What part of me trying to kill you gave you that impression?" I asked.

His look of bewildered disgust concerned me. Did he really think that I would flip? That I was going to just wake up and say, "Hey, today seems as good as any for a mass murder"?

"Anya, if we are not allies, we are enemies. Do you understand that?"

I was so tired of getting that threat. Before I could make a comment about his supervillain canned response, his eyes became like a winter storm and his mood changed to match.

I had a feeling that until just a few minutes ago he'd clung to a miniscule shred of hope that I would come around.

Sucked back, I slammed into something before it gave enough for me to sink into it. A light translucent box enclosed me. Strong magic poured into the small enclosure and I felt oxygen drift out. I gasped a breath. He concentrated as he stepped closer. Keenly focused on whatever magic he was doing, he kept moving forward until he was just inches from the little prison. I pressed along the lines of the entrapment. It bulged but never gave. I pounded the sai in it; the magic expanded and rebounded with even more force. Oxygen didn't seem plentiful, and I wasn't sure if it was the lack of it or the overwhelming magic, but my head throbbed and I felt light-headed.

He gritted his teeth and stepped closer. The lavender-colored box restricted me. I was silhouetted against its walls. My head no longer felt light, but it continued to beat hard, crowded by something—the massive headache that caused a ringing in my ears. It was then that I remembered Conner's promise that if I wouldn't go willingly, then he'd control my mind. He grabbed at it, trying to take it. His voice in my head was a gentle calm, asking me to release myself to him. An ethereal voice asked for me to give up control. It was a beneficent plea from a kind stranger. But I knew they were false feelings, false beliefs.

There was nothing angelic or ethereal about Conner. He was anything but. He was a demon, a monster, a magical deviant who wanted me by his side to rule with him. I pushed him hard with so much force his head lurched back and he winced.

"Anya, this is your own doing," he said slowly, watching me in the magical cage like I was an animal in a zoo. "What is so wrong with what I want? It's freedom for us. No more hiding from Trackers. No more feeling like we have to hide our magic and what we are. You fight it because you have never had it."

Conner didn't look much older than I was, so I suspected he'd never lived in that freedom, either—unless Vertu were immortal. Legacy weren't. We aged, grew old. But he dwelled on the time before the Great War as if he had been there, even though his fondness for it held the luster of one with a revisionist view of history. I wasn't there, I didn't know if it was all sunshine and daisies and a true heaven on earth. My mother had told a different story of the physical beauty of the homes, the gardens, and the people—the faces they presented to the public. But behind the genteel eyes, the soft voices and the odd-colored hair were dark souls that were reviled by the other supernaturals that they considered unacceptable and weakened versions of the Legacy. That would be kept as pets for entertainment or foot soldiers whose lives they would willingly sacrifice if necessary.

Not all Legacy were bad; some had resisted, and others had been foolish enough to get caught up in the rhetoric. I stepped closer to the magical wall. The pain in my head had settled since he'd stopped trying to invade it. Perhaps my glare was too hard to look at: the disdain and disgust a bitter reminder of how I saw him. He turned his back to me and looked out into the distance, taking the fallow land, the dead grass, the absence of beautiful flourishes like trees, exotic flowers, and waterfalls. If they were illusions, they were still beautiful. This place was dead, a forgotten dilapidated world right out of an apocalyptic movie.

He ran his hand through his hair, changing it to its burnt orange coloring, a little reminder of who we were.

When he turned around, I said softly, "You lost, Conner." A light smile of condescending disbelief slipped through his frown. "Several days ago, I came out. Everyone knows we exist." It was a limited view of "everyone" since it only consisted of the Magic Council, the SG, and my friends. But he got the point. "Most of your recruits are gone, and the rest are imprisoned." I kept my voice level. I was locked in a magical box, and I wasn't quite sure how he would respond.

"It will make things easier. Those that are in hiding will seek us out instead of us finding them. They know their roles. It seems that only you, Anya, are okay with your role of submission. Others have not settled as easily into such an acquiescent state. They haven't forgotten their history, their past."

Fine. Conner was beyond reason and rationality, and I made the decision to give up trying to appeal to his morality and common sense. "Okay, do what you want, Conner, but know that history is not on your side. Your twelve people were wiped out, and honestly quite quickly."

"Because of your betrayal!" he snapped. The box made spastic movements that matched his booming voice.

I had to get out of there, but I had no idea where "there" was. I knew I was behind a veil, not one often used—probably never used. But first I needed to get out of my magical cell. I called on magic. It didn't feel the same; it seemed weaker and probably was. I'd fatigued it with the constant use. I pushed aside the exhaustion and doubt and called for it. The colors were as vivid as usual, bouncing lazily in front of me. I gathered it, targeting it through my single sai, the other one still outside of my little cage just a few feet from Conner where I had embedded it the ground.

Concentrating, I forced so much through the sai that it ripped the box and I tumbled out, quickly rolling to my feet and pointing the blade at him.

"We are done here," he said, turning his back to me, and with a wave of his hand he blasted me out of there. The fine illuminated line of the wall remained open, allowing my one sai to come through. It soared out and landed in my leg. It was enchanted, unable to be used against me, but apparently that didn't include unintentional stabbing. Blood spurted the moment I pulled it out. I started to look around before I did magic to heal it, but then I realized that I didn't have to do that anymore. The sealed cut hurt like hell, but at least it wasn't bleeding. I scanned the area and it was definitely where Conner had taken me from. It was just as destitute and barren-looking as the place I'd left. I inhaled the air. I wasn't a shifter, but trees, dirt, and flowers were easy to smell. The only thing that I smelled was dirt—lots of it. It was now dusk and I didn't know how many hours I'd been gone. I vowed to learn how to transport.

I started walking, hoping I would get to a street soon. After ten minutes of walking, I did, but I wasn't sure which one and considered flagging down an oncoming car that was starting to slow. When it got closer, I recognized the driver, Gareth, and his passenger, Savannah. The car hadn't come to a complete stop before she jumped out. She gasped and then frowned. "Your hair."

Damn, why does Conner keep doing that? And how did he do it without touching me? I couldn't remember him touching my hair. I was out now, I could keep the color—but it wasn't me. I didn't want to stand out—I wanted to blend in.

"Do you need to see a doctor?" Gareth asked after he'd gotten out of the car. He knelt down to get a better look at the area under the bloodstain on my jeans.

"No, it's fine." I tried not to limp as I made my way to the car. I opted for the backseat instead of taking the front when Savannah offered. I lay back, resting my leg, which felt some-what better, but the day I'd had started wearing on me. I was so tired and hungry I took the banana and granola bar Savannah took out of her "quest bag" and was exhausted and famished enough not even to complain that it wasn't accom-panied by a burger or something that was on a farm at one

190

point. Then she handed me several Handi Wipes. As much as I'd teased her about her bag's name choice, I had to give it to her, I liked the thing. Resting back, I closed my eyes and fell asleep and didn't open them until the car came to a stop and the door opened.

"Slept like a smart-mouthed baby," Gareth teased, handing me a bag of food. They'd stopped for food. Real food, or as real as fast food could be—well, that was Savannah's opinion of it. If it satisfied my hunger, I considered it real. I winced when I turned to get out. The area where I'd been stabbed by the sai was really tender; I was going to feel it tomorrow.

With a half-smile, he asked, "Would you like me to carry you to your apartment?"

Challenged accepted. "Yes."

My smile mirrored his at his astonished response. "What?"

"Yes, I would like you to carry me." I was unable to keep the amusement out of my voice.

He lifted me with ease and I pulled a few fries out and started to eat them as he carried me to the apartment. "Are you enjoying this?" he asked.

"You're the one that's always trying to damsel someone. I'm just trying to be more amicable." Savannah held open the door, her lips pressed into a tight line, trying without success to suppress a laugh. He parked me on the sofa and sat to my right.

Clasping his hands behind his head, he waited as I finished my burger, watching me, his gaze roving over the strings of red that had come out of my braid.

"Do you plan to keep it like that?"

I shook my head. I wasn't foolish enough to think that now that I was out, people were just going to magically forget what I was and what my kind had done. There had to

191

be some backlash eventually. So, no, I had no intentions of keeping my hair that color.

He chewed on his lip for a moment in consideration and seemed to be choosing his words carefully. "Harrah thinks it's a good idea for you to come out not only to us but to everyone."

"No."

"I simply told her I would ask. Your answer is no."

Since he didn't push it, I had a feeling he didn't like the idea, either, and probably made the suggestion out of professional obligation.

I hadn't really had a moment to think or deal with it. People had seen me do Legacy magic in the middle of the street—you can't unsee that, and it was too late, probably unfeasible to find and wipe the minds of everyone who did.

"You agree with me?" I was shocked.

He looked at Savannah, who was perched cross-legged in the chair opposite the sofa. "Too many things are questionable. The Guardians of Order—"

"Trackers," I interjected. The Guardians of Order made them seem noble. They were mercenaries and assassins. They studied us, tracked us, and killed us. There wasn't any order, and they damn sure weren't Guardians.

"What happens now?" Savannah asked. "We have the Legacy who were willing to work with Conner."

"Conner is still on the loose, and he's the greater danger. Believe me, as long as he is free, he will try to get them out," Gareth said grimly.

"But there are only seven left. They aren't really a threat if he does," she countered.

"He has four of the five Necro-spears out there. I don't know how many other Legacy objects he has that can be used," I added. "He's going to try to get as many Vertu and Legacy as he can to ensure that he will be successful when he decides to strike. And he'll also try to recruit higher-level mages because they are strong enough to use the magic from a Necro-spear to assist." The idea that a mage would help seemed absurd, but he'd managed to convince one to help before. Who knew how many others would be willing to help for a chance at more power? The thought chilled me to the core.

Savannah blanched. "A high-level mage can do a Cleanse?"

I shook my head. "They can use the magic from the Necro-spear only after using it to pull magic from a witch, fae, and shifter. Even then it's not strong enough to do a global Cleanse, just a small one."

That wasn't much better, and it was displayed on her face. As much as I wanted to protect Savannah from everything, I couldn't. I was sure telling her that a high-level mage could do a small Cleanse if he was psychotic enough to perform three murders wasn't any better than knowing that Conner could do a global one.

"Finding others should be a priority. I think you can be of some use with that." I looked in Gareth's direction, and his eyes had narrowed to slits, feral anger sparking behind them; my words sounded as bitchy to him as they did to me. It wasn't intentional, but I had a Guardian of the Order in my home. It still bothered me, and he'd bested and even put iridium cuffs on me. What if he had stayed with them and was the Tracker that was sent after me? Protective magic coiled around me, roiled over my arms, danced across my fingers. I was having a hard time controlling it because I couldn't get the anger to settle.

I jumped up. "I really need a shower. Give me ten."

Yeah, Levy, be weirder.

I took more than ten minutes. I spent more than ten minutes thinking about a nice way to ask Gareth to leave. He wasn't the bad guy—I knew that. But he kept making me think of the bad guy, and I just needed a minute. My life had never gone this far off the rails and I just needed to figure things out: I was out of the closet and the Magic Council and the SG knew. Seven of Conner's crew were locked away, but for how long? Conner was still free and being Mr. Demagogue with one goal—to do a global Cleanse again. Apparently I was going to be his consort. He'd let me go—that was the issue that bothered me as much as Gareth being a former Tracker. He'd accused me of betraying him and then let me go. Who did that? His behavior didn't make sense to me.

I was dressed and sitting on the bed when someone knocked lightly on the door.

"Come in."

Gareth peeked his head in and then the rest of him. "My history with the Guardians of Order really bothers you, doesn't it?"

I shook my head; he frowned and sighed. "Do we need to go over the whole 'I can hear the changes in breathing, voice cadence, respiration, and heart rate' thing again?"

"Yeah. But it's my issue, not yours."

"It's mine. You want to know how I could do such a thing?"

"No." I lied.

A look of disappointment settled on his face. He crossed his arms and rested back against the wall. His eyes went to my wet hair. "It really fits you."

"No, it doesn't. You're eroticizing the whole idea of a Tracker and Legacy together. It's a forbidden fruit thing. Will they? Won't they? A made-for-TV movie scenario."

He chuckled. "I think they will."

And if by chance I ever forget how arrogant you are—you remind me within seconds.

Gareth's moving with the grace of a skilled fighter and

predator hadn't bothered me as much when he was just the head of the SG and a member of the Magic Council. Now it did when I thought about him as a Tracker. I suspected he sensed it, too.

He studied me for a long moment, and when he spoke, his tone was softer, regretful. "I was younger, self-involved and naïve, and I wanted to make a difference. I grew up hearing about the Cleanse and how it changed the world and that some still suspected there were more Legacy that existed. You weren't faces, you were an ideology: good versus evil. But it's never that simple, and when you're young, discerning those things is difficult. My parents would have killed me if they knew, and I was there for two years."

"Is it set up the way I imagined, with complex computers and data, cross searches of information and sightings?" I'd always pictured it as just a bunch of overzealous fake army guys in someone's bunker or basement.

His lips contorted to the side as he considered my question in an uncomfortable silence. Was I making him relive a part of his past that he wasn't particularly proud of? But he had an updated dossier, which meant he still had ties with them in some way.

"Something like that. There is a database, along with the dossier I showed you. Computers can be hacked, so they keep paper copies as well." Gareth pushed himself up from the wall and then took a seat next to me, holding my gaze, his shifter ring seeming to glint a little more than usual. "Ask your question, Anya."

"Don't call me that." I wasn't sure why it was a problem. It had been my name until I was five and the first time a Tracker found us. We'd moved to a new city, changed our names, and continued donning the walnut coloring on all our heads. Being out wasn't as freeing as it should have been. I jerked out of reach when he extended his hand to touch my hair. Quickly pulling his hand back, he stood, keeping his eyes on me the whole time as he made his way back to the wall to lean against it once again.

"Tell me what's bothering you. Do you not trust me?"

"I trust—" I stopped abruptly. I didn't need the whole "I can tell when you are lying" speech. "No. I don't. I can't stop thinking about what exactly drove you to join the Trackers."

Relaxing into the wall, he thought for a moment, and when he spoke, his tone was soft. "No one sees images of you or thinks of people like you when we think of your kind, especially shifters. It doesn't sit well with us, immune to magic, to have someone who defies the laws of magic as we know it."

"Animancers can," I offered.

"I've never met one. I'm sure they exist, but I've never met one, and one hasn't used his magic against me. And until the other day, I've never had magic used against me." In weighted silence he began to walk the length of the room, looking around it. I wondered if he was comparing our modest space to his. My room was half the size of his guest room, and while he seemed to be drawn to neutral and darker colors, I assumed because it reminded him of the forest, my walls were a light yellow. The light beechwood furniture comple-mented it and made it a little brighter. I didn't like the dark, so there was always a light or the TV on. Sometimes I would light a candle like the one that flickered now, filling the room with a light cucumber-melon scent.

Gareth kept pacing. I waited patiently for him to continue speaking, but his attention had drifted off to the window behind me. "Legacy killed a lot of our family and friends. It's hard to forget even when dealing with you. I know that you all aren't like that, but I can't help but wonder, where was the resistance when the idea was proposed? Why didn't they warn us? They didn't do anything until it was too late."

The guilt was always there; it wasn't mine to bear and yet it weighed me down as though it was my burden. "I didn't do it. Don't try to make me feel guilty about it."

He inhaled and blew out a slow breath and shook off the morose mood that the topic had put him in. "We had a big win today, let's celebrate. Let's get a drink."

I nearly said yes until I glanced in the mirror. I needed to color my hair. "I can't." I pointed to the flame-colored tresses.

"Wear a hat," he suggested. He grabbed the one he'd loaned me that was on the dresser. He put it on my head and it dropped low, covering the top part of my face, looking as ridiculous as it had the other day when I'd worn it.

"Maybe another time."

"Change it now, I'll wait. I just need to get out."

Had I at any point asked him to stay? He was free to leave. I was confused.

A lazy mischievous smile played at his lips. "We could do other things to distract us." He glanced at my bed.

"You *can't* be proud of that one?" I scoffed, coming to my feet, and as I passed him, I jabbed my elbow into his side.

"Actually, I am a little. Your face is now the same color as your hair," he teased.

I slammed that bathroom door. One look at my cheeks and I knew he was right. *Why the hell do I keep letting him get to me like this?*

We went to a shifter bar, which was interesting. I'd only visited two. I liked vodka, usually straight. Until I saw the bottle my shot had come out of, I was convinced it was grain alcohol. Gareth laughed at my second attempt to take the shot and left the small booth we were sitting in. He returned with two more glasses and put them in front of me.

"This should suit your delicate palate."

"I drink vodka straight—there isn't anything delicate about my palate," I said, grabbing a few fries off the large plate in front of me. In a vamp bar I was always leery that I was what was really on the menu, but in a shifter bar I had to figure out how to avoid getting alcohol poisoning. Shifters' fast metabolisms meant two things: the alcohol would be strong, and there was always food available. No one wanted to be around a hungry shifter. You wanted to make sure they weren't going to chase you down and make you food.

Gareth leaned into me, his lips brushing against my ear. "Sorry we have to talk like this, but we *are* in a room full of shifters." He kept his lips pressed against my ear too long and I could see the curve of his smile out of my peripheral vision.

"I have just the thing." I scooted over and dug in my purse, grabbed my phone, and then my fingers moved quickly over the keys. His phone buzzed and he looked at me.

"You can stop breathing that hot air on my ear and just text."

He grinned and slid his phone away from him. "I'm good." He moved over, putting a few inches between us as he regarded me for a long time. I suspected he wanted me to get a look at what I was turning down. And it *was* something to look at, as much as I wanted to deny it. He had a masculine beauty that was hard to ignore, and the more I was around him, the more obvious it was. I so wanted to believe that the carnal energy that existed between us was purely because he was a shifter. Being around them awakened a primal urge that was otherwise dormant, right? And the reason my eyes were fixed on his lips was because his tongue kept running over them. Right?

He leaned in and spoke with the ever-present self-assured lilt in his voice. "Okay, no more flirting. When you try to seduce me, I think I will let you."

I sneered at him. "At any point before you speak, do you think about what you say?"

With a mocking grin that made his eyes brighten with amusement, he said, "Alright, Levy, you win. All business." He shifted into the table but kept the distance between us and spoke in a low voice. I had to really lean into the table but refused to move closer to him. "We have four daggers we need to find, do you have any idea how to do it?"

Oh, we're back to business. Rightfully so. We should have been back to business; we were just two people who had a common goal—mine was to restore the reputation of the Legacy and eventually be safe now that I'd been outed, and his was to protect the supernatural world and make sure the Cleanse didn't happen again.

I stayed stretched across the table. He could hear me, but he spoke lower and lower each time, and eventually he was just a murmur over the noise. I looked around; most people weren't paying attention. As at the vamp bar, the shifter bar had its share of fangirls and boys, and they weren't hiding behind the flimsy excuse that shapeshifters ignited something carnal and rapacious in them. They came to the bar with the fuse in hand and handed their desired shifter a match. On the dance floor, many of the people and shifters were distracting and possibly breaking some decency laws.

At least Gareth attempted to control the grin when I slid closer to him. He took a sip from his glass. Bourbon was what he'd ordered, but it smelled just like the grainy alcohol I'd had earlier.

"Now, how difficult was that?"

Pride doesn't taste like chicken, I can tell you that for damn sure.

"I can try to find them. But if Conner keeps blocking them, I might not be able to."

"He'll be distracted," Gareth offered.

He was probably right. Conner would be distracted trying to figure out how to get the others out. "We have people guarding the place we sealed his followers in at all times. He'll show up, and the best thing will be to look for them then."

"We just wait?" I liked to be proactive. Waiting for a sociopath to strike and break out his sociopath friends didn't seem like a good plan. "I would like to try at least once. If he blocks it, then fine, but at least let me try."

He nodded slowly and took another drink. He waved for the waitress and lifted my shot glass, letting her know he wanted to order two more shots. He drew attention to my peach glass, I assumed making sure she knew to bring alcohol acceptable for human consumption.

"But tonight, we eat, drink, and see if Levy actually knows how to have a good time."

"Drinks and nothing else."

"Of course. With your attitude, I'm not going to let you see me naked. Now you're going to have to work for it."

I laughed. "Or I could just drive past Forest Township on any given day, where I'm likely to see your ass or some other shifter's." If you hadn't had lessons on general human anatomy, you could drive through that area anytime and were sure to get a crash course. "Why can't shifters deal with clothes? It's weird."

"Most people don't have a problem with it, why do you? They're just bodies. We see them all the time."

I wondered how long it had taken after the alliance for people to get used to seeing a naked shifter walking across the street as often as they saw a deer grazing on the side of the road. It had to be quite a sight at first, seeing one in human form, walking around naked without the good sense of shame afforded to others.

After several more drinks, I had enough liquid courage in

me to ask Gareth about Savannah. I suspected that a couple of the shots the server had brought weren't human specialty drinks. I told him about Savannah being approached by the Councils, and he didn't seem surprised by it at all. It was requesting that he discuss her being under the Shifter Council that seemed to shock him.

"This is something she wants?" he asked, surprised.

"We think it will be best." I didn't like debts, and this seemed like a hefty one I was incurring, requesting it. "Kalen and I were discussing you—"

His brow rose and a half-grin played at his lips. "You were discussing me?"

"Yes, I told him that you had to get your mommy to get you a reservation at Antonio's, and he couldn't believe that you didn't have the clout to do it yourself. It was shocking."

Chuckling, he took another sip from his glass and sat back in his chair. "You and Kalen were discussing *me* and then …"

This guy.

I wasn't going to take the bait. I ignored him and continued. "We figured it would be better coming from you. I don't see why she has to be under any Council, but apparently she has to."

"Encountering someone like that is so rare, whether she can really be considered a supernatural is definitely a gray line. I do believe she has a case to be neutral." Taking another long draw from his glass, he looked down at it once he set it on the table. "On second thought, I think her being under the Shapeshifter Council is a better idea. I think it will be the best case for Savannah."

"Thank you. I owe you one."

With a dismissive cast of his hand, he said, "You owe me nothing. I don't mind doing this if it will ensure Savannah is safe. We definitely owe her a thanks. That explains why you had that look on your face when we asked her to help. I should have considered that. I'm sorry."

———

It was nearly one in the morning when Gareth dropped me off at home. When I opened the door, all I could think was *Yeah, this is about how my life is right now*. Lucas was shirtless in our kitchen, his blond hair disheveled. His lips kinked into a devious smile as I stared at him. He probably thought I was taking in his sinewy, sleek frame, the lean striations of muscle that ran along his chest, arms, and abs, which I was. Besides wondering if vamps spent the day doing crunches, I couldn't take my eyes off the glass in his hands. Seeing a half-naked vampire in my kitchen, drinking *my* orange juice may have been one of the strangest things I'd seen, and my life was a string of strange things. He relaxed back against the counter, easing into his smile, as if he was doing me a favor by giving me a full view of himself. He put the glass down.

Before I could speak, he brought his fingers to his lips. "She's sleeping. She's had a trying night."

I really didn't need to know that. He responded to the confused look on my face. "She met with the Councils a couple of hours ago."

Why had she done that without me? What had happened? Why had she had a trying night?

Before I could pepper him with the many questions going through my head, he went to the fridge and placed the juice back in. Momentarily distracted, I just couldn't leave it unasked. "How are you drinking juice?"

"Levy, with my mouth of course." He shot a grin in my direction.

Now the hot zombie is a comedian, too.

"I know with your mouth. But I didn't think you could drink or eat."

He pulled back his lips, exposing fangs. "I have these, so of course I can eat. We can't survive on human food, and most things taste funny to us, so we don't bother, but I like juice."

I laughed. I didn't know what about the most powerful vampire in the city, maybe even the country, expounding upon his love for juice tickled me—but it did. And that coaxed a weird look from him.

"You are quite peculiar, aren't you?"

Any other time I would have pointed out that most people would have considered him far more peculiar than I was. Even though most of his mannerisms and speech were modern, certain things he did dated him, like the fact that him being shirtless in my kitchen was the only time I'd seen him out of a suit. Which reminded me again that I was in my kitchen with a half-naked vampire.

Several minutes had passed and I still couldn't find the right way to ask why he didn't have a shirt on.

"Why did Savannah meet with the Councils tonight?"

"She was quite distracted," he offered.

That didn't answer the question. It was then that I remembered that he was the Master of the city and probably unaccustomed to being questioned and definitely not used to follow-up questions from us mere mortals. But I couldn't make sense out of "she was distracted." He'd most likely never seen her with a book—the world ceased to exist to her. I was used to Savannah being distracted.

"She was distracted, and …?"

He shrugged. "She seemed worried and distracted by meeting with them. I sought to ease her discomfort and requested that the meeting occur sooner rather than later. They met with her; some were curious about her skill and she exhibited it. It was tiring for her because she is still a novice at it." Calling her holding someone's hand a skill was really taking creative license, but once again I kept my mouth shut. I focused instead on the most important part of the information: she'd met with them, and I was sure it had gone better with Lucas there than it would have with me accompanying her. Hot zombie was slowly moving up the list toward being one of my favorite people. Now if I could figure out where his shirt was and why he wasn't making an effort to go find it and put it on....

"Why don't the vampires have a Council?"

He scoffed and frowned as the word *council* rolled over his tongue with exceptional disdain. "We existed before trivial things like 'organizations' and 'councils' came into being, and I refuse to reduce myself to it. I have chosen for the vampires to be excluded from such frivolity—we remain a Seethe. They believe it to be equivalent to what they refer to as a *council.*"

"You get to circumvent the rules of having a Council because you're old. I think skirting rules and expectations with excuses like that only works for grandmas and grandpas."

He laughed. "You are indeed a delight, Ms. Olivia Michaels. A true delight. I see why Gareth is so taken by you." Then he leaned in and inhaled.

That's not creepy and weird at all, Lucas.

"And since his scent is on you, perhaps you find him equally entertaining." The mischievous grin on his face was hard to ignore, and it remained as he walked past me into the small laundry room. He returned with a wet shirt on a hanger. He inspected it. "Wine stain. I didn't think it would come out. I don't want to wake her, but make sure you let her know it came out."

The mystery of the missing shirt was solved.

CHAPTER 11

*J*didn't believe in luck, but apparently Gareth and I were having a string of it because I was able to locate the Necro-spears. Gareth might have been right about Conner being too distracted about his magical misfits to be thinking about blocking the locator spell I'd used to find them.

Now Gareth and I were at the location where Conner and his new recruits had stayed, ready to retrieve the Necro-spears. Having them in the possession of the SG wouldn't make everyone totally safe, but at least it would make things better. I'd somehow find the rest of the Legacy before Conner did and see what could be done. I still didn't like doing magic with an audience and especially not one as intrigued by it as Gareth. The magic from the veil was strong; I pushed into it with force and it rebounded, exerting that same amount of force. It wavered but didn't break.

That was Conner's game. It was reinforced, or maybe this was how it had been before and he'd weakened it to give me a false sense of security. I called on stronger magic. The overwhelming flood of it coursed through me, pricked at my being and slowly unraveled. I bolted a full charge of it at the veil. It bent in, stretched to the limits, the thick illumination reduced to a sheer lining that just needed another jolt of magic to rip it open. My fingers opened, magic sparked, and then a blast hit me in the shoulder, sending a piercing sensation into my arm. Pain—shrilling pain shot through me. Two more shots, but not into me. Gareth collapsed to the ground. His eyes were open but he wasn't moving. I didn't see blood. That was good, but why wasn't he moving?

Gareth, get up.

I watched him for a few minutes and he remained still on the ground, unmoving, eyes open.

I swallowed bile and clawed at the dart embedded in my arm. I tried to put a field up—nothing. Again I called magic that I hadn't tapped before, and nothing. Voices spoke off in the background. I rolled to my side, still twisting my arm to get at the dart. I yanked it out, rolled to standing, and looked for the person I planned to return it to by shoving it into them. Everything felt dull, even the magic. It was there, a remnant of it moved through me, but dull, languid, weaker. I waited for the torpor to pass, and as I looked around, I heard the voices but didn't see anyone. They were there, hidden behind the vast trees.

Come on. Come on. Come on. I felt the gentle warmth of my magic start to come back to life at a slow burn. I waited for it to be a roaring fire. Warmth enveloped me, and even if I couldn't see the vibrant colors of it, I could feel magic coiling together in kinship—my magic. I needed faces, not voices. I scanned the vast area; florets of green leaves obscured my vision. Cowards hid. Cowards shot from a distance. I didn't know what was burning in me more, the magic or the anger. I walked toward the forest, and the voices became louder and more fervent: giving orders. To my right I heard the crunch of a branch being stepped on. I shot a ball of magic in that area, and someone grunted. Then the same pain shot through me again. Then again. Magic dulled and my senses felt off. Then another shot of pain lanced through my leg. I clung to the light even though darkness came faster, merging with the flickers and light until it had snuffed out every bit of it and all I had was darkness.

The last thing I heard was "We have her."

"We have her." The words kept repeating over and over in my head. I kept my eyes closed and my face pressed against the cold hard cement floor and concentrated on the sounds and smells around me. But there weren't smells, there was just one smell—mildew. It seemed to dominate any others that might have existed. I opened my eyes into small slits and scanned the area. I was in a basement and my arms were cuffed behind me. *Fuck.*

I rolled to my side and sat up. I was in a large room with unfinished plaster walls. Minimal furniture, just an old gray sofa and a few chairs. Hats and other outdoor wear hung on a coatrack. Everything else was covered with a sheet.

I took another look around the area, hoping to find something I could use as a weapon. Since my hands were cuffed behind me, it wouldn't have helped if I had spied something. When footsteps descended the stairs, I flopped back onto the floor and closed my eyes. The footsteps were close. "I thought you said she was up."

"I thought I heard something."

I could feel the heat of a body coming closer. Human. Definitely human. That meant it probably wasn't a Tracker. I shifted noticeably and opened my eyes so they could see them.

"I told you she was awake. How ya doing? Do I look

mean enough now?" He did—it was the jerk that had been with Clive when they'd first attempted to recruit me to Humans First, and he looked plenty mad. I'd joked about him not looking menacing enough. He looked it now, and so much more. I winced as he yanked me up by the cuffs and jerked me over to sit in one of the few chairs in the room.

"Sit," he growled.

I continued to stand, refusing to speak.

"Did you hear what we said?" Another voice from behind me.

I didn't answer. The one thing that secured my fate was that they needed me; they weren't going to hurt me. But Mr. Wanna Be Mean Face kept the scowl on the whole time. He must have spent hours in the mirror perfecting it so that it could convey the right amount of malice. I wasn't going to point out that no one found dimples menacing.

"Do you hear us!" he shouted in my face.

I still didn't answer. He pulled on the cuffs with force, jerking my shoulder forward. The pain seared through me but I kept my face emotionless, refusing to allow him to see me in pain. I clenched my teeth and dealt with it.

The next time he got in my face I lowered my head. Like all bullies, he saw it as a sign of weakness until I jerked it up, slamming it into his nose. He stumbled back. I stomped his foot, swiped his ankle, and, when he hit the ground, I jammed my foot into his groin.

"Yeah, I heard you the first time." And then I plopped into the seat.

With a deep rumble of a laugh, the man who had spoken earlier revealed himself. It was the officer who had attempted to arrest me. His cheeks were sucked in, an attempt to keep from laughing. Then he glared at me.

"The next time you do that—"

"What you are going to do, abduct me, shackle me like an animal? Because you already did that."

"No, I'll put you in a cage and keep you there until you decide to cooperate."

"Big deal, a slow death opposed to a quick one," I responded.

"We have no intentions of killing you, Levy, if you cooperate. But if you don't … well, I can't guarantee what will happen to you. I guess your fate is really up to you. I'm sure we don't have to tell you what we want."

"How noble are you? You are one stand-up person."

"Look, you better be glad I don't end you right now. You killed an innocent man. A good man."

"Okay, unless we are living in some sort of world of opposites, Clive and Daniel weren't innocent, nor were they good people. They wanted the Cleanse to happen just like you jackasses. And when your objective is to kill a lot of people because people who possess magic are icky, you don't get to play the 'good' card. You're an asshole. Own it."

His face tightened. Pulled so tight it was unpleasant to look at.

"I know it's easy not to see it our way. I don't expect you to ever understand, but you and HF have a lot in common."

"Is that the speech they make you learn on the first day? Are you dumb enough to buy this garbage? Tsk, of course you are. Well, let me tell you how it will end. You want to do this to get back at Conner. I'll do the Cleanse, he'll hide behind a ward as strong as mine or stronger. He'll survive and be unaffected. Then he'll mobilize whatever army of Legacy and Vertu he has left. And from my understanding, I'm not that special; there might be many more of us out there. He'll use you for pets eventually. But honestly, you're so fucking boring, tired, and easily manipulated, I doubt you'll entertain him for very long. Then he will put you down like any animal. Because that is all he sees in you. I'll be fine. Will you?"

They looked at each other, and if my words were being considered, they didn't let me know. Instead they left me there in the chair, but not before zip-tying my legs together. While they were gone, I tried to use magic several times. Nothing. I hated iridium cuffs with a passion. I needed to find a spell to get rid of them. I didn't mind suppressing my own magic and limiting its use, but when it was done *to* me it felt like a violation. It didn't hurt, but the nagging irritation of it being there, welling inside of me and urging to be released, was agitating.

For such an expensive metal, it seemed like people were giving the cuffs out like candy on Halloween. I expected the Supernatural Guild to have it, along with a lot of iron, which restricted witches, fae, and mages. Silver subdued shapeshifters, and as much as vampires hated it and wanted to dispel what they considered a rumor and misinformation, holy water and a stake through the heart worked fine for them. Probably the cheapest of the weapons needed to apprehend a supernatural.

When they returned, they were agitated and tense but obviously not dissuaded from their goals. "We need you to do a Cleanse," Mr. Wanna Be Mean Face's friend informed me.

"I can't do it." I had to disabuse them of the notion that I could achieve their dream.

"That is going to be a problem, Ms. Michaels."

They glared at me as their faces twisted in disgust at my refusal.

"It's a spell, a strong one. What do you think, our family pulls us aside on our thirteenth birthdays to teach us how to perform a spell that will destroy half the population?"

I understood the retelling of our existence painted us as

ruthless, heartless monsters, but did anyone ever think that some of us were better than that?

"Then we have no use for you." I heard the threat that lingered over the words and the dismissive way they looked at me. My fate had been decided. They believed that I had killed one of theirs and the only way they were going to absolve me of it was if I could do this for them. I tugged at the cuffs again—nothing.

I tried to do magic. Nothing. When they walked a couple of feet away, I was sure to discuss what to do with me, I looked around the room. Hands shackled and legs restricted, I didn't have a lot of options.

"Conner." I blurted the name. "Daniel and Clive were working with him. If you let me get in touch with him, I will help. I just ask one favor."

"What is that?" the police officer asked.

"Let me take Kalen with me. Let me protect him." I wanted to ask for Savannah, too, but they didn't know she was considered a supernatural of some sort, and I wasn't about to put her at risk. If they found out, they'd try to exploit her. They knew who Kalen was, and if they'd done any research, they would have known he was a fae. It wasn't like he hid it. If a shirt advertising the fact wasn't so tacky, he would have worn one.

They turned from talking low. I figured they wouldn't do it—I wouldn't have. But desperation often makes fools of people, so I continued to see how true the platitude was.

"I can't keep doing this. You know people will not accept me. And you'll keep trying, so I might as well help you and get it over with, right?"

Neither one answered; instead they assessed me for a long time. I hated lying, but I was good at it. I'd lived most of my life under an assumed name, claiming to be human.

Being good at lying was the hallmark of a sociopath, but it was also the behavior of someone who needed to survive.

"Conner is who Daniel and Clive dealt with. They didn't trust him, and rightfully so, but you all want the same thing." I sighed. "I don't want this, but I don't have a lot of options. The Magic Council doesn't want me around any more than you do. At least you'll give me a chance at surviving—they won't." I wasn't sure how much of that was a lie. Perhaps Lucas and Gareth were on my team, but when it came down to how Legacy were portrayed to humans, I speculated that they would throw me under the bus, and not figuratively, if I became a liability that they needed to eliminate. Harrah cared only about how things played out in front of the cameras, and I knew how cold and calculating she could be.

"If you uncuff me, I can use magic to call him," I offered.

The policeman's eyes narrowed to slits studying me, and if he were a shifter I would have been nervous. It probably worked with suspects, and it was intimidating, but when you were fighting for your life, a sharp look just wasn't enough.

"You can do that?"

No. Of course I can't. How the hell did you get this gig as the leader? I nodded. "I think so." I looked around the room again, taking in the exits. I had worked out my plan. I just needed the cuffs off. Then the footsteps came. Heavy, pounding steps that lacked grace and were all power. The man who came down the stairs matched the sound he made—hard, cold, ominous. Pale blond hair was a stark contrast to his face, darkened by a short beard. The rounded planes of his face should have softened his features, but they were stone hard, cold. If he was part of HF, he was missing the human part, or it was so far removed that he was more animal than man. But he was human, or as barely human as one could be and still be considered one. If he was considered the face of HF, then they could no longer be considered an innocuous group that was all rhetoric and no action. He *was* action.

"Being able to call a supernatural is news to me. A new skill? Please tell," his low, rough voice inquired.

"I can do it." I kept the same calm voice. "But not like this."

It took so long for him to answer, I was convinced he didn't believe me. The cool grin faltered too many times, but his eyes stayed on me.

"Of course. If you can, call Conner. The more the merrier."

Oh. Nice, a true psycho.

Then he went to the corner, pulled out a tranquilizer gun, and took his time loading it in front of me, never letting his eyes leave mine. *Can't help but love a showman.*

"Just in case you're lying. We are really going to make sure you're not lying, Olivia Michaels. Shall I ask you again? Can you get Conner here?"

There was nothing like playing chicken with a sociopath. I was just playing on the dark side; this man dwelled there for kicks and giggles.

I nodded.

"Good. I've heard so much about him."

And for the first time since I'd met a person from HF, the group with the silly name that made me think of a bank, I was scared of them. They were supposed to be the "humans are special" cheerleaders, with silly visions of a magicless Utopia where all the little critters that had something to do with magic went away. They clung to that without a way in hell of making it happen. Not this guy.

Following his example, the other policeman took out his weapon—not a tranquilizer gun. They wanted me alive—I was sort of sure of that. He was all show. But Wanna Be Mean Face was still bitter about me kicking him in the groin.

He stood just a few feet away. The twisted sneer had become as much of a uniform as his black shirt and dark jeans.

When he moved closer to me, I kept my attention on the new arrival. The imperturbable new arrival. He was calm, which meant he wasn't new to this. He was kept hidden, because he was anathema to everything that Humans First presented to the world.

I rubbed my wrist as the cuffs came off. The idea that supernaturals were "allergic" to the various metals was wrong. We weren't allergic, we just had an aversion to our magic being inhibited.

"Do it," he commanded.

"Can I stand up first and get my bearings?" I asked, stalling. The cop was directly in front of me, pointing his gun, and Wanna Be Mean was to my right. The policeman wasn't going to shoot me—I hoped I wasn't underestimating him. I kept an eye on the new arrival, Mr. Personality, who was positioned to my right.

"Be prepared, he may not be very hospitable being summoned," I warned.

"I don't care if he has an attitude as long as he does what he said he would."

"And you do the Cleanse here and then what? You think the Magic Council—"

I stopped because if the Cleanse was successful there wouldn't be a Magic Council. There wouldn't be a Supernatural Guild, there wouldn't be a Fae, Witch, Mage, or Shifter Council. There wouldn't be a Master of the city. *Fuck.*

He nudged me with the end of the gun. "Hurry up." Not only did I want to get out of there, I needed a way of doing it successfully after kicking Mr. Personality in his man parts. That was going to be a lot harder, but I wanted to make sure it happened.

"I need a knife," I told him.

"For what?"

So I can shank you with it. "My blood has to be shed to call my own kind."

Wanna Be Mean was the first to move, pulling out a knife. I reached out for it and he gave the contemptuous look that I expected.

"Give me your hand!" he ordered and took great pleasure in slicing it. Blood welled and I said the invocations. As the final word fell, embers of light glowed in the small space as a diaphanous map displayed in front of me. Mr. Personality stared at it with interest, sucking in a rough breath. For people who hated all things about magic, they couldn't deny that there was something wondrous and intriguing about it. An elusive beauty that easily belied any aversion to or hatred of it. First pastels swept over the odd map, covering it, and then each color pulled from the mélange, something different than what I had seen before. And then it changed to slate gray, which it usually did before divulging its answers. A ripple of darker colors inched over it. This wasn't me—this magic was different. It had been taken over. *Damn you, Conner.*

"What's happening?" Mr. Personality asked.

Happy that I wasn't dealing with a shifter who could probably see through my BS, I said, "The magic is working."

"How long will it take?" the officer asked, his voice coarser than before. I wasn't sure if he was unhappy that it was taking so long or that he was seeing magic differently. It didn't fit into one of the neat boxes that he'd constructed: Humans—good. Magic—bad.

"It has to find him first," I said. They were distracted looking at the map, trying to discern the colors to track the illusive Conner. Wanna Be Mean leaned closer when I did, mirroring my movements, trying to see what I did, and it was all I needed. The magic stopped, and I pushed the police

215

officer against the wall, pinning him there, his gun still in his hand. He turned out to be more resilient than I'd anticipated. But he was fixed against the wall—out of the way. I yanked Mean's arm and pulled him to me as a shield from the tranq gun pointed in my direction. He had several inches on me and was definitely stronger. He clawed at the hand I had pinned around his throat, leaving long red marks.

The officer struggled to release himself from the wall. Mr. Personality was going to take the shot. Two if he needed to get to me. I didn't have to deal with predators on a regular basis to know that I was dealing with one now. He had one target. Me.

He squeezed the trigger. I shoved Mean aside, let the officer drop to the floor, and hit him with a jolt of magic at the same moment the tranquilizer dart impacted my shoulder. Pain. Searing pain. I yanked it out, but it was too late and I started to feel light-headed, vision blurring. I needed to leave, and willing it wasn't enough. I bolted for the stairs. I intended to bolt, anyway. My movements were sluggish, and I lumbered up the stairs, blinking back the water in my eyes and the lethargy that wouldn't fade. *Get to a door.* Fresh air had to help. I sprinted for the door, heavy footsteps behind me. *Door. Get to the freaking door.*

I pushed through it. It was still light outside, and I scanned my surroundings through blurred vision. The drugs settled in my system. Blinking several times, my eyes flickered as I tried to push back the hazy feeling that was starting to overtake me. I performed a healing spell. Ensorcelled by magic, I still felt like I was fading in and out. Afraid to close my eyes, I forced them to widen.

"Levy." I turned toward Gareth's familiar voice. For once I wasn't in a rush to find out how to block his ability to find me. He cleared the distance between us in several steps. He was in front of me and then he wasn't.

The grass bristled against my back, and when I opened my eyes, the tiredness had subsided. I'd expected to feel hungover or feel some effects of being drugged, but I didn't feel anything. How long had I been out?

"You haven't been out very long," Conner said. I followed the voice, which seemed to be farther away than he was. When I pushed myself to stand, he moved close. Very close, just inches from me. My gaze narrowed on him, and I wondered if he could read my mind. Doubtful, because if he could he wouldn't have stood so close.

I looked around. It didn't look like the dank, dark, barren hellhole he'd brought me to before. Large oaks with tapering branches were off in the distance. A thick bosk of trees with leaves enhanced to vibrant rich oranges and reds, although it wasn't fall yet, complemented the lush greenery of the oak trees. Exotic colorful flowers snaked around the periphery of the land. In the middle of the vast area of grass was a small pond with ducks. And water lilies decorated it.

"It's beautiful, isn't it?"

It was, but I wasn't going to admit it to him. He'd made the uninhabitable land a magical nirvana. It wasn't real. It was magic. He was trying to distract me from the ugliness of his magic with beauty.

He stepped away from me, sensing danger. I wasn't feeling violent but confused. The poison in my system was gone. Had he done that?

"I was shot," I whispered.

"Not a bullet wound, just bad human magic. They aren't good at a lot of things, are they? It was quite easy to fix." In a pair of khakis and a pear-colored shirt, he didn't look like a monster who wanted to kill all the supernaturals. He didn't seem like a demagogue with delusions of creating a new world where only what he considered the purist form of magic existed. In front of me stood a man that belied any distrust others might have had and entreated a level of empathy and understanding. Despite all the things that I felt or didn't feel, his magic was strong. He didn't seem to have a shield to mask the aura of magic, and if he did it wasn't very effective. It roiled off him, a light brisk wind. He didn't walk over to me, but teleported—a display that didn't go unnoticed. How could I stop someone whose magic I had limited knowledge of? All I knew for sure was that he was stronger than I was.

My curiosity about his capabilities was rising. He'd mastered magic, and I needed to learn to master mine. Not from a mage, witch, or fae, but from my own kind, or at least someone with similar magic.

He was so close I could just reach out and touch him, but I didn't. I hoped he didn't touch me, either. It seemed as though we had settled into an unspoken truce.

"How do you do that?" I asked.

He teleported just across the vast area and was back in front of me within moments. "That?"

I nodded.

"Would you like me to show you?" His tone held the same wisp of humor that had curled his lips into a miscreant smile.

I nodded again. It was exactly the look I expected. Sheer surprise. But why wouldn't it be? Each time we'd encountered each other had been rife with virulence and violence. Now I was asking for a favor. Truce. My request wasn't really instilled with the benevolence that he seemed to think it was. I needed to know more about my magic. I understood why my parents had elected to teach me just defensive magic and cognitive manipulation. It had served me well. Before they could teach me more, they had been killed, when I was a teenager. I was curious about Conner and the others whose magic was far more advanced than mine.

"Of course, I will do this for you." He extended his hand for me to take; I stared at it as if it was poisonous. Taking it was as good as an assignation with the devil.

"Anya," he said softly. I cringed at the use of the name. That *was* my name, but I was so far removed from it and all that it represented that it wasn't who I was. I was Olivia Michaels and not a Legacy. For a brief moment I didn't really know what it meant to be a Legacy, other than the Cleanse. What was my magic really like? All of it. Was I capable of creating a world with a wave of my hand, like he had? Did I have access to the same type of magic?

"What would you like to do, Anya? Whatever you need to do and learn, I will teach it to you."

I was positive he couldn't read my mind, but it didn't take an auteur of a mind reader to know that I had to be curious. If Savannah was right, I wore my emotions prolifically on my face. I was like any magic wielder and wanted to know the extent of my magic.

"Trust me, I will do this for you, Anya, for us."

That snapped the curiosity right out of me. There wasn't an *us*. We were on different sides of a volatile and destructive issue.

"A man who wants to kill a group of people can't be trusted. I watched you kill two men, and for what reason? Because you wanted to. So there isn't any trusting you."

I noticed a small lifting of his lips, but I didn't know if it was from dark amusement or ominous excitement. He clasped his hands behind his back and slowly paced in front of me. "You see me as your enemy."

"Should I see you as anything else? If you were to succeed, what do you think will happen to me? I will not be immune to the magic and with everyone else I will fall. And what about the others like us? They will die, too. You are my enemy."

He stopped walking and assessed me with an odd mélange of derision and appreciation. "You'll try to stop me."

"I'll be fighting for my life. I'm sure that I have no intention of *trying* and every intention of succeeding." I sighed. Attempting to appeal to his humanity hadn't worked in the past; perhaps he was devoid of it and nothing more than just magic, which explained why standing next to him felt like grabbing a live wire. The magic that came off him was stronger than even that of my parents, who had been quite powerful. Perhaps I was naïve, but I wanted to believe he could be reasoned with. I needed to because of the way we were portrayed in history books, in the tales that I'd heard, in the dystopian movies that were an artistic interpretation of what Conner presented. We had to be more than that. *He* had to be more than that.

"I had to hide most of my life. I was fifteen when Trackers killed my parents, and I had to live in foster homes until I was eighteen. The first time I met you was the first time I'd ever met a Legacy, and you were trying to do the very thing that made us the most hated people in the world. It might not have been our doing, but we carry the taint of the crimes of our parents. I lived isolated from other Legacy for fear that if there were more of us in the area, I was likely to be found. We're out—although you don't seem to care, given the magnitude of the destruction you're causing. The Magic Council knows of our existence and they are okay with it."

I didn't have to wonder about his look or what he was thinking this time, because derision was aptly displayed on his face. Disgust. Superiority. Revulsion. "You think I care whether the Council thinks I should exist? They are nothing more than a diluted version of who we are. The bastards of magic do not have a say in my existence, but *we* have domain over whether or not they exist." The frown beveled even deeper and his magic was more than a live wire—it was the blistering sirocco. Reasoning with this guy was out of my wheelhouse. I didn't have words to cater to his massive ego and I didn't want to.

"How many of us are there? Twenty, maybe thirty, children of the fallen and failed. I suspect most of them are like me, with just a rudimentary understanding and grasp of our magic. The Cleanse is a powerful spell; do you believe we can succeed?"

The faint smile didn't belie the cruelty of his gaze as it fastened on me. "I assure you there are more than enough to accomplish what is needed. Anya, we will not have this debate each time we meet. In fact, we will not have this debate again. I've done all that you've asked of me and I expect your alliance. You are my chosen consort, it is time that we put aside our differences and move forward."

"Put aside our differences! We aren't disagreeing about which is better, coffee or tea. We are talking about lives. Even if you consider the other supernaturals our bastards, fine. They are ours. We have a duty to protect them, not kill them. Don't make the same mistake—"

"Enough. This discussion is over and …"

I stopped listening because I knew exactly where it was going. The same "either you are with me or against me." The first line on the first page of the tyrant handbook.

"Will you stop being the cardboard cutout of every Lex Luther or Magneto in the world? I've seen all the movies and know all the lines. Yadda yadda yadda … with me or against me … I am insert name and I need to rule. You are a tired, boring cliché."

He grinned. "And you are tenacious and obstinate and have proven yourself as worthy of me."

Screw it. He hadn't earned my compassion or the energy it

took to try to reason with him. The strongest magic I could call struck into his chest and he flew back nearly ten feet, exhaling a gush of breath. As he struggled to breathe and come to his feet, I hit him again with another strike just as powerful. Ire sharpened his features and chilled his eyes as he glared at me. I guessed I'd lost my position as consort and had moved to the list of people he wanted to destroy. I kept going, strike after strike, exhausting myself, but I didn't have a choice. I would use all the reserves I had, fight until I couldn't stand. He couldn't be reasoned with, and he was the head of this mess. The leader. To destroy a regime, you had to take out the leader.

Weaponless, the only thing I had was magic, and I'd never used it to kill. I didn't know how, but there had to be a spell. Before I could attack, magic smacked into my chest and I crashed into a tree and he fixed me against it. Pinned to the tree, I tried to recall all the spells I had seen in the books that Blu had given me and the ones that my parents had shown me. I was sure there had to be some rule against teaching someone death magic. I used the spells in the arsenal of those I had at my disposal. I would manipulate his mind—make him forget. I wished I could steal his magic. For any other supernatural, that would have been a death sentence. Magic was as vital as blood and breath for a supernatural; take it and you might as well remove the heart because they were as good as dead. Legacy magic couldn't be taken.

Using magic, I finally freed myself from the tree. I approached the situation with caution. Quickly the spell fell from my lips, losing any of the care I'd used with others. I wasn't going to manipulate his thoughts—I doubted if I could—nor did I plan to modify them. I was going for a clean sweep. Remove it all: his memories of spells, intentions, life. When I was done he wouldn't remember his name. I suspected he'd have preferred death dealt by my twins.

I tugged at his thoughts, my magic migrating to them indiscriminately and wiping at them to remove them from existence. I pushed; he blocked and pushed back harder. Heat rose over my face from the struggle. He moved back and rested against a large tree just a few feet from me without any signs of distress. A cynical smile flourished and he watched me with interest. I pushed more, wrangling the magic and gathering it until it was a bigger force, something to contend with, but he fought it with ease. When I attempted it again, he pushed back harder, and it felt like someone had thrashed something into my head. I fought. Magic to magic, I didn't have a chance. My eyes swept over the area looking for a weapon. Nothing—he'd created the perfect world, with nothing I could use against him.

"Have you given up so quickly?" he asked with a hint of mirth in his voice. "Anya, I've asked you a question."

Desperate, I'd been reduced to barbaric tactics. I moved him slightly from the tree and then slammed him hard into it, again, and the third time, he pushed back with force. I tumbled back and rolled into a stand. He released himself from the tree. Each step he took was measured, slow, lithe. The foreboding way he looked at me—disappointment, anger, revenge. It all mixed together to become what existed between us. I expected him to attack again, but instead he erected a ward. Using magic, I pushed into it. A sheen of light flickered off the diaphanous wall that enclosed him. Once he was in reaching distance he grabbed me, and we were gone.

When I blinked again, I was in front of my apartment and he was several feet away from me. I'd used too much magic. I didn't have it in me to go another round with him. He stood, but his appearance had lost its vibrancy as well. He might not have been as weak as I was, but he wasn't at his full potential. Could I go against him again?

A second became a long drag of minutes before he finally

spoke. "A warrior. I chose well … but you didn't. I have a fitting end to your existence." And then he was gone. *What the hell kind of threat was that? Why can't he just threaten to kill me like a regular psychopath would?*

Somewhere between being abducted and fighting HF and Conner, I'd lost my keys and phone. I knocked on the door. Lucas answered.

Yeah, why not? For all I knew he now lived with us.

His eyes widened at my appearance. I had to look like I felt, and based on his frown it was probably worse.

"Who did this to you?"

I gave a quick explanation before he stopped me and pulled out his phone and told Gareth I was at the apartment.

Gareth leaned against the wall, eyes narrowed on Savannah, the shifter ring dancing around his pupil, his brow raised, and his face contorted into a confused frown.

Savannah's arms were crossed as she paced back and forth in front of him. Lucas had a similarly confused and amused look on his face.

"She was with you. You, Gareth. The moment she wasn't, I expected a call. I didn't receive a call! Why is that? Is your phone charged? Do you need another charger? We can get you another charger." Savannah's voice was high-pitched and sharp.

Oh, this was so going down.

Gareth was the head of the Supernatural Guild and a member of the Magic Council and considered one of the most powerful people in the city, and he was being chastised by the quarter magic, petite Bikram cult member. It was hard to imagine that someone dressed in a tangerine t-shirt and cropped yoga pants and sporting a messy ponytail could command the room, but she did. And everyone looked confused by it.

Lucas's deep, rich voice was low when he started to speak. "Savannah—"

"And you, fella. Humans First have been a problem all along, running around town, clowns in black." Savannah was officially angry, because she had reduced her dialogue to that of a 1920s gangster. I suspected she was going to start tossing out antiquated words like *dame, craw, toots,* and *caper.*

"I call them fake spy—" I was silenced with a quelling look before she turned her attention to Lucas again.

"Why were they allowed to do this? Now they're abducting people and trying to rid the world of supernaturals. You do realize you fall in that category? Immortals aren't immune to the Cleanse, you know that, right?"

He started to answer but she gave him a look. She was on a roll, and eventually I became the next target. "And you. You sneak out of the house without even telling me that you're going to do something so dangerous. How dare you! Then I spend hours calling a phone that apparently you couldn't answer because you were too busy being poisoned and abducted. I could have helped, but as usual you had to go at it alone. I am very disappointed in you, Levy. Very."

A Legacy, a vampire, and a shapeshifter sat in a living room—that sounded like the beginning of a lame joke. Not the beginning of a tale where they are locked in with a petite blonde getting their collective asses handed to them. Gareth still seemed to be in the thrall of the shock of being dressed down by someone who wasn't his superior. Lucas seemed to be experiencing the same confusion.

Lucas's tone was honey smooth and gentle as he

addressed her, his arms spread out over the back of the sofa, somehow finding a place of ease with the situation and Savannah castigating him. "You are correct, we did take Humans First too lightly, and that is something that we need to address."

Savannah relaxed some, but tension remained over her lips, still pulled into a small frown. Gareth looked even more confused as Lucas, the Master of the city, attempted to appease her. I doubt he was any more intimidated by her rant than Gareth was; he was trying to assuage her anger and frustration at her friend being placed in a dangerous situation. She'd assigned some of the culpability to us in some way. I realized that it had to be unnerving for Savannah to go from rooming with a woman she'd met through an ad to finding out that the woman she'd lived with for three years and become best friends with was a Legacy. And then to find out she was a ignesco. She would have never openly admitted that it might be a lot for her to deal with.

I followed Lucas's example. "I'm sorry. I should have told you even if I didn't think it was a dangerous situation. It had the potential to be, and it was terrible of me to make you wait."

She nodded into a sigh, and the frown gave way to a small smile.

Gareth's gaze bounced from me to Lucas and then to me again. Submission, even pseudo-submission, was a problem for him. After a few more moments of strained silence, he finally spoke, his voice a deep, low rasp. "Savannah, this was a situation that I wish could have been avoided. I agree Humans First is becoming a situation that needs to be addressed."

That seemed to be the final thing she needed to hear. She was better, or as good as I thought she could have been at that moment. Relaxing into a plaintive smile, she unfolded her arms and took a seat next to Lucas. He moved closer to her and then rested his hand on her leg. If she was trying to get out of the supernatural world, whatever she had going on with Lucas was heading in the wrong direction.

"Have you called someone to change the locks?" Gareth asked.

She nodded. After I came in the house, she'd interrogated me. By the time I'd come out of the shower, and before Gareth arrived, she had called a locksmith and had my phone turned off and the number changed, all the while stewing in her anger. I'd come in the living room to find that she had relegated Lucas to the sofa and Gareth to the wall.

"What exactly did Conner say? What exactly is his endgame? It is only him now?"

I shrugged. I had no idea. Thirty Legacy or more. I didn't want him to get to them first. I needed to get to them.

"What will you do with the others?"

"Harrah has made several attempts to communicate with them, but they aren't very open now that they have been moved and braced."

Braced. Rendered powerless using the iridium cuffs. Being magically neutered wasn't a good feeling, and I wondered how they were handling that. I guessed they had to move them; they couldn't manage the manpower to constantly watch them, especially since Conner knew where they were.

"And the triplets? Have you found the third?"

Gareth shook his head. I was sure it wasn't a priority. Without the power of the three of them together they weren't that dangerous. Just bad-tempered mages—nothing more.

"We were able to get the Necro-spears. Now I want Conner," Gareth finally stated. It was a relief that at least something good had come out of this disaster. But I couldn't help but wonder how much of the problem *was* Conner. Humans First was just as bad and militant now. Conner seemed more calculating in his dealings than I had given him credit for. He'd orchestrated a situation that forced me out of the Legacy closet. I assumed he thought it would cause an alliance between us. All it did was cause problems. The SG knew of my existence and so did the Magic Council; it was only a matter of time before it became common knowledge that we weren't the rantings of the crazy Guardians of Order.

"Humans First will be easier to address. It is being handled by the human police after their attack on me." Gareth made a face. It was obvious he would have preferred to handle it himself. He didn't seem like the type of person who could let something like that go.

"I don't know if I can find Conner again. In the past, he wanted to be found. I don't think he wants me to find him again. You try to kill someone one too many times and they start to take it personally," I said with a shrug. Dismissing Conner's threat was hard to do. He'd released several dangerous supernaturals just to get me to out myself. Now that I wasn't on his short list of potential consorts, I could only imagine what he had in store for me. Anticipating it was futile because I couldn't get into the mindset of someone like him.

I hated the "wait and see" plan, but that was pretty much what we were left with.

"Are you okay?" I finally asked Gareth once we went somewhere to speak privately. Lucas was in the living room, trying to get back in Savannah's good graces, which I suspected she was milking for all it was worth. If he gave it a day or two, she'd be right back on Team Hot Zombie. She was his number-one fangirl. I still wasn't sure there was anything I or anyone else could do to cure her of her odd fascination with vampires. I often wondered if it was the immortality thing. Most shapeshifters physically didn't disappoint, and if you could look past the aversion to clothing, narcissism, and overconfidence that had them on the very narrow line between jerk and complete jackass, it was easy to become a fangirl of theirs, too. But for some reason Savannah only seemed enthralled by Gareth—or rather oddly invested in *me* becoming enthralled by him.

"I was about to ask you the same question." He took a seat in the small chair across from my bed.

"Confused?" I said.

"By HF, Conner, or the Magic Council?"

"The Magic Council."

"What confuses you about the Council?"

I expected to be tired but I was on high alert. Instead of sitting, I paced the floor. "What happens next with me and the others?"

His teeth gripped his lips as he considered my question for longer than I expected. Was he coming up with a palatable way to say things?

"With you—nothing. I will make sure of that. There isn't a reason not to trust you. But there are others that aren't like you, Anya."

"Don't call me that. Are you ever going to tell me how you found out that an attempt was made on me? How is the information about me so thorough, and yet they didn't have Conner?"

"They did have him, they had his human pseudonym. He and his compatriots seem to have done quite a good job of hiding who they really are."

229

I didn't show any signs of being disturbed by how much information he had about us. "Is his family still alive?"

He shook his head, and I stopped my line of questioning because the more I identified with Conner the harder it would be to do what was necessary. But it was too late—I knew my only goal was to catch him, let him have a trial with the Magic Council, and get him put away, not kill him. Without the help of others he wasn't a big threat. Okay, that was a huge understatement—Conner was as dangerous as hell. But he was still a person who had been in hiding all his life. I wondered at what point he had woken up and thought it was a good idea to turn his tragedy to wrath against others.

"I'm sure when the original Legacy and Vertu were floating the idea around about the Cleanse, there were people who dismissed it as improbable. When do you think they decided to take them seriously? I'm sure it was too late then," Gareth said in a gentle voice. "I don't think you can give him the benefit of the doubt."

I nodded. "He won't be able to be found until he wants to be. For now, I think we need to find the others before he does."

"At least we have the Necro-spears, and the magic from those can't be used." Knowing that only higher-level mages could use them to do the Cleanse didn't bring comfort because we'd already seen that some would betray their own for the right price. Even if that price was just more power.

"We have them now and they will be destroyed."

We were on the same page. Why risk them being stolen again?

Gareth clasped his hands behind his head and slumped back in the chair, eying my room again.

"What?"

"I've been in here a lot," he said with a sly smile.

"Are you counting the times you were uninvited?"

"It's just an observation. Seems like you should have tried to seduce me by now."

He might have said it with a hint of amusement, but I had a feeling he wasn't often invited into bedrooms to just talk. "That didn't last long."

"What?"

"You know, the whole 'you're going to have to work hard for it' plan."

"I just wanted you to know you still have a chance. Don't give up so easily."

He stood and stretched, quite possibly for the visual effect. He didn't need to—his shirt molded over the muscles of his chest and the delineation along his abdominals, and since I'd seen him wearing less far too many times, I didn't need to use my imagination to know what was underneath. But I refused to stroke his ego by ogling him, so I found things in my room to focus on.

His light chuckle floated throughout the room. "Am I distracting?"

I nodded. "I feel smothered by your humility. I rarely find myself in the presence of shifters as humble as you are. I'm sure it's quite the task to maintain it." He'd stepped closer and I took a few steps back to keep the distance I needed from him. There was an attraction, but I was going to stick with the tried and true statement: it was primal attraction and I'd be feeling the same way if there were a different shifter in the room.

He started for the door. I wasn't sure if it was intentional or not, but he hadn't answered my question about the Trackers. Was he hiding something?

"You never answered my question." I dropped my voice, rougher, more serious. I didn't want him to flirt with me to try to redirect me.

His lips were still lifted into an amused smile as he turned toward me. It faltered and then quickly vanished.

"What question?"

"How do you still know so much about us and the attempts on us? Who was killed by the Guardians—I mean Trackers." I refused to make what they did seem as elite and dignified as the title they had given themselves. They tracked people down and killed them.

His fingers scrubbed over the light beard that had started to form. "I'd like you to trust me, and I think I've given you enough reason to do so."

This is the introduction to something dreadful. I simply nodded but couldn't make any promises.

"I'm still in contact with two people in the Guardians. One is a cousin."

I sucked in a sharp breath as the anger sparked inside me. I'd known that he was still in contact with them, but it still hurt to hear him say it, and having an active Tracker for a cousin made it worse. I closed my eyes briefly and tried to grasp what he was telling me. He was in contact with one and related to the other.

The last one that had come after me was a shifter. I assumed a wolf, but he hadn't shifted. Was it his cousin? I didn't need to speculate—I could get the answer right there. "I had one come after me a couple of weeks ago, I guess it's safe to assume you knew him, right?"

He barely moved into his nod, and his usually vibrant blue eyes seemed dulled by regret and intense thought.

When he took a step closer, I moved back to maintain the distance between us. The warmth from my rising anger was becoming an inferno that was difficult to manage. My gaze flitted to the left, where I kept my sai sheathed, and so did his. His stance changed. It quickly went from something casual to something dangerous. Really dangerous.

"Let's not have a repeat of the other day," he said in a gentle but warning voice that didn't have the desired effect. Instead of calming me down it just added fuel to the fire. The familiar prick of magic laced around my fingers. Defensive magic worked pretty much like the autonomic nervous system and awakened when I felt the fight or flight impulse. But it was only reasonable that it did. As in other supernaturals who wielded magic it was ingrained into our existence and biology. I didn't like that I felt like I needed to protect myself from Gareth.

"Why are you hanging out with these people and not arresting them?" I snapped.

"It's not that simple, Anya...."

"Don't call me that!"

"It's not that simple, Levy." His voice was softer, gentle and a direct contrast to mine. "We start to arrest them, then it pretty much gives credibility to their claims that Legacy exist. You are out right now. Savannah, the Magic Council, and the SG are the only ones who know that others exist. Can you imagine the panic when people know that there are more? Enough to possibly do another Cleanse? At least I know the Trackers and I'm familiar with their ways. There would be mass pandemonium if I arrested them and it gets out why I'm doing so. You think you're being tracked now? Imagine when scared citizens are doing it. The organization considers me a friend, which works. I'm able to feed them false information, and I've been able to prevent some attacks on Legacy. I can't do that if we arrest them. Some of them *have* been arrested and stopped, but for things unrelated, mostly possessing illegal magical objects."

The uncomfortable tension between us didn't end. I'd questioned whether I could trust Gareth, and this didn't help things. "What happens next, with me? I can't be blamed for what the others have chosen to do, and it's not like I can untell people what I am. Conner is getting bolder." I wasn't sure if he was more desperate or just indifferent about being discovered. Either way he needed to be stopped.

"Do you think Conner will lie low now?" he inquired.

"Apparently his goal is to have a fitting end for me," I offered, referring to his departing words. I had no idea how to figure out the inner workings of a crazy person's mind.

Gareth's brow furrowed. *Good, at least I'm not the only one confused about things.*

"You do have a way of getting into men's heads, don't you?"

Once again, he'd closed the distance between us, and I let him. With the anger gone, I felt other things I wasn't entirely comfortable with around Gareth.

"I need your dossier," I said.

He nodded.

"I'll bring it to you tomorrow." Moments passed before either of us moved. He didn't seem nearly as uncomfortable with the proximity as I was. A hint of a smile demonstrated that he was enjoying my dilemma a little too much.

"You keep looking at my lips, is there a reason why?"

I nodded. "Just wondering how long it would take for something egotistical to come out. It took a little longer than I guessed."

He stepped back. "Yeah, that's the story you should go with. And if you actually believe it, then at least one of us does." A haughty smile over took his appearance. After a few minutes, he turned and left.

Gareth wasn't gone too long before Lucas followed and I had the opportunity to tell Savannah about Gareth and his link to the Trackers. The bridge of her nose was still a ruddy color, which meant she was still frustrated, but I wasn't sure if it was just the situation or if some of it was directed at me. When she took a seat on the couch, scooted to the end, and patted the side next to her, I knew all was forgiven.

"Why don't you feel like you can trust him? He could have told you any story, but he told the truth, right?" I considered Savannah biased when it came to Gareth. She'd decided he was a good guy after her one-person protest to get me released from the Haven several weeks ago. She had been asked to leave and given ultimatums that were just nicely worded threats. She said that Gareth was the only one who was polite to her, which had earned him a place on her favorites list. She was Team Gareth for more reasons than I would ever understand. It was as if she turned a blind eye to his other qualities, like his conceitedness and narcissism, which didn't seem to bother her.

She was gazing out of the window behind us. The moonlight streamed in through the trees, and things didn't seem so bad, but they were.

"If Conner is ever successful at this, you know I'll die," she said in a low voice.

"So will I." I knew it wasn't much solace, but it was the truth. I was now his enemy and would have the same fate as everyone else with magic.

I told her about my concerns regarding the Magic Council knowing what I was.

"I don't trust Harrah," she admitted. Which made me trust Harrah even less. When Savannah didn't like someone there was usually a reason.

For a long time she sat in thoughtful silence. "Just be careful with her. Don't ever be alone with her if you can help it. I watched her at Devour, after the incident with the mages. She was able to do magic with such ease that it was scary. She walked in and everyone who came in contact with her for a moment had a glazed look in their eyes. I know she was doing the memory thing, but every time I've seen others do magic there was some effort. Their hand moves or their mouth; their eyes widen or they show some hint that they're doing something. Not with her."

"How did she not get to you?"

"I slipped out the moment I noticed it and didn't come back until she was on the other side of the room near Gareth."

"Please just stay away from her."

Harrah was the one person on the Council I planned to avoid the most. I really needed to fix things, too many things. Keeping Conner from being successful with his goal was a priority. Compounding the difficulty of that was the need to do it as quietly as possible, and Conner was bolder now and didn't seem concerned about being discovered. That would become a problem for Harrah.

"I need to find the others. Make sure they never side with him. He's still dangerous even without his followers. And it needs to be done discreetly."

Savannah added plaintively, "Yes, *we* need to." Before I could correct her she added, "The Shapeshifter Council called earlier. I'm going to meet with them on Tuesday."

Gareth worked quickly. She didn't have the same look of apprehension and fear that she'd had when we'd discussed her meeting with the other councils, which was a relief. She seemed anxious and excited. It was comforting to know she would be allied with a group immune to magic and political manipulation. All the traits most people hated about shifters were the very ones that made them great allies. Allies I was glad Savannah would have.

CHAPTER 12

*L*ess than twenty-four hours later, Gareth wanted to work on finding Conner. We couldn't give him more time to either devise a plan to get his remaining followers or start recruiting more. The goal was to apprehend him—and I didn't have any plans of leaving without succeeding.

I wasn't sure what game he was playing, but I could feel Conner's magic before I came into the area. I should have expected it: when I did a locating spell, the light fluttered an odd color. He taunted me with a magical invite. I had my sai in hand, circling. The SG had surrounded the area, everyone in pursuit of him. In the back of my mind I kept wondering if he would and could be cruel enough to do a spell and wipe us all out. Desperation made people unwise. I wasn't sure if Conner was desperate yet, or just angry. He'd prided himself on the loyalties of others and it had emboldened him. I'd fractured his ego when I wasn't easily persuaded.

"Anya." I didn't cringe at the sound of my name or the rough way he said it. He spit it out with the same disgust one would spoiled food. Nearly forty feet away, he cleared the distance when he disappeared and reappeared less than a foot away with a sword in hand. I assumed a defensive position, sai in hand ready to strike. The goal was to apprehend him. That was the SG goal—I wasn't sure it was mine. They wanted him arrested and forced to wear iridium. I wished I could say that I believed that would change things, but I didn't. It would only compound his contempt for supernaturals.

I gripped the sai as Conner and I slowly circled each other, his sword held casually at his side.

"Are we really going to do this?" he asked. He stopped and studied me, piercing gray eyes boring into me, studying me with a renewed interest. A smile played at his lips.

"I don't want to," I admitted. That wasn't the truth, but telling him I wanted to hurt him so bad it made my palms sweat was a little tacky.

"Then why are you doing it?"

"I need you to stop. I tried to reason with you. Nothing." He was the end of this. I hated it, but it was where I stood with this. I had to sever the head to kill the monster. I hadn't decided if it was going to be literally or metaphorically. But it was up to him.

"Well, you have me at a disadvantage. You want me dead, I don't wish such a fate for you."

Which was my advantage. But I refused to be a part of his nefarious adventure to do the Cleanse over again. And I would do whatever was necessary to stop it—even kill. It was never going to sit well with me that I had to kill—even worse, my own kind, or someone close to it. The gnawing guilt was there and it shouldn't be. Conner had made his choice. I'd given him more than enough chances to concede. If death was the ending, it was his own doing, not mine.

Conner's eyes narrowed on me; sparks of magic wrapped around his body and the aura of it was strong. He was stronger; I couldn't defeat him using magic. I wasn't sure if I was a better fighter, because he seemed to have been playing with me before. I had a feeling playtime was over.

"I don't want to kill you, but I will. And your little friend, Gareth, is it? Savannah will be an easier—"

I lunged at him, the blade of the sai barely missing him. As he turned around, I turned in time to miss the edge of his sword. He smiled. Was he testing me again?

"You fight well," I said.

"It is unfortunate that I do. But we had to learn, didn't we?"

I lunged at him and jabbed at him with my right sai. With a quick and graceful turn, he dodged it. I struck with the other and missed him again. My third attempt caught his left side. He sucked in the gasp and stumbled away.

Touching his hand at his side he pulled back crimson.

"You stop this." It was my last attempt at reason. I needed to know I'd done everything I could to stop him before resorting to murder.

His sword came down again. I blocked it with one sai and the other sank into his abdomen. Shock eclipsed his face, more red colored his shirt. I ripped the sai out, and he howled in pain. I cringed at the sound. Assassinating my kind felt wrong; we'd had it done to us so many times. Memories of my parents flashed in my head and I tried to push them aside. This wasn't the same. It wasn't.

Another quick lunge, and he spun away. Then he disappeared and reappeared several feet away from me.

"You would have been a great one for me to have. Your life will end the same way that you've lived it." He bowed his head.

Then I was surrounded by trees and tall grass. I looked past the thick bosk, and in the far distance there was open land but nothing else. Where the hell had he sent me? I moved slowly around, negotiating the crowded area. The only sounds were my footsteps. For nearly a mile, that was all I heard. But I was close to the land, maybe forty or fifty feet away.

As I moved closer to the edge of the forest, I heard more footsteps. They were light at first. I stopped and had to strain to hear them. One step, two steps, three and then the paws poked out before the three heads. Dagger-sharp fangs and a massive body. It moved quick like a feline but had thick, sinewy muscles. Each head was different: one a lion, another something wolflike, and the last a serpent. I had no idea what the hell it was. I watched the sinuous movement of the snake, because it had a longer reach than the others. Its tongue darted out, tasting the air. I wondered which head was the most dangerous. Didn't matter, it was attached to one body. I just needed to get to the body.

I moved back slowly. I needed to get away from the trees, give myself room to fight. The forest had too many obstacles and dangers of falling. I didn't need to have this creature over me.

It continued to take slow, deliberate steps toward me as I focused on the snake that went out to the side, wrapped around, and moved independently of the other two heads. Too much movement—less restricted than that of any snake I'd ever seen. Was this one of the "special" places where the Magic Council sent creatures they were unable to contain? Would it increase in mass like the minotaur had once it had fed? Nothing else was present, so the only thing that could feed them was me. Was this creature so dangerous that it was housed by itself?

It was slower than a lion but quicker than a wolf, and it took on small traits of all three animals, including the sinuous movement of the snake. Then it stopped, assessing me as if it was trying to decide whether I was predator or prey. Sai in hand, I waited for it to move. Prey. The snake recoiled back and finally struck, its reach nearly seven feet longer than I expected. A sharp jab with my sai impaled its scaly flesh. It recoiled back, freeing itself, and seconds later the wound closed. It healed itself. Like we healed ourselves. It wasn't a shapeshifter. *Fuck.*

The snake snapped out to the side, a distraction as the wolflike creature snapped at me. With a smooth, quick under arc strike, the sai sank in under its chin. It howled; I jabbed again with the other. The creature stumbled back several feet and jerked itself off the weapon. Blood spurted, but it wouldn't be long before it healed itself. I didn't wait.

I ran out of the forest, hitting open land and turning in time to miss a strike from the snake's tongue. At least I thought I did. When something bumped into my side, I retreated back. The three-headed creature made its move, lunging at me. I jumped to the right, but its claws grazed my side. When I jammed my sai into the offending paw, the thing made a sound that was a disturbing combination of a howl, hiss, and roar. A loud, deafening shriek that reverberated and rang in my ears. It tried to pull away; I kept the sai in it, throwing it off-balance. The snake struck at me again. I dodged back, and it hit air. The other sai went into its throat this time, and another deafening sound filled the air. I gritted my teeth and bore it, refusing to let go. I pulled both sai out and moved back, avoiding the pools of blood that covered the grass.

Changing my strategy, I went on the offensive and attacked, lunging at it, dodging around the striking snake head, whose second wound was healing slower than the first. It was weakening—healing magic required a lot of energy. It slowed, and losing the grace of movement, it lumbered to get away from my next attack. I thrust into its chest, and it stumbled back. A diaphanous wall formed around it, coming down weakly with very little use of magic. The creature's breathing faltered to ragged gasps. It barely moved. Stepping back slowly, I watched it carefully for any more movement. There wasn't any.

Then I moved quickly toward the outskirts of the field, looking for an exit. It wasn't hard to find, a live wire of magic that violently strummed against me. My magic pushed into it lightly; it gave. I added a little more force. I didn't want to use more magic than necessary because I wasn't sure what was waiting for me on the other side. Conner was playing his little games and I needed to be prepared and at my best. The wall wavered and finally gave, or rather it spat me out as though I'd worn out my welcome. I wondered if the creature had anything to do with it. I tumbled through the wall, spilling at Conner's feet.

"Is my pet alive?"

Pet. Yeah, that's about right.

He frowned at my silence.

This was going to end. I pushed him back hard, slinging strong magic into his chest. He recovered in time for the sai to sink into the flesh of his abdomen. His teeth clenched, but he wouldn't give me the pleasure of showing any more signs of pain. I swiped his leg, and as he crashed to the ground, I pulled the gun from my back holster and took the shot before he could move. It wasn't the pain of iridium being shot through his body, but the restriction of magic that bothered him. It was the first time since I'd encountered him that he'd shown anything other than confidence and haughtiness. He struggled with being divested of his power, if only for a few minutes.

I had no idea where I'd landed and if Gareth could get to me in time. Six minutes would be the longest break I'd have before he'd have his magic back, and I wasn't sure if anyone would be able to find me. I wished I could have handled the cuffs, but I couldn't and use magic. I didn't want to be magic-less going up against Conner. His eyes blazed with a new fury. My title changed: no more consort, probably mortal enemy. The minutes moved by faster than I anticipated. I pulled the sai out of his abdomen and prepared to engage if Gareth didn't arrive in time. Conner disappeared. *Dammit.*

Magic hit me hard and I slammed face-first into the ground several feet away. My sai sprawled off to my right, one barely out of reach, the other several inches away. I rolled to my feet and grabbed one in time to block the sword swinging at me. I needed to move more to get to the other. Enchanted so that they couldn't be used against me, they weren't of use to Conner. He drove me back and kicked it out of the way.

"This isn't how it should have been." His deep voice was laden with anger and contempt.

I stepped back several steps. "Tell me—what should have made me swoon over you—the idea that you wanted to deci-mate a group of people, or that you locked me up with your freaky pet in hopes that it would kill me? Neither is on the short list of how to get a woman."

He slowly circled me and stopped when he reached the spot where he could place himself between me and the other sai. "You have the others," he said in a low, ominous voice. "You will have them released."

"No. I guess you haven't been paying attention. They chose the wrong side, and so did you." The more I thought about the situation, the more frustrated it made me. If he'd succeeded, so many people would have lost their lives, and for what—so he and the others could be the only magic wielders? In the end, this all came back to his ideology and the very one that had led to the Cleanse.

The magic came at me quick and the ward that I'd erected barely stood after he attacked it with several more charges of magic. It wavered, bulging in, strained and preparing to fall. I didn't expect it to survive another one and I couldn't waste the energy to try to hold it. When he hit it with another blast of magic I let it fall, lunging to the right and rolling close enough to grab the other sai. The twins in hand, I sprang at him, wedging one through his blade and holding it. I thrust out the other and caught him in the side of the leg. I withdrew and attacked again next to the wound. He stumbled back, but I kept going. Strike. Parry. Jab. Crimson colored his shirt. He panted and I allowed him to move back several more feet. When he placed his hand over his shirt and the blood still remained, I knew he was weakened. I pushed all the magic I had into one sai and he tumbled back. Another jab came from the cave lion that attacked him from the left, hitting him hard enough that he crashed to the ground. Before he could recover, cuffs were placed around his arms by another agent. Conner collapsed to the ground, and not from any of his injuries. Being rendered magicless was a bigger injury than anything I could have given him.

"What the hell?" Gareth gasped once he was in human form again. He moved my arm, and with adrenaline sinking down, I finally felt the injuries. There was a gash on my stomach, snakebites on my arm, and cuts on my thigh. I thought they looked worse than they were. They weren't. I sucked in a breath and held it. I wasn't sure why, because that sure as hell didn't help with the pain.

Don't pass out. And I said it over and over again, but my body wasn't taking direction. Bile crept up and I felt lightheaded.

"Can you at least heal the wound on your stomach? That looks the worst." Based on the blurred grimace on his face, it wasn't by much.

"Just a minute." I lowered myself to the ground and lay back. I'd used more magic than I ever had in a fight. My intention was to rest for a moment and then attempt to heal myself. If only it had worked out that way.

The bed that I woke up in wasn't mine, but it was comfortable enough. I looked around the room: pale yellow walls, generic art of the wilderness and children playing on the walls, a small TV mounted to the wall, and in the chair next to me, Gareth, with a frown etched so deeply on his face it looked painful. I had several bouquets of flowers ranging from simple roses to orchids and lilies. And a gift basket that I planned on emptying as soon as I could get near it.

"I have a couple of questions," I informed Gareth. "Who sent me all the flowers, and can you hand me that gift basket?" His brow rose and then he stood, grabbed the basket, and handed it to me. I took out the two chocolate bars and started eating them.

He rolled his eyes in the direction of the flowers. "You wake up in a hospital, and those are your first questions."

I nodded.

He grimaced and then shook his head. "As you probably guessed, the flowers and the basket are from Lucas. I can only imagine what the room would look like if you dared to be here more than two days."

Two days explained the hunger. I wondered why they hadn't tried to feed me intravenously.

"The mage saw fit to let me starve?" I asked.

"No, they tried to insert an IV but couldn't get past your wards. I guess after they stuck you the first time to give you intravenous meds, you didn't like it. You put up a ward each time anyone came near you. Is that typical?"

I shrugged. "I've never been unconscious before, and I don't know what I do in my sleep."

"You put up wards in your sleep," he offered with a half-smile.

"I have another question. Is there any way I can get a cheeseburger and fries?"

He laughed and shook his head. "You don't want to know about the poisonous snakebites, the three large claw marks on your leg, or the gut wound?"

I thought about it. "Hmm. Yeah, how did that go?"

"How did that go!" If he didn't calm down, he was going to need a pill or something. "How did it go!"

Maybe something stronger.

"It's maddening, isn't it?" Savannah asked as she came through the door. "She does it all the time." Then with a dramatic roll of her eyes and an over-the-top gesticulation of her hands, she did a poor impersonation of my voice. "'It's just a ten-inch gash, I'll live.'"

"Well, if everyone is finished mocking the injured woman, can someone give me some clothes so I can go home?"

I waited to see which one would be more appalled by my request. Savannah won. She shrugged and handed me a bag of clothes she must have brought for me. "Of course, why not let the near-dead woman go home the moment she wakes up? Nothing bad can come from that. Why not?" she prattled on in a huff. But she didn't insist that I stay.

The mage physician told Savannah I was fine and wouldn't have any side effects from the medication they had given me for the venomous bite. The other injuries had been healed using mage magic. What she heard was I was an invalid, had an incurable disease, and only had days to live—or rather that was how she'd treated me. I had to keep reminding her what the doctor said. Showing her a scar-free leg and abdomen helped. Kalen was calling every hour on the hour to check on me because Savannah was the one who'd called to let him know why I wasn't at work and had given him her version of the story. He was convinced that the Grim Reaper was coming any day to claim me. Two days after I was released from the hospital, she was still my shadow. I needed to get away from Nurse Savannah, which made accepting Gareth's invitation to dinner a very easy choice. Spend another night with Savannah, the overzealous nurse, or Gareth?

I looked around the restaurant and was glad I'd let Savannah convince me to change into a black halter dress, pin my hair up, and wear the small jeweled necklace Kalen had given me for Christmas in hopes that I would don more than my Converses and plaid. I hadn't heard of the place, and when I'd looked it up online, the pictures hadn't done it justice. Cascades of billowy silk drapes decorated the large floor-to-ceiling windows. Pendant lights set a mood that hinted at exclusivity. And if that didn't provide enough clues, the elegantly dressed waitstaff in their all-black suits definitely conveyed it. It was another restaurant that was hard to get a reservation for and had a hefty price for the privilege of doing so.

Several times I looked up from the menu to find Gareth's gaze planted on me. "How are things at home?" he asked with a faint smirk.

"You know how things are. Savannah's bat crap crazy. I swear I expected her to bring a wheelchair into the room and make me use it."

He smiled. "She's quite enthusiastic, isn't she?"

"The words you are looking for are *overbearing* and *over-protective*. Not *enthusiastic*. That makes her sound like she's

Mary Poppins singing me nice little ditties while we clean up or something. She was a freaking drill sergeant forcing me into bed to recover."

His voice dropped, low, concerned. "Your injuries were bad. Worse than they looked once they weren't obstructed by your clothing."

I glossed over the bad injury information and went straight to the part about my clothes being removed.

His brow lifted at the same time one corner of his lips did. "Now who's the arrogant one? You think I'm so desperate to see you naked that I'd do it while you were injured?"

Warmth pricked at my cheeks, and I hated that it did. He smiled, leaned into the table, and dropped his voice to a low purr. "I'm sure when you're ready for that to happen, you'll let me know."

And then he leaned back in the chair once again like he was giving me a view of him. Why did he have to be so full of himself? *Oh, because he's probably actually been near a mirror to look at himself.* I rolled my eyes away from him.

"Things with Savannah could have been worse."

"I doubt it."

"She's an associate of the Shapeshifter Council now, given right of protection and assistance when necessary. If she felt she was in danger or needed any form of assistance, including an obstinate roommate who is in danger and in turn putting her in danger, one call and she could have had a houseful of shifters there to offer assistance." Amusement made its way to his eyes and added a sparkle to the indigo shifter ring along his pupils that already shimmered as the light hit. "I wonder if she knows this. Hmm, perhaps I should tell her."

Me glaring at him from across the table only added to his amusement.

It wasn't until we had eaten dinner and I was slowly slipping into a chocolate-induced euphoria from the dessert that I relaxed back against my chair.

He slid my glass of wine to me and I took a drink.

"What?" I asked after several moments of him watching me.

"I like you like this," he said quietly.

"What, slightly buzzed and coming off a sugar high?"

"No, relaxed. You don't seem to do it often."

My life wasn't necessarily full of relaxing moments. I relaxed too much or became too comfortable, I could possibly die. But I didn't say that. I simply shrugged and smiled.

"The Necro-spears were taken again, and we have no idea how it was done. They were stored behind magical barriers and a restriction was placed on them to keep them from being located," Gareth said in a low voice edged by irritation and frustration.

"You think Conner is behind the theft?"

He made an exasperated sound. "No, he said he didn't have any knowledge of it."

"He's a sociopath, of course he would lie about it. He has to know who has them."

He shook his head and sighed. "Not while he was braced and being questioned by a fae. He couldn't use magic to block it. So we got the truth."

There were other players involved. But who? It had to be someone with magic, who could get past wards. And then the realization hit me—with Conner and his accomplice Legacy detained and rendered magicless, there had to be someone or *someones* with equal or stronger magic to locate the Necro-spears and break the magical barriers surrounding them.

"We have to find the other Legacy," I said.

It wasn't as cut-and-dried as I wished it were. Unlikely

alliances were formed. HF would do anything to get rid of supernaturals and so would another group—possibly Legacy and Vertu; they all had to be stopped.

I became very aware of the way Gareth's firm hands pressed into my back. His thumb lightly stroked there and I liked it—a lot. I really wanted to blame the two glasses of wine I'd had with dinner for my inviting him in once we'd pulled up to my apartment. The devilish look that shadowed his appearance and the wicked smile that beveled his lips were all signs to proceed with caution. Was there ever caution with Gareth? At the moment I really didn't care.

You want to come in for a drink or something? Had there ever been a more BS line spoken? *Let's have a drink* seemed classier than saying: "I just kicked Conner's ass, possibly saved most of the supernaturals from being murdered, escaped from Humans First, and survived a fight with a mutated hound, and I want to feel the warm lips of a very sexy man on me and possibly see him naked. Let's do this."

The moment I opened the door, Gareth pressed me against the wall; his lips caressed mine. His hands moved over the lines of my body. Clawing at his shirt, he eased back just enough to pull it over his head. Settling in to me, the weight of his body pressed me harder into the wall. He inched my dress up my thighs as my legs curled around him, pulling him closer to me. He tugged at my dress as he kissed me hard, sparking a need for more. He pulled away as he nipped at my lips, tasting them. Holding me to him, he started to carry me toward my bedroom when his phone buzzed. He ignored it and it eventually stopped but then started again. He ignored it again. A voice called his name over the speaker. I made a mental note never to accept a phone from the fae. Holding me close to him, he snatched it from his hip. "What!" he growled into it.

As the person on the phone spoke, Gareth's hold on me loosened and he lowered me to my feet. When he hung up, a look of anger, fury, and betrayal was displayed prolifically on his face. Knowing he was a shapeshifter and predator capable of carnage and destruction was one thing, but witnessing it unfold in him was something else. Scary. Protective magic pricked and started to slowly roil over me, ready to protect me if necessary.

"They're gone. Every one of them," he said through gritted teeth.

I knew who.

A look of betrayal quickly overshadowed Gareth's other emotions. "The Guardians of Order helped get them out."

Emotions brewed in me, too, but mine came from a place of confusion. Why?

Before I could ask, he'd turned around and left.

―――――

For notifications about new releases, *exclusive* contests and giveaways, and cover reveals, please sign up for my mailing list and join my group.

Reviews are very important to authors and help other readers discover our books. Please take a moment to leave a review. I'd love to know your thoughts about the book.

MESSAGE TO THE READER

Thank you for choosing *Obsidian Magic* from the many titles available to you. My goal is to create an engaging world, compelling characters, and an interesting experience for you. I hope I've accomplished that. Reviews are very important to authors and help other readers discover our books. Please take a moment to leave a review. I'd love to know your thoughts about the book.

For notifications about new releases, *exclusive* contests and giveaways, and cover reveals, please sign up for my mailing list at mckenziehunter.com.

Happy Reading!

www.McKenzieHunter.com
www.McKenzieHunter.com

85410435R00158

Made in the USA
San Bernardino, CA
19 August 2018